Forbidden Steps

A BOYS ON THE BRINK NOVEL

JAMIE DEACON

Ink Lane
Publishing

Forbidden Steps

Published 2024 Ink Lane Publishing
First Published 2022 by Beaten Track Publishing
Copyright © 2022–2024 Jamie Deacon

All rights reserved.

Paperback ISBN: 978 1 0686249 4 0
eBook ISBN: 978 1 0686249 5 7

Cover Design: Natasha Snow
www.natashasnow.com

Editing and Formatting: Debbie McGowan
www.inroadpublishing.com

To all my readers who have lived through divorce, and who understand just how messy and complicated families can be, this one's for you.

CHAPTER ONE

TAYLOR

"YOUR STEPBROTHER'S COMING HOME today."
This had been Mum's greeting when I slunk into the kitchen that morning, having pried myself out of bed to investigate the noise. No 'Did you sleep well, darling?' or 'Let me make you a nice cup of tea.' Just that single statement, delivered with the unique blend of impatience and accusation she reserves especially for her children.

Your stepbrother's coming home today.

Thanks so much for the reminder. I mean, just for the teensiest fraction of a second, that fact actually slipped my mind.

Hours later, Mum's words continue to buzz around the inside of my skull like a fly attempting a fruitless exit through a closed window. I'm stretched out on the bed that's masquerading as mine, curtains drawn tight against the July afternoon, trying to bury myself in a *Peter Grant* novel…and failing spectacularly. Not even Aaronovitch's world of magical law enforcement can distract me from the frenetic banging and clattering echoing up the stairs. Mum's been on overdrive since the crack of dawn, dusting away every last cobweb and pursuing poor Buddy from room to room with the hoover, guzzling up any hairs he has the audacity to trail in his wake. Anyone would think she was tarting the house up for yet another prospective buyer rather than preparing to welcome the stepson she's never met.

I let the book slump onto my chest. Sunshine filters through the navy curtains, drenching everything in a watery haze. Until now, Ben hasn't existed for me in any real sense. He's been a name, an abstract concept that has no bearing on my life. Soon, though, he'll be here, reclaiming his territory, devouring the space with his living, breathing presence.

I shouldn't care; it isn't as if this room could ever feel like mine. All the same, it's been my sanctuary these past months, a place to escape, somewhere I could shut the door against the rest of the house and everyone in it.

I glower at the only photo in the room, posing centre stage on the top shelf of the bookcase. His features blur together in the dimness. Still, I imagine my stepbrother watching me, all blue eyes and broad smile. A prefect badge gleams on the lapel of his school blazer, and he's standing shoulder to shoulder with a group of equally wholesome-looking young men. No wonder Mum's half in love with him. Ben Willoughby has 'perfect son' written all over his sweet, freckled face.

I avert my gaze, reaching up to trace the bumpy metal train track that follows the curve of my ear. Each stud represents a tiny act of rebellion, a middle finger aimed at Mum's need for control.

A breeze nudges through the open window, bringing with it the sugary scent of baking. Would Mum be going to so much effort if it were me returning from a year backpacking in Australia? Hardly. If anything, she'd bribe the Aussie authorities into extending my visa. She certainly wouldn't be channelling Mary Berry, whipping up scones and lemon drizzle cake.

Not like she is for Ben. Ben, with his prefect badge and his let-me-kiss-your-arse smile. Ben, who didn't even come to the fucking wedding.

The bedroom door opens, and Buddy's head edges into view. As always, at the sight of this Old English Mastiff with his soulful eyes and lumbering walk, my heart thaws.

"Hey, Bud." He ambles over, tail wagging, and I scratch him behind his floppy ears. "That witch still on the prowl?"

Buddy pushes his nose into my hand in answer, then hauls himself onto the bed and collapses beside me with a long-suffering sigh. Pressed up against the wall, I run my fingers through his soft fur until his breathing turns to snuffling snores. Gradually, my resentment fades to a background itch. In the nine months since we moved into the Willoughby house, Buddy has been one of the few things that have made my fuck-up of a life bearable.

Our peace is short-lived. A determined tread sounds on the stairs a moment before Mum appears in the doorway.

"I thought I told you to sort out this mess." She crosses to lean over me, yanking open the curtains. "God, it's like a subterranean cave in here."

I throw up an arm to shield my eyes from the onslaught of sun and dazzling sky. Even the weather's pulled out all the stops to welcome my stepbrother home. Besides glaring at Mum from beneath my forearm, I don't respond. It's a game I play, seeing if I can endure an entire conversation with my mother without uttering a word. Entertainment's thin on the ground these days.

Mum's freshened herself up since her last spot check. She's the picture of polished efficiency, her bob newly highlighted and brushed to a light-brown sheen, the crisp linen of her dress devoid of creases. It isn't hard to see why Martin valued her so much as his personal assistant. So much, in fact, that he whisked her from under Dad's nose and married her.

Hands on hips, Mum assesses the damage in a sweeping glance. "You haven't even started, have you? This room is a disgrace."

I drop my arm, eyebrow raised. To hear her talk, you'd think the floor was littered with condoms and used needles rather than a few piles of books and discarded clothes.

"And what's that animal doing in here?" Mum rounds on me. "How often do I have to say this? No dogs on the beds."

She seizes Buddy by the collar and tugs. He lifts his head, fixing her with a reproachful stare, but otherwise refuses to budge.

"For heaven's sake!" Mum gives an almighty heave. "I've told Marty a thousand times. This dog is unmanageable. Come on. Off!"

With a weary harrumph, Buddy allows himself to be manhandled from the bed and over to the door. Mum shoos him onto the landing, then turns back to me, mouth set. "I mean it, Taylor, I want this lot tidied up. How do you think Ben will feel, coming home to find his room in such a tip?"

The look I shoot her is one of purest venom. I'm amazed it doesn't eat into the doorframe, causing the fresh paintwork to bubble and blister. *Ben's room.* Like I need reminding. Like I haven't spent every day since we moved in feeling like an intruder, a cuckoo in another family's nest. I could live here for a hundred years and it would never be home.

Mum goes to leave but can't resist a passing dig. "Oh, and take off that ridiculous make-up before Ben arrives. I want you to make a good impression."

Right. Wouldn't want me showing you up in front of the golden boy, would we?

Mum retreats onto the landing. I squash the urge to snatch up the bedside lamp and hurl it at her rigid back. Don't know how much more of this I can take. It isn't as though she's ever been the touchy-feely type, the sort of mother who spits on her thumb to wipe a smudge from your cheek, who swears she'll be proud of you no matter what. Just do your best. No, Mum's always had high standards, always obsessed over what others think, and since my parents' marriage imploded, I can't seem to do anything right. Not in her eyes. It's as if she blames me for everything that went wrong between her and Dad.

With Mum's last snipe smouldering like a discarded dogend in my belly, I launch myself off the bed and over to the chest of drawers. Here, I slap on an extra-thick layer of eyeliner and mascara. I started wearing it soon after Dad left, on the same day we found out we'd lost the house. It was just another way, along with the piercings and dark clothes, that I could show my mother—show the whole damned world—how pissed off I was. Then I discovered I liked it. I liked how it made me look, bold, defiant, until I fooled even myself.

"You are not," Mum said the first morning I sauntered into the kitchen with my eyes made up, "going to school like that. People will think you…that you're—"

"Gay? Well, that's good, because I am." I slammed out of the house, burning with vindictive triumph, blissfully unaware that this would be the last time I ever set foot there. Not the most tactful way I could've come out, but it did the job. Mum barely spoke to me for a week—a huge improvement, as far as I was concerned.

From downstairs, a key rattles in the lock. Imogen, back from school. Only my sister closes the front door with such careful quiet. If she hoped to slip in unnoticed, however, she's out of luck. I wince as Mum's voice carries up to me, berating Imogen for dumping her schoolbag in the hallway. A moment later, light footsteps climb the stairs and a door at the far end of the landing snaps shut.

I study my reflection in the mirror above the chest of drawers. A boy returns my stare, brows furrowed, purple bruises beneath shadowed eyes. I scarcely recognise him. With a shrug, I turn away and contemplate the mess, crumpled T-shirts strewn like mounds of ash amidst an avalanche of toppled books. I prod a few odd socks under the bed with my toe before losing interest. What's the point? When my stepbrother sees what Mum's done in here, my dirty underwear will be the least of his worries.

I slide my feet into flip-flops and head along the landing to tap on Imogen's door. I wait a beat, then crack it open. "Hey."

My sister's seated cross-legged on the floor, still wearing her school uniform, a jumble of cogs and screws spread out in front of her. She glances up, brushing the midnight curls away from her face, and offers me a small smile. I translate this as an invitation and advance into the room, squeezing past her in the cramped space. As the youngest, having turned thirteen in April, Imogen got lumbered with the boxroom. Not that she complained; she hardly ever does.

I perch on the edge of the bed and scan the electrical innards arranged on the carpet next to the toolkit Dad bought Imogen for her tenth birthday. "What're you working on?"

She flips over a flat metal plate, and I recognise the clock that usually sits on the mantelpiece in the living room. It looks old, ornate numerals picked out in gold on an ivory face. As far as I know, it hasn't worked since we've lived here.

Irritation sparks in my gut. "That's Martin's. What're you mending that for?"

Imogen sighs but doesn't bother telling me to give our stepdad a chance; we've been down that road too many times already. She simply tilts her head and fixes me with her dark eyes—the eyes we've both inherited from our Turkish dad. "Because it's broken."

For my sister, it really is that simple. Something's broken and she has the ability to mend it. If the only thing standing between her and death was the fact that her enemy's gun was in pieces, Imogen would put it back together. I don't think she could help herself.

"What about our family?" I want to demand sometimes. "Why can't you fix that? What about me?"

I flop onto her pillows and change the subject. "So, how was your day?"

Imogen shrugs, her attention on sorting through the various metal parts. "Double English."

I grimace in sympathy. It isn't that Imogen dislikes learning. Hell, from the moment she could talk, my sister has displayed a hunger for knowledge to rival that of Annabeth Chase. She's a genius problem-solver and consumes documentaries the way other people binge on reality TV. Also like Annabeth, though, she's dyslexic. She has always struggled to keep pace in lessons and tends to suffer in silence rather than speak up.

I fiddle with an embroidered daisy on the duvet cover. Mum's choice, not Imogen's. "Still, at least it got you out of the house. Mum's been a nightmare all day. You'd think she was expecting Wills and Kate to show up on the doorstep."

"He might be all right. Ben."

"What? With Abby for a sister?"

Imogen's mouth quirks in a sheepish grin. The reason she doesn't mind her relegation to the boxroom is that it saves her from having to share with our stepsister. If the girls had been forced to sleep within ten feet of each other, it would've been a race to see which of them could murder the other first.

Imogen goes back to sorting through the clock's intestines. "You never know."

I turn away to stare up at the ceiling. Maybe she's right. I might be judging Ben unfairly, branding him as the male equivalent of his goody-goody sister, although I doubt it. Either way, it doesn't matter. Mum might have thrown out her old family, upgraded to a pristine, bug-free version, but I want no part of it.

My chest constricts. I had a family once. Not a perfect family. It had cracks, sections of rickety boards that sagged and creaked when you put too much weight on them, but it was solid enough...or I thought it was. I certainly didn't expect a single blow to bring the whole structure crashing around us in a shower of disillusionment and fragmented dreams.

BEN

DAD'S WAITING FOR me in Arrivals, face half hidden behind a copy of the *Daily Mail*. At the sight of him sitting there, it hits me with a pang how much I've missed him. I've missed all of it—eating pizza in front of rubbish Saturday-night telly and playing elaborate drinking games with the lads before sleeping in till noon. I had to go, or that's how it felt. I needed to escape, to get far away from what happened.

Far away from him.

Dad glances up, gaze searching the eddy of tourists and home-comers. When he spies me weaving through the crowd, he immediately jumps to his feet, newspaper sliding to the floor. I push forward, swerving to avoid a rowdy family reunion. My heart bangs against my ribs. After everything, I can't be sure of my reception.

"You made it," Dad says when I'm a few feet from him. He closes the distance between us, arm outstretched. For a moment, I'm sure he's about to pull me into a hug. I actually go to return the gesture, but then he grasps my shoulder instead. "Good to see you. Flight OK?"

"Yeah, fine. Just long." I brush aside the sting of disappointment. Stupid. Dad's never been a hugger, not with me, and especially not since I came out to him and Mum when I was fifteen.

"Good, good." He releases me and steps back to give me the once-over. "You, uh, look well."

I seriously doubt it. After more than a day's travelling, of hanging around airport terminals and being crammed into a seat in economy, my eyes are gritty with exhaustion and a layer of sweat sticks my clothes to my skin. Then again, Dad's probably remembering how I looked when I left. Compared with the boy who boarded that plane twelve months ago—pale, shell-shocked, his heart in smithereens—I must seem a different person.

"Me?" My grin costs more effort than it should. "What about you?"

Dad's put on weight while I've been gone. His face is fuller, the buttons of his crisply ironed shirt straining against his stomach. It suits him.

He chuckles, more relaxed than I've seen him in…well, since Abby and I were little. "Ah, Lindy's taking good care of me."

I wince at his use of the pet name and swallow the bitter tang of resentment. How mean-spirited can I be? I should want Dad to be happy. I do want that. I just wish he could have been happy without tearing our family apart.

"Shall we get going then?" Dad asks, and we move towards the carousel.

Once I've been reunited with my trusty rucksack, scuffed and battered after our shared adventures, I follow Dad from the airport and out into the summer-afternoon warmth. I blink, momentarily dazzled. Only yesterday I bade farewell to the cool drizzle of a Melbourne winter. It feels much longer, another lifetime. While Dad tracks down the car—he always forgets where he's parked—I inhale great lungfuls of air. Even flavoured with tarmac and exhaust fumes, it tastes like home.

On the motorway, crawling through the Friday rush hour, there's nothing to distract from the awkwardness that has never wholly eased since I told Dad I was gay. It insinuates itself between us, as impossible to ignore as an unwelcome third passenger. Dad isn't homophobic; this is just something he can't relate to. He has no idea how to talk to me anymore.

He's trying, though, I'll give him that. He bridges the distance between us with small talk about Abby and the weather, and I summarise the plot of the Ben Affleck film I watched on the plane. We avoid any thorny topics—the chaos I left behind and what had sent me fleeing across the world. I'm pretty sure Dad blames himself, that he thinks the break-up was responsible for driving me away. It wasn't. Still, better he believes that than know the truth.

"How's Esmerelda?" I ask during a lull in the conversation. Thousands of miles away, I'd scarcely given a thought to the shadow-black Ford Fiesta my parents bought me for my seventeenth birthday. Now, after months of rattling bus journeys and hitching rides with friendly locals, I'm itching to get behind the wheel of my own car.

"Who?" Dad looks blank for a moment. "Oh, she's just as you left her. I've been starting her up every couple of weeks to keep her ticking over. I did wonder whether Taylor might want to borrow her while you were away. With your permission, obviously. He has his licence, and it seemed a shame to let a perfectly good car go to waste, but he, well, he didn't seem comfortable when I suggested it."

I turn to stare out of the window. The idea of some guy I've never met driving my precious Esme, flicking through the radio stations, using the footwell as a dumping ground for crisp packets and empty Coke cans, causes a twisting sensation in my gut.

After several more miles have passed in silence, Dad clears his throat. "Lindy's really looking forward to meeting you."

"Is she?" This seems unlikely, given my refusal to fly home for the wedding.

"Absolutely." His face lights up. "She's making your favourite fish pie to celebrate."

"That's nice of her." I cringe inwardly. If my stepmother's hoping to win me over, she's missed the mark. I haven't been able to stomach seafood since I ate a dodgy prawn vindaloo in Sidney and spent the night throwing up.

Perhaps Dad picks up on my scepticism because he says, "Lindy's been very good to me. To Abby, too. Give her a chance, eh?"

I stare out at the rolling fields, an expanse of impossible green beneath the brilliant sky. Dad knows I'm not the sort to make trouble. Failing to attend the wedding is the most rebellious thing I've ever done—unless you count deferring my uni place for a year while I took my backpack and shattered self-esteem along the Australian coast.

"Look," Dad continues as though following my train of thought, "about the wedding. Lindy said I shouldn't bring it up, but—"

"Dad," I cut in, then stop. What can I say? That I'm sorry I didn't stick around to watch him move another family into our home and marry his PA? But I'm not. It was no secret that my parents' relationship had been rocky for a while; the arguments and door slamming were somewhat of a giveaway. Still, until Linda came on the scene, a childish part of me believed they would work things out.

Dad saves me from having to answer. He swallows, the sound audible in the air-conditioned hush. "I just wanted you to know…I understand. We both do."

"Really?" Not the reaction I expected. I study his profile, searching for a sign that he means it.

A crease appears between his eyebrows. "You mustn't think I don't realise how hard this has been on you, on all of you, but I'm hoping we can put that behind us. Look to the future. As a family."

We already had a family, before you decided it wasn't good enough and traded it in for a newer model. I bite my tongue. Good old Ben. You can always count on him to keep the peace.

"So?" Dad darts me a tentative smile, his round face eager. "What do you say? Fresh start?"

Weariness drags at me, and I let my head loll against the seat. I wish things could have been different. I wish Dad had never appointed Linda Solomon as his personal assistant, that he hadn't been seduced by her efficiency and sexy filing system. But he had. This is how life is now, and wishing it otherwise won't change anything. Besides, it's only for one summer. I don't want to head off for uni on a sour note, not after the way I left last July.

"Yeah, fresh start."

Dad removes one hand from the wheel to pat my leg. "Good lad. I appreciate it."

We fall quiet again, although it feels like a less charged quiet. Dad switches on the radio, and something mellow and classical washes over us. I drift between dozing and gazing out at the changing scenery. We leave the motorway and enter the outskirts of Brookminster. The cathedral grows steadily nearer, its spire picked out against the cloudless blue. Familiarity mixed with nostalgia tugs at me.

Almost there.

As he steers the car into our road, Dad says, "Before we go in, I should probably warn you. Your stepbrother's been finding things somewhat...difficult."

I resist the urge to roll my eyes. Of course he has. He's lost his home and spent nine months living in another family's house. 'Difficult' hardly covers it.

"We're hoping," Dad adds, "Lindy and I, that you'll have better luck getting through to him, being close to his age and having...certain things in common."

Even after four years, Dad can't bring himself to discuss my sexuality outright. He prefers to skirt around it, if he's forced to mention it at all.

"I'm not expecting miracles," he assures me. "Just talk to him, see if you can help him settle in, all right?"

"Sure." I shrug, too busy drinking in the sight of my street to pay much attention to what I'm agreeing to.

Fairfield Avenue snoozes in the late-afternoon warmth, neat and orderly with its mown lawns and clipped hedges. It's a galaxy away from the haphazard impulsiveness of the past year. And there it is, the house I've lived in for most of my life.

Only...it isn't.

The moment Dad pulls into the driveway, its entrance marked by a large 'For Sale' sign, I'm flinging open the passenger door and clambering out. I scarcely register the stiffness in my limbs. I'm too busy staring at number twenty-four, struggling to reconcile what I'm seeing with the home I remember. Gone is the cherry-red front door, the terracotta pots overflowing with their riot of pansies and busy lizzies. Instead, fresh paintwork gleams a blinding white, and a pair of ornamental trees flank the front steps. If not for Esmerelda basking like a sleek, black cat in a patch of sunshine, I'd swear we've come to the wrong address.

Behind me, Dad cuts the engine and climbs from the car. I'm about to make some comment about the changes when a mass of brown fur hurtles around the corner of the house from the annex and collides with me, covering every millimetre of exposed skin in ecstatic kisses.

"Someone's glad to see you," Dad says, chuckling.

My heart swells. I thought Buddy might have forgotten me, but I should've known better. I hug him, laughing, not caring that he's knocked the wind out of me.

"Sweetheart, you're home!" Mum hurries after Buddy in a swirl of skirts, oblivious to the gravel beneath her bare feet. She holds out her arms, beaming. "Hey, you."

She pulls me close, enveloping me in a cloud of White Musk and wild curls, and squeezes the breath from my body.

"I've missed you so much," she says in a fierce whisper against my ear. "So, so much."

My throat closes. I bury my face in her shoulder, unable to speak. Seeing my mum after all this time, leaning into her the way I longed to when I was at my lowest, makes me realise more than anything else could have done just how homesick I've been.

In the midst of the activity, Dad retrieving my rucksack from the boot while Buddy leaps around us and generally gets in the way, I glance over Mum's head. My heart stumbles. A boy with spiky hair and an earful of piercings stands in the shade of the hedge, thumbs hooked through the belt loops of his jeans, watching us.

Taylor. I recognise him from the few wedding pics Dad sent me. Even through my numbness, I'd registered the fact that my stepbrother was attractive, albeit in a surly, unsmiling sort of way. Yet no photo could have prepared me for the sheer force of him. Every angle, every taut muscle oozes sensuality. I take in skintight denim sculpted to slender hips, the toned stomach peeping from beneath the hem of a black vest, the dark hollow at his throat. Finally, my gaze rests on his face, all cheekbones and stark beauty.

Mouth dry, I offer him a cautious smile. Taylor doesn't return it. His eyes meet mine, the expression in them leaving me in no doubt that he resents everything about me. Then, without a word, he turns and vanishes from view.

CHAPTER TWO

TAYLOR

WHEN WE FIRST moved into the house on Fairfield Avenue, I fully intended to avoid Martin's soon-to-be ex-wife. Not that I expected her to seek me out. It was my family who'd driven her from her home and into the annex, after all. I assumed she hated me. How could she not? Half the time I hated myself.

Then, on a drizzly Sunday morning in October, I escaped the house to go for a walk at the same time as a figure turned into the driveway. She was lugging a Pardo's carrier bag in each hand and her raincoat created a splash of crimson against the overcast sky. Shit. I pressed myself against the wall, trying to melt into the brickwork, and waited for her to pass.

Instead, she smiled without a hint of accusation and came over. "Hi, you must be Taylor. I'm Poppy."

I nodded, scuffing the gravel with the toe of my trainer. What was I supposed to say? *Yeah, that's me, the son of the woman currently swanning around your home like she owns the place.* God, let a sinkhole open up under my feet and drag me into its depths.

"Why don't you come in for a cuppa?" she asked. "Unless you have somewhere to be."

I didn't, but neither did I relish the prospect of a cosy chat with my mother's predecessor. On the other hand, between Mum's nagging and the daily torture school had become, it felt like forever since anyone had seemed pleased to see me.

"Uh, all right." I followed her around the side of the main house, where Poppy unlocked the door to the annex.

I hadn't given much thought to how Martin's wife might be living. If I had, I would have pictured somewhere lonely and bleak, a dreary bedsit bare of comforts. The open-plan room Poppy led me into was nothing like that. It was warm and bright with books everywhere and photographs on small side tables.

Poppy carried the shopping through to the kitchen area at the far end, refusing my offer to help put it away. "No, no. You make yourself comfortable and I'll pop the kettle on."

I still wasn't convinced I should be here, but I did as she said, perching on a sofa piled with velvet cushions in shades of coral and turquoise. A desk stood against the opposite wall, half buried beneath a computer and stacks of colourful notebooks.

"My work." Poppy glanced over to see me eyeing the clutter. "I write steamy romance novels. Well, when I'm not drinking tea and watching *Homes Under the Hammer*."

She flashed me a conspiratorial grin. If Poppy felt remotely awkward playing host to her husband's future stepson, she showed no sign. As she filled the kettle, she chatted easily about the insane queue at the supermarket and the adorable Boxer puppy she stopped to pet on her way back.

"And how are you settling in?" She handed me a steaming mug before sitting beside me.

I avoided her eyes and stared into my drink. This was precisely why I'd wanted to steer clear of her. If I told the truth, that I despised everything about living here, I'd sound like an ungrateful arse. If I lied, enthused over her beautiful home, I'd come off as tactless.

In the end, I merely shrugged. "OK."

"It must be hard," Poppy said gently. "This has been a massive upheaval for you."

I couldn't get my head around it, the fact that this woman, who had more cause than anyone to be resentful could find it in herself to be kind to me. Mum's idea of compassion was to tell me to stop whining and get on with it.

Indignation kindled in my chest—indignation on Poppy's behalf. "How can you stand it? If I were you, I'd loathe the sight of me."

"Don't be silly." She shook her head, fox-red curls falling across her face. "None of this is your fault. Things had been difficult between Martin and me for a while. I'd already moved into the annex to get away from the rows, so it's not as if you turfed me out."

"It can't be easy, though, us taking over your home."

"Not easy, perhaps, but I'm happy where I am for now, and you had nowhere else to go."

True enough. After my parents' marriage broke down, we were on the verge of homelessness. If Martin hadn't insisted we move in with him, we'd probably have ended up in a bed and breakfast. Still, I would've preferred that. Anything other than feeling like an interloper in someone else's family home.

"Besides," Poppy added, eyes twinkling, "if me being here makes Martin uncomfortable, that can only be a good thing. It'll encourage him to get his act together and sell the house."

SINCE THAT DAY, the annex has become my refuge. Whenever things pile on top of me, when Mum's criticism gets too much to bear, I head next door for a cup of tea and some sympathy. As well as listening to me rant, Poppy's been incredibly supportive of my ambition to work in publishing, and we've lost countless hours obsessing over books. Without those cosy chats, the two of us curled at either end of her squashy sofa, I think I would've lost my mind.

So, before Mum can start on at me again about the state of Ben's room, I steal downstairs and collect Buddy from his bed in the utility. We evade Mum, who's hoovering the living room for what must be the fourth time, and let ourselves out of the house. Buddy trots ahead of me, leading the way along the path to the door of the annex, which we find propped open with a stack of Jilly Coopers.

Poppy's seated in front of her computer, but she looks up with a smile as we approach. "Hello, lovely boys. Come on in."

Buddy ambles over to greet her, tail windmilling, but I hesitate on the threshold. "Sure we're not interrupting the literary masterpiece?"

"I wish." She sighs, closing the document she was working on. "I haven't got much done today. Can't concentrate."

Poppy turns to me, eyes shining. She might not be challenging Mum for the title of Domestic Goddess of the South East, but there's no mistaking her excitement. Jealousy, cold and hard, solidifies in the pit of my stomach. For the first time, it hits me that Poppy will have less space for me in her life once she has her own son home. Not that I blame her. I just don't know how I'll survive without this haven to escape to.

"I was going to put the kettle on," Poppy says, going through to the kitchen, "but I think I fancy something stronger. How about you?"

"Hell, yes." I collapse into my usual spot on the sofa. Immediately, Buddy clambers up beside me and sprawls across my lap. "Mum's being a fucking nightmare. 'Tidy your room, Taylor.' 'Take that ridiculous make-up off, Taylor.' 'Kindly stop breathing before you blow the air a millimetre out of place, Taylor.'"

I break off, embarrassed. Thoughtless prat. Like Poppy needs to hear about another woman getting ready to welcome her boy back from his travels.

She merely laughs, though, splashing Bacardi into two glasses and topping them up with Coke. "You're terrible. Your Mum wants to make a good impression, that's all."

I snort. Poppy returns with our drinks, handing me one, and I take a huge gulp. Of course Mum wants to make a good impression. That's all she cares about, what other people think. She has to be seen to be perfect at everything she does—the perfect PA, the perfect mother, the perfect wife.

"You'll like him, you know," Poppy says, sitting next to me. "Ben, I mean."

I nod, but only so as not to hurt her feelings. The fact is, if my stepbrother remotely resembles the Boy Scout in his photos, I doubt we'll hit it off. Not that it matters, seeing as I won't be getting to know him. If it's one lesson this past year has taught me, it's how fragile relationships can be. Families disintegrate and even the people you trust most in the world can toss you aside as easily as they would an empty Starburst wrapper.

I relax into the cushions. The rum begins to work its magic, draping my brain in a fuzzy blanket. I just need to make it through this last summer and then I'm out of here, off to London and university. If not for Imogen and Poppy and the great lump of a dog currently cutting off the circulation in my legs, I might never come back.

Unfortunately, Poppy knows me well enough by now to read my silences. When she speaks, her tone is soft and far too understanding. "Just give him a chance, OK? For me?"

The purr of an engine rescues me from making a promise I won't be able to keep. We swivel towards the window, and a moment later, early evening sunlight flashes off Martin's silver BMW. Faster than I've ever seen him move, Buddy bounds from my lap and out through the open door, barking madly.

"Oh, they're back." Poppy's on her feet at once, abandoning her barely touched drink on the floor. She beckons to me, face alight. "Come on. Come and say hello."

Without waiting for me to follow, nor even pausing to slip on her sandals, she races from the annex after Buddy. Shouts of welcome drift to me from the driveway, all jumbled up with laughter and ecstatic barks.

I have no desire to be part of this reunion. I slip outside, meaning to retreat unnoticed to the relative peace of the back garden. Yet, some masochistic urge draws me towards the group, and I hover in the shadow of the hedge to watch.

It's like witnessing some skewed re-enactment of *The Railway Children*, those closing pages where the train brings their father home unexpectedly and Bobby rushes to meet him, crying, "My daddy. Oh, my daddy."

Poppy has her arms around a tall young man with strawberry-blond hair, squeezing him so tight I'm amazed his ribs don't crack. They're both laughing, heedless of Buddy's attempts to bowl them over in his enthusiasm.

Envy gnaws at my stomach. I've seen enough. I'm about to creep away when Ben looks up. His eyes are bluer than they appear in his photos. They flicker over me, bright with interest, before grazing mine. Then he smiles at me—a smile of comradeship. It's like he thinks we're on the same side, that we're in this together.

We're not.

I rebuff his smile with my best blank stare. It's the visual equivalent of a ten-foot fence topped with barbed wire and a glaring NO TRESSPASSING sign. Ben's expression falters, and I harden my heart. It's better this way. Turning my back on the touching scene, I slink around the side of the house.

BEN

THIS IS ALL wrong.

After Dad closes the front door behind us, I simply stand there, thrown off balance. It's laid out the same, the L-shaped hallway with the stairs curving away to my right, and yet everything has changed.

Gone is the jumble sale of odds and ends—shoes, coats, umbrellas—that always filled the nook under the stairs. In their place is a swanky telephone table set with a brand-new cordless and a vase of lilies. Gone, too, is the cheerful wallpaper with its pattern of bright-yellow daffodils. The family photos and display of artwork dating back to Abby's and my nursery days have been taken down, and the sole decoration relieving the off-white walls is a mirror in a brass frame. My own face stares out at me from the glass, confused and disorientated.

I should've expected this. I knew my parents had agreed to sell the house as part of their divorce settlement. Dad told me during one of our rare phone calls that Linda was helping him spruce the place up ready to put on the market. Still, none of that prepared me for the shock of barely recognising my own home. It even smells different. That indefinable, utterly familiar scent is buried beneath the sweetness of baking and the cloying fragrance of the flowers.

A woman hurries around the corner from the kitchen, smoothing her bob behind her ears. In her cream dress and pearl earrings, my stepmother is every bit as perfectly groomed as she was in her wedding photos. She might be on her way to a royal garden party.

"Ben, welcome home. I'm Linda. It's wonderful to meet you." She embraces me, all sharp angles and floral perfume.

It takes everything in me not to flinch. I'm nowhere near ready for this level of intimacy, not with this woman I've barely met. Perhaps I never will be. All the same, I force myself to return the hug. "Thanks. You, too."

Linda releases me and turns to Dad. "Good day, darling?"

"Not bad. Busy." He smiles at her. "Miss having you there to keep me in line."

"Oh, shush." She waves his words away, although her cheeks grow pink under his gaze. He's looking at her with such tenderness that my insides squirm, as though I've stumbled in on a private moment.

God, I'm itching to escape to my room, if only for a few minutes. I reach to take my rucksack from Dad. "Here, I'll dump my stuff upstairs."

"Oh, don't worry about that," Linda says. "You must be worn out after your flight. One of the others will do it. When they finally get themselves down here, that is." She moves past me to the foot of the stairs. "Girls! Taylor! Ben's home."

"Really, they don't—" I start to say, then stop.

My sister appears on the landing, hair pulled into a strawberry-blonde ponytail, tanned legs emerging from the navy-blue pleats of her school skirt. When did she get so grown up? The gangly fourteen-year-old I left behind a year ago has morphed into this graceful, long-limbed beauty who looks far older than fifteen. Abby saunters down the first few stairs, the picture of cool, before she drops the pretence and hurtles the rest of the way into my arms.

"Hey." I squeeze her tight, inhaling a combination of sun cream and citrus shampoo. She's softer than I remember, as though the past months have sanded her rough edges. "Wow, I think you actually missed me."

"Yeah, like a face full of pimples." Abby retreats a pace, rolling her eyes in a superb display of disdain.

I laugh and tug her ponytail. "Oy, you'd better be nice to me, otherwise the present I bought you will mysteriously end up on eBay."

"You wouldn't dare." She gasps in mock horror, then leans up to hiss directly into my ear. "If you ever disappear like that again, I'll hunt you down wherever you are and drag you straight back home."

Too choked to speak, I can only smile. Abby cuffs me on the shoulder, returning my smile, and it all comes flooding back—the teasing, the late-night confidences, the bickering when one of us used the last of the hot water. How could I have stayed away for so long?

"Imogen, there you are," Linda says, a bite of impatience in her voice.

I look up to see a girl of around twelve or thirteen descending the stairs, her bare feet soundless on the plush carpet. My stepsister hesitates a few steps from the bottom, dark eyes peering through a thicket of curls. She has a smudge of something that could be grease on the end of her nose.

"Here." Linda relieves Dad of my rucksack and thrusts it at her. "Take this up to the boys' room and tell Taylor to come down. Oh, and wash your face while you're at it. You're filthy."

If Imogen minds being treated like a hotel porter, she doesn't show it. She merely accepts the rucksack, darts me a shy glance, and slips back upstairs without a word.

Linda turns to me with a warm smile, irritation evaporated. "Come through to the garden, and I'll make us a cup of tea. Then you can tell us all about your adventures."

There are several things I'd like to do right now. I'd like to stand under a hot shower until every atom of dirt and sweat has swirled away down the plughole. I'd like to crawl into bed, luxuriate in the sensation of smooth sheets and plump pillows after a year sleeping in hostel bunks. Most of all, I'd like to run from this house that no longer feels like mine and seek refuge with Mum in the annex.

Of course, I don't do any of that. For one thing, Dad's casting me a warning look as if he can sense I'm about to bolt. For another…well, I suppose I really am a good little boy at heart. Be polite. Don't cause trouble. Keep your head down and go with the flow, no matter how strong the urge to fight against the current.

The image of my stepbrother flashes into my mind, the way he watched me from the shadow of the hedge, arms crossed, face belligerent. I saw him for only a few seconds, but I got the distinct impression Taylor Solomon would have no qualms about rocking the boat. He'd rock it so violently the whole damned thing would capsize, sending everyone crashing into the turbulent waters. I envy him.

In the kitchen, the whiff of smoked haddock has my gut churning. Again, my stepmother's handiwork screams at me from every direction, but I'm allowed only a fleeting glimpse of white gloss and gleaming chrome before she leads us out into the garden.

I pause on the back step, savouring the smell of grass and sun-baked earth. Here, at last, is something familiar. True, the lawn is tidier than usual, but Mum's always been a keen gardener, and the rainbow of colour spilling from every border is all her.

Linda tells us to take a seat, then disappears once more into the kitchen. The plastic furniture that's been a permanent fixture on our patio for as long as I can remember has vanished, replaced with a posh wooden set beneath a striped umbrella. We pull out chairs at the table, and Abby entertains us with a story about a girl in her science class who'd accidentally set fire to her textbook, until my stepmother re-emerges bearing a laden tray.

"Lindy, that looks delicious." Dad eyes a golden sponge, glistening with icing and oozing lemon juice.

"Oh, well." Linda beams as she unloads a plate of scones, pots of jam and clotted cream, and a china teapot with matching milk jug. "I wanted to do something a little special. Tea, Ben?"

"Thanks." I shift in my chair. She really didn't have to go to all this trouble. Not for me. Maybe I'm being ungrateful. It's just that this all feels kind of over the top, as if we've landed on the set of *Downton Abbey*.

I accept a slice of cake, trying not to imagine how different this homecoming would have been if Mum and Dad were still together, the jokes and easy laughter. Instead, I'm on my best behaviour. I answer Linda's endless questions, giving her the censored version of my year abroad—mixing cocktails in beachside bars and picking bananas on a farm in Tully, snorkelling with whale sharks off the West Coast and watching the sunset over Sidney Harbour.

"What an incredible experience," she gushes, "and so brave to do it all by yourself."

I focus on chewing my mouthful of sponge, the lemony sweetness bursting on my tongue. Linda's admiration could be genuine, or she might be laying on the charm thicker than the cream Dad's piling on his scone. Either way, she wouldn't be looking at me with such approval if she knew the whole story.

"You've missed out the most important part," Abby says, as though reading my thoughts. "What about the hot boys? Bet there were tons."

I grin, nudging her knee with mine. "More than even you'd know what to do with. All those bronzed surfer's bodies...you would've been in heaven."

Abby slumps onto the table in a dramatic swoon, and I snort into my tea. She's insanely bright, my sister, Oxbridge level bright. Focused, too. She's wanted to be a barrister ever since becoming addicted to *Silk* on BritBox. Yet even with all her drive and after-school study groups, she finds the energy to fall in and out of love at least twice a month.

Abby's eyes, hazel like Mum's, gleam with excitement. "We'll have to rethink our pre-uni summer trip. Lauren wants to go to Thailand, but I'm sure I can persuade her to do Australia instead. Or maybe we can fit in both."

"In your dreams," Dad says, reaching for a second scone. "If you're lucky, I'll let you go to Eastbourne for the weekend."

"Dad!" Abby sits up with a cry of outrage.

"Humour him, darling." Linda leans across the table, voice lowered to a stage whisper. "You know your father can't cope with the idea of his little girl growing up."

"I heard that." Dad's doing his best to sound stern, but the twinkle in his eyes gives him away.

My sister and stepmother share a complicit glance. All at once, I feel like an outsider. I hadn't expected this, that Abby might have bonded with Dad's new wife. Stupid, really. It isn't as if she and Mum have ever been close. Abby's too organised, too grounded in the real world to have much patience with Mum's dreamy abstraction. Still, my mouthful of sponge takes on a bitter tang.

Imogen appears like a shadow at my shoulder. I hadn't heard her approach. With a mother like Linda, perhaps you learn not to draw attention to yourself. She snags a chunk of cake and moves around the table to sit next to Dad.

"Plate," Linda snaps. She plucks one from the stack, sliding it across to Imogen in time to catch the shower of crumbs. "Where's Taylor?"

Imogen shrugs, her mouth full of lemon drizzle. Her expression remains untroubled. She must be so used to her mum's nagging that she no longer hears it.

"For heaven's sake." Linda bats at a wasp buzzing around the jam. "I asked you to fetch him. If he thinks he can skulk in his room all evening—"

"He wasn't there." Imogen cuts her off mid-rant. The wasp lands on her forearm, and she studies it with mild curiosity.

"What do you mean, he wasn't there? Where else would he be? I'm so sorry about this, Ben." Linda turns to me, cheeks flushed. "I specifically told Taylor to be here, but he must've slipped out behind my back."

"Really, it doesn't matter." My gaze flickers to the shed at the end of the garden. I have a pretty good idea where my stepbrother's hiding. No one but me noticed him on the driveway—or saw him retreat along the path to the side gate. If he didn't enter the house through the back door, there's only one place he can be. However, Taylor made it clear he wants nothing to do with Linda's little tea party, and I have no intention of giving him away.

CHAPTER THREE

TAYLOR

A T THE END of the Willoughbys' garden, between the shed
and the yew hedge that backs onto the house behind,
there's a strip of concrete, barely eighteen inches across. It's
where I come whenever I need to escape but don't have the
energy to walk the streets. Not the most comfortable hideout,
but it's peaceful.

I've spent hours out here over the past months, wooden slats
sheltering me on one side, dense foliage on the other, while the
wind rustles the leaves and distant traffic whooshes by on the
Brookminster Road. Normally, I can lose myself in the stillness.
I'll let my thoughts wander and simply…be. Not today.

I lie on the hard ground, arms cushioning my head, and glare
up at the slice of pastel sky. What was I thinking? I should've
lurked around the side of the house while everyone was on the
drive, then crept out once they went indoors. Instead, in my
haste to avoid the reunion, I've landed myself a prime spot to
overhear the entire disgusting charade.

The breeze picks up, carrying snatches of conversation
to me from the patio. I try to tune them out, but they worm
their way into my ears—Mum spewing platitudes over
Ben's tales of Australia, laughing with Abby about Martin's
overprotectiveness. Was she ever this relaxed, so full of

unquestioning approval, with Imogen and me? Maybe, when we were little. I don't remember.

As if to prove my point, Mum's tone sharpens. "For heaven's sake, I asked you to fetch him. If he thinks he can skulk in his room all evening—"

"He wasn't there," Imogen says.

"What do you mean, he wasn't there? Where else would he be? I'm so sorry about this, Ben. I specifically told Taylor to be here, but he must've slipped out behind my back."

Good. If Mum believes I've gone out, she won't send anyone to search for me. I'm safe, at least for now.

After an eternity of mindless talk, Mum announces that she needs to put the dinner in the oven, and gradually the others follow her inside. Quiet settles over the garden. Still I don't move, reluctant to face the inevitable interrogation. I stay where I am, listening to the pigeons coo to one another and the delighted shrieks of children from down the street.

I must have drifted into a doze. When my eyes flutter open, the sun has gone in and the sky deepened to a hazy mauve. Goosebumps skitter over my skin like the legs of a hundred tiny insects, and there's a figure blocking the gap between the shed and the hedge.

"Thought you might be here," Ben says.

I blink at him through a fog of drowsiness. From my supine position, he appears much taller than he had on the driveway so that he seems to tower over me. I struggle to sit up, wincing at the soreness in my back and shoulders. Why did he have to catch me like this, at such a disadvantage? Come to that, how had he even known where to find me?

Ben must sense my unspoken question because he raises an eyebrow. "Come on. I've lived in this house since I was five. You think I've never hidden back here to avoid a telling off?"

"I'm not hiding." Fuck, I sound like a petulant child. My face heats. I draw my knees to my chest, wrapping my arms around them.

"Whatever." Ben runs a hand through his hair. It sticks up in damp spikes, and he gives off the clean scent of musk and sandalwood. "Just don't feel you have to shut yourself away on my account. I promise I'm not that scary."

He smiles at me, a hesitant smile free of judgement. My stomach pitches as though I've plunged several floors in a fast-moving lift. That's what I get for not eating since breakfast. I regard him in stony silence. Damn him for being so bloody nice. He's hot, too, much less preppy than in his photos, his hair shaggier, his arms more muscled. Damn him to the fiery depths of Mount Doom.

When I don't respond, Ben's smile fades. His gaze drops. "Anyway, thought I'd tell you dinner's almost ready. It's none of my business, but your Mum'll probably burst a blood vessel if you don't show."

He turns and walks away, leaving me to glower after him. I punch a fist into the concrete; pain shoots across my knuckles. Shit. Ben had wrong-footed me, ambushed me when I was half asleep and scrambling to form a coherent thought. He must think me incredibly immature, a kid playing hide-and-seek.

Well, so what?

If Ben weren't my stepbrother, if we'd met at a club or while I was walking Buddy, I might've checked him out. He would've offered me that same hopeful smile, and rather than rebuffing him, I'd have flashed my most charming grin. As it is...

One last summer and I'm out of here.

These words have kept me going, kept me sane, since my life went to hell. Now, they give me the strength to push myself to my feet and brush the grit from my jeans. Then, squaring my shoulders, I stroll out from behind the shed and up the garden path.

The moment I enter the kitchen, the reek of smoked haddock punches me in the face. Mum drops a colander of broccoli into the sink with a clatter and rounds on me. "Where do you think you've been?"

"Out." The single syllable scrapes my parched throat. I saunter past her, heading for the fridge.

Abby's seated at the kitchen table, a sheet of newspaper spread out in front of her, painting her nails the same baby-pink as her sleeveless top. She smirks at me through a shining curtain of hair. My stepsister never seems to tire of watching Mum lay into me.

"How dare you show me up like that?" Mum pursues me across the room, keeping her voice low. "I expressly told you to be here to welcome your stepbrother. How must it have looked to Ben, you disappearing like that, no one knowing where you were? I can't remember when I've been more embarrassed."

Really? Let me help you out. It would've been the last time I did something that insulted your idea of how I should behave. That's my sole reason for existing, after all, to be an utter embarrassment of a son.

Feigning deafness, a feat I've become expert in over the years, I grab a bottle of water from the fridge and lean against the worktop. The first ice-cold mouthful quenches my thirst, although it does little to soothe the burning resentment.

"Well, I'm disgusted with you, that's all I can say." Mum turns away as though looking at me causes her physical pain. "And don't you even think about disappearing again. I'm about to dish up so Abby can eat before she goes out."

I snort into my drink. Like I need reminding that my world now revolves around Mum's new family. Ben's favourite meal. Abby's social life. The combined stench of fish and nail varnish has my gut roiling, and I take another gulp of water.

Mum goes back to straining the broccoli. She glances over at Abby, features softening. "That's a gorgeous colour, darling."

"Thanks. I bought it the other day to go with my outfit. I'll paint your nails tomorrow before we go shopping if you like."

"Ooh, would you? I thought we could grab some lunch while we're out, make a proper day of it."

Who is this woman? The one who gossips with Abby over mugs of coffee while the two of them flip through fashion magazines. It certainly isn't the same person who raised Imogen and me. Then again, Abby's like a younger version of Mum, so maybe it's no surprise they get on so well. I doubt anyone would believe they aren't actually related.

Ben wanders in from the hall, pausing when he sees me. Wariness steals into his expression, though his tone is friendly enough. "Hey. Imogen was just showing me her DVD collection. She's an even bigger Brian Cox fan than I am."

I twist my bottle around and around in my hands, watching the way the liquid sloshes against the sides. So, Imogen's decided to become a fully paid-up member of Team Ben. She's finding it far easier to adjust to this new situation than I am. Still, that's for the best. Knowing my sister will be OK means I don't have to feel guilty about my desperation to leave.

"Need me to lay the table or anything?" Ben asks Mum. The suck-up.

She beams at him. "That's sweet of you, darling, but everything's done. Would you tell your Dad and Imogen to sit up?"

Ben nods, and a moment later, his voice carries along the hallway as he calls up the stairs for Martin to come down. Mum smiles after him, stars practically dancing in her eyes. She must think she's won the fucking lottery marrying Martin—big house, a husband who wouldn't dream of cracking inappropriate jokes during a dinner party, and the kind of children she's always wanted.

I can't do this. I can't sit at the dinner table, forcing down forkfuls of revolting fish pie with this family I never asked to be a part of. Tossing my empty water bottle into the recycling bin, I head for the back door.

Mum's hand shoots out to seize my arm. "And where are you off to?"

"Out," I say, shrugging from her grasp.

The fact is, I don't know. Maybe I'll stop by KFC, commandeer my favourite park bench, and eat my way through an entire bucket of chicken. Or maybe I'll find a secluded corner of a pub garden and, anonymous in the Friday-night crowd, drink myself into a stupor. I don't care, so long as I'm anywhere but here.

"Taylor Solomon." Mum's tone holds all the lethal intent of a poisoned blade. "If you take one step out that door—"

"You'll what? Ruin my life? Newsflash, Mum, you already have." And before she can stop me, I'm out of the house and through the side gate, hightailing it into the dusk.

BEN

"So, WHOSE PARTY is it?" I ask Abby as we head onto the driveway to wait for her lift.

She perches on the low wall facing the street. "Lauren's brother's. It's his eighteenth, and Thomas said she could invite a few friends. Don't tell Dad, will you? He wouldn't approve."

I sit beside her, listening while she catches me up on all the little dramas in her life—Lauren's break-up with her boyfriend of fifteen months, Michaela's disastrous attempt to bleach her hair, the afternoon Hannah got her tongue pierced for a dare. As Abby talks, I'm hit with a wave of nostalgia for the normality of it all, the routine of school and homework, parties and hanging out with friends. Even before I fled to Australia, I'd missed out on so much of that, shunned it in favour of secrecy and illicit encounters.

I thrust the thought away. No point picking over my mistakes, wishing I'd done things differently. I force myself to focus on the here and now, on being home, sitting with my sister in the lavender warmth of a July evening.

"You and Linda seem very chummy." I mean to sound offhand, but accusation creeps into my tone.

Abby nudges my shoulder. "Linda's all right once you get to know her."

I scuff my foot back and forth on the pavement. My stepmother seems nice enough. She certainly couldn't have been more welcoming. Still, I can't shift that sense of wrongness, the resentment at having a strange woman in our house where Mum should be.

"She's just…a bit much."

"She wants you to like her, that's all. She'll calm down. And look how happy she makes Dad."

It hurts to admit it, but she's right. The last years of my parents' marriage were fraught. Dad spent them in a permanent state of anxiety, shouting at Mum whenever she got so caught up in her fictional worlds that she forgot to take his suits to the dry cleaner's. The time she dyed his best white shirt pink after accidentally putting it in the wash with her red scarf, they didn't speak for three days. It's easy to see how this clutter-free life with its sparkling surfaces would suit him.

"Ah, there's Hannah's mum." Abby slides from the wall, smoothing her skirt, and hurries to meet the white Lexus as it pulls up to the kerb. Before joining her friends in the back seat, she tosses me a wave over her shoulder. "Enjoy your night in. Don't wait up."

I stick my tongue out at her, and she giggles. Once the car has rounded the corner onto the Brookminster Road, I get up and make my way around the side of the house to the annex. The door stands open in welcome. I pause on the threshold, blinking.

It was once a garage, but when Granddad Howes died and Nana was struggling to cope with being alone, my parents had the space converted into a self-contained flat. In the last years of Nana's life, the large kitchen/living room had burst with her familiar things—the cut-glass fruit bowl that was always stocked with pears and satsumas; the vases of tulips and sunny daffodils on their lace doilies; the toby jug Abby refused to look at because it gave her the creeps.

After Nana passed away, the annex became a games room where my mates and I would play Xbox and drink forbidden cans of Foster's. Now, I hardly recognise it. I'd known Mum was living here, of course; she'd retreated to the annex more and more in the weeks before I left. Still, ten thousand miles away, I found it impossible to picture. I exhale. The tightness that has been coiled around my insides all evening relaxes its hold. This cheerful collection of rugs and patchwork throws, ornaments and books, feels far more like home than the show house next door.

I cross to the kitchen area where Mum's forearm-deep in washing-up water. The draining board displays all the evidence of a single life—one plate, one bowl, one set of cutlery. A pang twists my stomach. All through dinner, while I choked down second helpings of fish pie and Linda disguised her annoyance at Taylor's absence beneath a layer of chatter, I was conscious of Mum bare metres away. I imagined her eating alone on the other side of the wall and felt like a traitor.

"Hey, sweetheart." Mum smiles at me, drying her hands on a tea towel. "I was just about to make a coffee."

Once we're curled on the sofa with mugs of instant, she insists I fill her in on the highlights of my trip. Unlike the edited version I gave Linda, I recount all the best bits—the beach parties that began in the late afternoon and went on till dawn; skinny-dipping in a cannabis-induced haze; one-night stands with young men from as far afield as Torquay and Tallahassee. Mum absorbs my words with the same entranced expression she gets whenever she has inspiration for a new story.

"And did you meet anyone special?" she asks. "Some gorgeous Aussie desperate for you to move into his seafront apartment?"

"No, no one special." I look away, down into my empty mug. Those first months in Australia, I was too heart sore and homesick to think about getting involved with anyone. I don't say any of that, though. I can talk to Mum about almost anything, but not about that.

She leans in to me, resting her shoulder against mine. "Much as the romantic in me loves the idea of you being swept off your feet, I'm glad you won't be going to live on the other side of the world."

"Yeah, me too." And it's true. For the first time since that afternoon when Dad and I pulled into the driveway, I really feel as though I've come home.

Mum gets up to make more coffee. When she returns with our mugs, I take mine from her, searching her face for any hint of strain or unhappiness. I don't find it.

"You OK?" I don't say *with Dad's new wife playing lady of the manor*, but Mum's wry smile tells me she heard my unspoken question.

She sits back beside me, tucking her legs beneath her. "I'm fine, sweetheart. It's made a nice change, actually, being able to please myself. I can write whenever I like without worrying I'll forget to put the dinner on or take the washing out of the machine. And of course, Abby's just next door, and Taylor stops by most days for a cuppa and a chat."

Mum's face softens when she mentions my stepbrother. An image scrolls across my vision—Taylor seated right where I am now, chatting with Mum over endless mugs of tea, filling the space my absence had created. Scalding fingers squeeze my chest. Like I have any right to be jealous. After all, I was the one who left.

"He's good company," Mum continues, oblivious to the petty struggle going on inside me. "He lends me books, lets me bounce plot ideas off him."

"Really?" I can't keep the scepticism from my voice. It's hard to imagine the surly boy I'd discovered skulking behind the garden shed being anything other than hostile.

"Really." Mum grins, expression knowing. "He can come across as a bit…prickly at first, but give him a chance. He might surprise you."

It's late when I finally leave the annex. Despite being worn out after the events of the day, I was reluctant to tear myself away from Mum. Eventually, though, I lost the battle to keep my eyes open and admitted defeat.

When I let myself in through the front door, the house is quiet save for the murmur of the TV. I poke my head into the living room where Dad's watching Sky News. "Hey, Dad. Abby home yet?"

"Ah, there you are." He blinks a few times as though waking from a doze. "Your sister got back a little while ago and went straight to bed. Said she was tired. I hope she hasn't been drinking. She seemed a bit odd, cagey."

Given that it was an eighteenth birthday party, I'd bet the whole lot of them were drinking, including Abby. Still, Dad doesn't need to know that.

"Don't worry about Abs. She's way too sensible." I stifle a yawn. "I'm going to head up. Night, Dad."

It's all I can do to drag myself up the stairs to my room. Only…it isn't just my room anymore. It's our room, mine and Taylor's. My bed—the big, cushiony double I've been fantasising about since I got off the plane—has vanished, along with my

Star Wars posters. If not for my collection of DVDs arranged on the bookcase and a few athletics trophies on the top shelf, I could be anywhere.

Taylor has returned from wherever he's been all evening. He's propped up in the bed under the window, reading by the glow of the bedside lamp, yet another of Linda's additions.

"Hey." I push the door shut and sink onto the end of my new single bed.

Taylor nods without looking up from his book. Well, I didn't really expect a response. It's tempting to give up, but I remember Mum's words of earlier. She's clearly fond of my stepbrother. There must be more to him than this silent animosity.

"What're you reading?" I try. Not that I'm much of a reader. I've scarcely opened a novel since we read *Of Mice and Men* for GCSE English, but judging by the pile of books on the bedside cabinet, this seems like a good conversation starter.

Without glancing at me, Taylor holds up the book to show me the title. *Foxglove Summer*.

Still clueless, I ask, "Any good?"

"Yeah." He lowers the book again and turns a page, all without raising his head.

So much for that.

The softness of the mattress calls to me. All I want is to crawl fully clothed under the covers and sleep till the following afternoon. With an effort, I push myself to my feet and start to undress. As I strip down to my boxers, I sneak a peek at the beautiful, belligerent boy framed in the lamplight. Though he puts on a good performance of being engrossed, the tension in his shoulders betrays him.

"I know it must be weird," I say. "Me being here, I mean, after you've had this space to yourself."

At last, Taylor looks at me. His eyes appear vulnerable without their shield of make-up, and the shadows beneath them stand out like bruises against his light-brown skin. "Whatever. It's your room."

My gaze takes in the oil slick of black T-shirts spilling from the laundry basket, the tubes of eyeliner and mascara on the chest of drawers. I shake my head. "I think it's safe to say this is our room now."

Taylor's expression, already unreadable, goes utterly blank. Without a word, he returns to his book.

I huff out a breath. I'm way too tired for my stepbrother right now. Pulling aside the covers, I collapse into bed. After a year of sleeping on hostel mattresses, the luxury of cotton sheets and downy pillows is as close to heaven as I can imagine. I roll onto my side, facing away from Taylor. At once, sleep begins to draw me under. My parents might be keen for me to give my stepbrother a chance, but that can wait. We have the whole summer, after all.

Something tells me it will be a long one.

CHAPTER FOUR

TAYLOR

I ROLL OVER, REACHING for my phone to check the time. 5:58. Shit. I'll have to get ready for work in an hour. No point trying to go back to sleep. Doubt I could, even if I wanted to. I haven't slept well since we moved in here. It's hard to relax when you feel so completely out of place in what's meant to be your bedroom and damned near impossible with the legitimate owner of that bedroom snoring in the next bed.

I sit up, rubbing the grit from my eyes. Pale light seeps through a chink in the curtains. The other bed is empty, the duvet flung aside to reveal rumpled sheets. Ben must be in the bathroom. Determined to be gone by the time he gets back, I hurry into my running shorts and an old vest, unearth my trainers from behind the laundry basket, and creep along the landing.

The moment I reach the foot of the stairs, Buddy pads out of the kitchen to join me, expression hopeful. I crouch to pat him. "Sorry, Bud, not now. I'll take you for an extra-long walk after work, OK?"

He licks my cheek in forgiveness. I scratch him under the chin before pulling on my shoes and getting to my feet. When I open the front door, I almost fall over someone perched on the top step.

Ben looks up from tying his trainers, eyes widening. "Uh, hey. What're you doing up?"

"Could ask you the same thing." After all, he's the one who's just flown across the world.

"Body clock's up the creek. Woke up and couldn't drop off again."

I don't respond, didn't come out here to talk. No one else was even supposed to be awake. I lower myself onto the bottom step, careful to keep an arm's length between us, and tighten my laces.

"Thought I may as well go for a run," Ben says. "Usually helps me relax. You, too?" His gaze takes in my running gear.

I lift one shoulder in a half shrug; my clothes speak for themselves. Standing, I fish my iPod from my pocket and start up the driveway.

"Taylor?"

I pause, turning. Ben's got to his feet, arms hooked behind his head in a stretch. Christ, he's in good shape, far more built than in his photos. I noticed as much last night while he undressed. What was it he told Mum he'd been doing in Oz? Picking bananas? Well, it's certainly done wonders for his physique. I'm already checking him out when I remember he's off limits. Hastily, I peel my gaze from his long legs, the muscles rippling beneath bronzed skin, only to get an eyeful of his biceps. Warmth flares in my cheeks. I stare down at my iPod, fiddling with it in a show of disinterest. Why does he have to be so fucking attractive?

"Mind if I run with you?" Ben asks. If Buddy could talk, he'd sound something like my stepbrother, all good-natured eagerness. "Since we're both out here."

"Whatever," I tell him, although I do mind. I mind a lot and curse myself for not saying as much. If it had been anyone else, I would have, but Ben's genuine friendliness is making it far harder to keep my distance than I expected.

Pathetic.

I turn and break into a run, not waiting to see if Ben decides to follow. He draws level with me a short way along Fairfield. I focus straight ahead, attempting to lose myself in the rhythmic thud of my trainers on the pavement. It's a perfect morning, the air crisp and fresh. Translucent threads of sunlight trail from a sky the colour of washed-out denim. Without slowing, I slip my earphones in and attach my iPod to my waistband.

Before I can switch it on, Ben makes another stab at conversation. "Any plans for your day, besides getting up at the crack of dawn?"

I let out a frustrated breath. He really doesn't know when he's fighting a losing battle. I keep my hand on my iPod, hoping he'll get the hint. "Working."

"Oh, right. Where do you work?"

"The Inkwell."

"The bookshop on the high street? Makes sense."

What? Because you've shared a room with me for one night and now know everything about me? Not that he's wrong. When I trawled the high street in search of a summer job, The Inkwell was my first choice. I've lost whole afternoons over the years among its shelves, feeding my insatiable appetite for stories. The family-owned store has often been my refuge, especially these past months.

I increase my pace, rounding the corner onto the Brookminster Road. It's quiet this early on a Saturday, only the occasional car zipping by towards the city centre. My feet pound the concrete and send a tingling ache up my calves. If my curtness won't convince Ben to abandon this pointless exercise, perhaps I can simply shake him off.

He matches my stride without visible effort. "You're good. Were you on the athletics team at school? Where did you go, by the way? Not Bhelmead."

This statement, tossed out with such certainty, immediately gets my back up. No, my parents didn't earn enough to send Imogen and me to private school, but Dad wouldn't have let us go even if they had. He's never agreed with paid education; it's one of the many things he and Mum argued about.

"The grammar," I tell him, my tone flat.

"Ah, yeah. I would've remembered if I'd seen you around at school. You're a bit of a brainiac then."

"No need to sound so surprised."

"I...I'm not." Ben falters. It's the first time he's appeared rattled. I accept it as a victory, however small. He sucks in an audible breath. "Anyway, you must've been on the athletics team."

"Nope."

"You're kidding."

"Sure, I can hardly speak for laughing." Enough with the fucking inquisition. My finger hovers next to my iPod. All I want is to drown myself in some mindless techno and forget everything for a while.

"But that's crazy," Ben says, panting slightly. "My coach at Bhelmead would've snapped you up. Did you not try out?"

I don't dignify this with a response. The truth is, up until a few weeks into my final year, I was on the athletics team. If I hadn't been, I might never have met Liam Knowles and these past months would've played out very differently. Why my stepbrother thinks this is any of his business, though, is beyond me.

"For God's sake." Ben skids to a halt. "What is it with you?"

It's so tempting to keep running, to put on a spurt and leave him coughing up dust, but I resist. Since Ben flatly refuses to take the hint, I'll have to spell it out, lay down the ground rules in a way not even he can misunderstand. I slow to a stop and spin to confront him, arms folded.

"I'm doing my best here." Ben glares at me. "Can't you meet me halfway?"

I glare back. The sunlight picks out the freckles dusting his nose and catches the red in his hair so that it gleams like gold shot through with copper.

"Here's the deal," I say. "Neither of us asked for this, and I sure as hell didn't want it. So how about you leave me alone and I'll do the same for you?"

Ben flinches as though I've slugged him across the face. Then his expression hardens. "Fine. If that's what you want."

"It is."

"Fine." Without another word, he moves past me and continues jogging along the road.

Guilt, sharp and unexpected, jabs me in the ribs. I brush it off and hurry after him. It would've been easier to go home, but these morning runs help clear my head and keep me sane. We jog side by side, the silence stretched taut between us, until we reach the next intersection. Then, by unspoken agreement, Ben peels off to the left and I veer right.

BEN

ONCE I'M SURE Taylor has left for work, I risk padding along the landing to have a shower. The water, cranked as hot as I can stand, kneads the soreness and frustration from my muscles. I'm finished with my stepbrother. Talking to him is like trying to befriend a wolverine with zero social skills. My parents can go on at me until their tongues drop off about how he's having a tough time adjusting. Do they really think it's any easier for me? I just don't feel the need to be an arse about it.

I close my eyes and tilt my face into the spray. An image of Taylor, perspiration moulding his clothes to his hard, toned body, imprints itself on the inside of my eyelids. I thrust it away before *my* body can react. My stepbrother might ooze sex appeal from every pore, but he's spinier than an entire prickle of hedgehogs. He's also decided I'm the enemy, and I won't waste one more joule of energy convincing him otherwise.

Back in my—our—room, I pull on jeans and a T-shirt before going in search of breakfast. As I reach the top of the stairs, the bathroom door opens and Abby slinks out, hair tousled, rubbing the sleep from her eyes.

"Hey." I grin at the sight of her. "Good night?"

"Oh my God, it was amazing." She moves towards her bedroom with a smile I can only describe as dreamy.

Curious, I follow her inside, then choke on the alcohol fumes. "Jesus, Abs, it stinks like a vodka distillery in here."

"Shit. Linda will kill me. I've cleaned my teeth. Can you smell it on me?" Abby turns to exhale a cloud of mint-scented breath into my face.

"You're fine." I squeeze her shoulder and cross to throw open the windows. "A bit of air and our stepmother will be none the wiser."

With a sigh of relief, Abby collapses onto her pillows and snuggles under the covers. I perch on the edge of the bed and look around. This room is just the same, everything in its place, textbooks stacked neatly beside Abby's laptop, not so much as a stray sock on the floor. I'm reminded of all the times we've stayed up late into the night, sharing our crushes and dissecting the growing tension between our parents.

"So." I nudge her leg under the duvet. "Amazing, huh?"

Her shining eyes meet mine. "I think I'm in love."

"Not again. Who with this time?"

"Don't take the piss. I've fancied boys before, but I've never felt anything like… Stop laughing."

"As if I would." I conceal my smirk beneath what hopefully passes for a serious expression. "Who is he?"

Abby's scowl vanishes. She gazes up at the ceiling, her dreamy smile back in place. "His name's Carl. He's one of Thomas's friends. I've met him before, obviously, but last night was the first time we really talked, and we just…clicked, you know?"

"Yeah, I know." Or thought I did. With an effort, I keep my mind from veering off track. "Come on then. What's he like?"

"Honestly, he's one of the nicest boys I've ever met—kind, funny, smart. Well, he's just left Brookminster Grammar, so he must be."

"Taylor went to the grammar," I remember. "He might know him."

Abby scoffs. "Trust me, he and Carl hang out in very different crowds. Taylor doesn't even have a crowd. He's too much of a prick for anyone to want to be friends with him."

"Don't be a bitch." I slap her playfully on the leg, although she has a point, at least if his antagonism towards me is anything to go by. "Tell me more about dream boy."

"God, he's totally gorgeous—blond, blue eyes, this incredible rugby-player build. You'd definitely swoon over him."

"Nah, he's all yours. I prefer my guys dark." And with compact runners' bodies. The memory of Taylor saunters unwelcome into my mind, and I blink to dislodge it.

Before I can quiz Abby further, my stomach gurgles and she gives me a gentle shove. "Go eat, and tell Linda I'll be down in a bit."

I leave my sister to her daydreaming and follow the aroma of freshly brewed coffee. Not a smell I'm used to in my house.

Linda descends on me the moment I enter the kitchen, perky and immaculate in linen trousers and a pink blouse. Probably the closest she ever gets to casual. "Morning, darling."

"Morning." I suppress a wince at the endearment. It's all too much, coming from this woman I only met yesterday.

"How did you sleep?" She brushes something from the sleeve of my T-shirt. "What did you think of the new pillows? I bought them specially. They were part of Harcourts' luxury range, filled with Siberian goose down, apparently."

I blink at her. Filled with what? "Yeah, they were… I slept fine. Thanks."

"I'm so glad. Can I get you a cup of coffee? There's plenty in the pot. Or I can make tea if you'd prefer. It's no trouble."

"Coffee would be great." Christ, is she always this manic? I appreciate her making an effort, I do, but if she keeps this up all summer, we'll both be dead from exhaustion.

Seated at the kitchen table, Imogen mimes throwing up into her bowl of cereal behind her mum's back. I catch her eye, and the corner of her mouth lifts in a lopsided grin. Oblivious, Linda busies herself with the fancy coffee machine. Mum's fancy coffee machine. The one Dad bought her for Christmas a few years ago. My fists clench. I almost snap at her to take her hands off my mum's stuff but bite my tongue. It isn't as if Mum ever used it; she's far happier with the kettle and a jar of instant.

I raid the bread bin and pop two slices of wholemeal into the toaster. Through the window, I glimpse Buddy on the patio, sprawled like a furry beanbag in a patch of sunshine.

"I'll do that." Linda presses a steaming mug into my hands and nudges me towards the table. "You sit down. You had a long day yesterday."

I'm more than capable of making myself some toast. I want to protest, but this isn't a battle worth fighting. Not today.

I pull out the chair across from Imogen, who's poring over a thick book between spoonfuls of cornflakes. "Hey."

She raises her spoon to me in a salute, still examining the page in front of her. I get the sense Imogen doesn't talk much, although the perceptiveness in her dark eyes suggests she doesn't miss much, either.

"What're you reading?" I ask.

Imogen turns the book to show me a diagram, the inner workings of something mechanical. "For a project."

"Yeah? What sort of project? Something for school?"

She shakes her head, her secretive smile making it clear this is all she's prepared to say.

As the smell of toast fills the kitchen, Buddy's nose edges into view around the back door.

"Out!" Linda swipes at him with the tea towel. "Go on, shoo."

The nose beats a hasty retreat. My stomach tightens. The way Linda treats Buddy is already starting to grate on me. I'm amazed Dad stands for it, to be honest.

"Buddy's allowed toast," I say. "Mum always gave him toast and Marmite with his breakfast."

"That explains a lot." Linda whisks the slices from the toaster and begins buttering them with unnecessary vehemence. "No wonder he's so fat and badly behaved. Toast and Marmite. Ridiculous."

She sets a plate of buttered toast in front of me, then goes to work with the dishcloth.

I reach for the raspberry jam in its silver pot—no unsightly jars for my stepmother—and vow to slip Buddy a piece of toast when she isn't looking.

Linda glances at the clock on the wall beside the door. "Abby should be up by now. Perhaps I'll take her a cup of tea."

"It's all right," I cut in. The fresh air should've blasted the reek of alcohol from Abby's room, but I can't risk Linda barging in there, just in case. "She said to tell you she'd be down in a bit."

"Oh, good. I'd like to hit the shops before the car park fills up." Linda bustles around, straightening the tea towel on its rail attached to the oven door, rubbing at non-existent smudges with her dishcloth. "Ben, darling, your dad's had to go in to work today. He wondered if you'd like to meet him for lunch at Harcourts."

"Did he?" I try to swallow, but the toast and jam has turned to cement in my mouth.

"Only if you want. There might be a summer job going, too, if you're interested. He said not to feel obliged, but he knows how much you enjoyed working there last time. Of course, I told him…"

Her voice fades to a meaningless buzz, drowned beneath the thrum of blood in my ears. I can't go back there. Not so soon. Not when it's taken me months to reassemble the broken pieces of my life. Dad has no idea why I'd been so enthusiastic about working at Harcourts two summers ago, nor why the thought of ever setting foot in the department store again has a steel vice closing around my heart.

CHAPTER FIVE

TAYLOR

"THAT'S SEVEN NINETY-NINE," I tell the girl at the counter. She fumbles in her purse, showering the scuffed surface between us with a cascade of loose coins and crumpled receipts. "Oops, sorry."

Her face, already pink from the July warmth, flushes a deep scarlet. She ducks her head, mousy hair swinging forward to hide her embarrassment, and begins scooping everything into her shoulder bag. A few pennies slip from her grasp, bouncing off the carpet. "Blast."

She bends to retrieve them, looking close to tears.

"Here." I duck around the counter to help. In a matter of moments, we've gathered up the scattered money and I'm packing up her purchase—the latest Robyn Carr. To be on the safe side, I drop her change into the bag as well, then push it across to her with a slight smile. "Be careful with that, yeah?"

"I will. Thanks so much." The girl darts me a sheepish glance. Still blushing, she clutches the book to her chest like a child with a favourite stuffed animal and hurries from the shop. The door shuts behind her and quiet descends once more.

"Someone has an admirer." Dean emerges from the storeroom with an armful of colouring books. To judge from his smirk, he's followed the whole exchange.

"Jealous?" I quirk an eyebrow. "Because there's no need. You know you're much more my type."

Dean turns almost as red as the girl beneath his tufty fair hair. He escapes along the closest aisle, burying himself in the arts and craft section.

I grin and return to *Foxglove Summer*, which I have propped against a display of promotional bookmarks. Beside the fact that this is one of my favourite places in the world, working at The Inkwell does have its perks. No one expects anything of me I'm not willing to give. All I have to do is scan customer's purchases, look stuff up on the computer, and sometimes offer recommendations. Compared with being at home, where everyone seems to want something from me, it's like being on holiday.

When business is slow—which, let's face it, is most of the time—winding Dean up provides some added amusement to my day. I shouldn't, really. His parents own The Inkwell, and a single word from Dean could have me out on my pierced ear. After all, I'm only filling in until his best mate gets back from Devon or Cornwall or wherever he's spending the summer. He's just so easy to provoke, I can't help myself.

This is our second Saturday working together, and Dean clearly doesn't know what to make of me. He's polite enough, but beyond the occasional suspicious peep at my eyeliner and mascaraed lashes, he avoids my gaze.

To prove my point, he reappears from between the shelves and gestures towards the till without meeting my eye. "I'll take over if you want to have your lunch break now."

"Cheers, babe." I stand and turn to leave, although not before I register Dean's wince.

In the poky office off the storeroom, I collect my lunch and head out through the back entrance. It's quieter here away from the high street, and the blocks of flats lining the road create an oasis of shade.

I settle on my usual bench and bite into a sandwich. Tuna. I almost gag. How could Mum have been the best PA Martin ever had and yet always forget her only son hates fish? Unless she does it on purpose. I've told her countless times I'm more than happy to make my own lunch. You'd think she'd be grateful to have one less thing to do…but no. Apparently, I leave the kitchen in too much of a mess. There's no pleasing some people.

I'm forcing down another revolting mouthful when a bark of laughter echoes along the road. Shit. I swallow too soon and a barely chewed lump of bread lodges in my throat. I'd recognise that laugh anywhere. So far this summer, I've managed to avoid CJ Farmer and his gang, but it seems my luck's run out. I look up…and there he is, silvery-blond hair gleaming in the sun, the guy who's been a constant pain in my arse all year. I scan his companions and my heart skydives. With him is the only person in the world I want to see less than CJ.

"Hey." CJ spies me, his mouth curling into a delighted sneer. He elbows Liam in the ribs. "Look who it is."

Pete and Syed, both rugby players built like Gregor Clegane, snigger behind their hands. For an instant, Liam's gaze brushes mine. A trace of something—fear? regret?—flickers in his blue-grey eyes. Then he looks away, dismissing me. Regret knifes me in the stomach. I thought I was over it. I *am* over it. Still, seeing him like this, when I'm totally unprepared, blindsides me.

"Oy, fag boy." CJ ambles over, Pete and Syed flanking him. "Fancy meeting you here. Waiting for a customer?"

He emphasises the last word just in case I might misunderstand. Fat chance. Even the first time, that joke was more threadbare than the knees of my jeans.

"Nope, it's your lucky day. I'm all yours." I feign nonchalance, intensely aware of Liam standing at a safe distance. He's examining the toes of his trainers, mahogany fringe falling over his forehead, apparently deaf to CJ's taunts.

CJ grabs my shoulders and slams me into the bench, punching the air from my lungs. He puts his face close to mine. "Say that again."

"You heard me." My back throbs where it connected with the wooden slats. I will myself not to flinch and scan the deserted street for an escape route. They might outmatch me in the strength department, but I can outrun them, no problem.

This must occur to them, too, because the three of them close ranks. Their combined bulk hems me in. Beyond them, Liam stares into the distance, shoulders hunched. The message is clear. He won't take part in this, but nor will he step in to defend me.

CJ shoves me again, cracking my head against the brick wall. Before I can stop it, a gasp hisses through my clenched teeth. I try to shrug out of his grip, but Syed laughs and kicks me in the shin.

"Watch it." CJ spits at me. "That smart mouth will get you into trouble."

Syed snorts. "Bit late for that."

"Yeah," Pete says, leering. "So, fag boy, how much did you offer Liam for the privilege of sucking him off?"

I ignore the jibe, glaring past him at Liam. His fists are clenched, and a crimson flush has crept up his neck. Good. He fucking should be embarrassed.

"Is there a problem out here?" Dean emerges from The Inkwell's back entrance, expression harder than I've seen it. I could kiss him, and not purely for the fun of watching him squirm.

At once, CJ steps away from me and flashes his charming smile. "No problem. We were just catching up." He punches me on the arm, the gesture carrying a thinly disguised threat. "See you around, Tay."

He beckons to his mates, and the four of them continue along the street. I watch Liam's retreating back, but he doesn't glance my way again.

Dean frowns after them. "Are they hassling you?"

"No more than usual." I rub the back of my head. A lump has started to form, but my fingers come away free of blood.

"CJ's an arsehole," Dean says. "I've played rugby against him. Never seen anyone get away with as many fouls." He turns to study me. "You sure he wasn't giving you grief?"

"Only a bit." With a sigh, I toss my uneaten sandwich into the nearby bin. "Nothing I can't handle."

BEN

"WHAT A MORNING." Dad picks up his knife and fork and attacks his plate of Bolognese. "I'm telling you, my department's been a shambles since Lindy left."

Mouth full of spaghetti, I do my best to appear interested while searching the surrounding tables. He isn't here. Of course he isn't. For one thing, Buddy will sprout wings before Sebastian drags his tailored backside into the store on a Saturday. For another, he never eats in the staff canteen. He'll be holed up in a corner of some fancy restaurant, enjoying a long, liquid lunch, his hypnotic eyes snaring those of the young man opposite, luring him under his spell. My gut twists, but I ignore the pain. I'm over him. I am. I've been over him for months.

"Chloe's a sweet girl, don't get me wrong," Dad's saying, oblivious to my distraction. "Pretty little thing, very eager to please, but where her head is most of the time, I have no idea. You'll never guess what she did the other day."

With an effort, I give Dad my full attention. "I don't know. Add Tipp-Ex to your coffee instead of milk?"

"Lord, what a thought. Then again, that might do me a favour, get rid of some of this flab." Dad chuckles, gesturing at his stomach. "No, this was far more embarrassing. Sales in the cosmetics department have dipped recently, so I asked Chloe to schedule an appointment with Annabelle to discuss the latest figures."

Annabelle. A mouthful of pasta sticks in my throat at the mention of her name. I reach for my glass and gulp down some water. Annabelle, head of marketing at Harcourts—beautiful, brilliant, ambitious. Annabelle, wife to Sebastian and the woman who stole my dreams.

I swallow. "She's back at work then?"

"Oh, yes. Handed the baby over to a nanny the moment she pushed it out. You know how career-minded she is, unlike that scrounging husband of hers."

Dad has never concealed his contempt for Sebastian, only child of the Harcourts and their sole heir. Once, hearing him talk about Seb like this would have annoyed me. Now, I can see him for the entitled brat he is, abusing his position as HR manager to fund his extravagant lifestyle while doing as little as he can get away with.

Annabelle, on the other hand… I'm not surprised she scorned the notion of maternity leave. With her cool professionalism and flawless make-up, she never struck me as the motherly type, probably why the news of her pregnancy was such a shock.

"Anyway," Dad continues, "Chloe contacted Annabelle to arrange a meeting, copying me in on the email. Imagine my horror when I glanced through my inbox, only to discover she'd asked Annabelle Harcourt if she could meet with me to discuss the performance of our make-out."

I snort into my plate, causing a group of glamorous young women at the next table to turn in our direction.

"It isn't funny. Put yourself in my shoes, having to explain the mix-up to Annabelle. God knows what she must've thought." Dad shakes his head, though his lips quiver.

It's unexpectedly companionable, sharing Bolognese and crème brûlée with the dad I haven't seen for a year, the two of us seated by a window that has a panoramic view over the rambling grounds of Brookminster Symphony Hall. Even before I left for Australia, it had been a while since we really talked. Dad was too busy stressing out and arguing with Mum. Now, as he has me in stitches over Chloe's daily blunders, there's a definite twinkle in his eye. Much as it galls me to admit it, I can't deny my stepmother must have put it there.

"Lindy told me not to pressure you," Dad says when we emerge onto the corridor outside the canteen, "and I promise that isn't what I'm doing. I just want you to know there's a summer job here for you if you'd like it."

I force a smile, stomach sinking. "Thanks, Dad, but I might chill out a bit before uni. I managed to save some of my wages while I was away, so I should be all right."

"Of course. Make the most of the holidays. The offer's there, though, if you change your mind." Dad claps me on the shoulder, tells me he'll see me later, and heads towards his office.

The moment he disappears from view, a prickling unease crawls over my skin. I need to get out of here. Need to get out and never come back. Resisting the urge to run, I push through the set of swing doors to my right and into a small hallway that houses the stairs and staff lifts. The doors close behind me with a muted thump. Without the hum of conversation from the canteen, the silence presses uncomfortably against my eardrums. I jam my finger on the button to summon the lift. Come on. Come…on.

"Hey, baby boy."

The lift door slides open, promising escape, but I can't move. That voice—silky, caressing, horribly familiar. It's the voice every part of me ached to hear during those first agonising months in exile. The voice I'd later come to dread. Only the fear of being trapped in an enclosed space with him stops me from hurling myself into the lift. Instead, feeling as though the contents of an ice bucket have been emptied into my chest, I turn to face him.

He stands before me, all rumpled hair and mocking smirk. His eyes glitter like obsidian, and he has his suit jacket draped over his shoulders with a casual elegance only the rich and beautiful can pull off. Sebastian Harcourt. My nemesis. Star of both my fantasies and my nightmares and the only man I've ever loved.

How had he got the jump on me? I glance towards the stairwell. Either I somehow failed to notice him lurking in the shadows or he crept up the stairs with the stealth of a panther stalking a deer.

Sebastian's mouth—the full, sensual mouth that had propelled me to the extreme heights of pleasure—quirks in amusement. "You look like you've seen an axe-wielding maniac. Aren't you just a little pleased to see me?"

He advances, assaulting my senses with his musky scent, his animal sexuality. I stay where I am, cemented to the spot. Hostility wars with the traitorous desire to sink into him, to let him devour me with his kisses and deceit.

"You are." Triumph flashes in his eyes, and he reaches out to trail a finger down my cheek. "It's written all over your face."

Heat flares at his touch. I flinch, suspended somewhere between arousal and disgust. "Don't."

"Aw, no need to be like that." He moves even closer, his body a mere whisper from mine. "I've missed you, baby boy, and I bet you missed me, thousands of miles away. Go on. Tell me you didn't lie awake thinking of me every single night, all alone in some sleazy hostel bed."

His words snap me from my trance. Memories of Oz, of the betrayal that sent me fleeing my home city, come flooding back. I jerk away, putting several feet of space between us.

"Baby—"

"Don't call me that." I glare at him, fists balled at my sides. "How's your wife?"

Seb waves a dismissive hand. "Annie's…well, Annie. Doesn't care about anything but her precious career. Let's not talk about her. She isn't important."

"She was important enough to have your child. Congratulations, by the way."

"Babe—"

"I told you not to call me that."

"Fine." Sebastian crosses his arms, features tightening. "I explained all this before."

"No, you lied to me. I thought we had something, that you cared about me, and all the time you were…" My voice shakes, disintegrating.

It hits me in a wave of remembered pain and anger—Seb's assurances that his relationship with Annabelle was nothing more than a marriage of convenience; his promises to leave her as soon as the time was right; my shock when I discovered she was pregnant and the rows that followed…the tears, the explanations, the heartache.

Sebastian puffs out a long breath. "I never lied to you. My marriage is a sham, a public display to keep my parents happy. Now I've fulfilled my duty, produced an heir, I'm entitled to some fun."

"Yeah." I rub my forehead where a dull throb has started. I want to go home. "Yeah, that's all I ever was to you, isn't it? A bit of fun. You were never going to leave her, were you?"

Sebastian opens his mouth, doubtless to spout yet more lies, but then he shrugs. "What does it matter? It's a marriage in name only. I don't love her, never have. All I've ever wanted is you, and I know you feel the same." He crowds me again, his gaze hungry on mine. "What do you say? Shall we pick up where we left off?"

"What? So I can be your guilty pleasure while you play the perfect husband and father?" I turn away in disgust. "Thanks, but no thanks."

Before I can dart for the stairs, Seb hooks a finger into the back pocket of my jeans. I wrench myself free, but when I spin to confront him, he already has my phone in his hand.

"Hey!" I grab for it, cursing myself for never bothering to secure it with a passcode.

Sebastian holds it out of reach, chuckling, and taps the screen. A moment later, the opening chords of a Nora Jones track drift from the depths of his jacket. 'Turn Me On'. One of Seb's favourites. An image so vivid it blinds me blazes across my vision—sitting in the passenger seat of Sebastian's car, his hand on my leg, 'Come Away with Me' pouring from the stereo as we drove through the night to some out-of-the-way hotel. I blink, and the memory fractures into a million sparks of colour.

"Thanks for giving me your new number." With a smirk, Sebastian slides my phone back into my pocket. His lips graze my earlobe. "I'll be in touch, baby boy. By then, I'm sure you'll have changed your mind. In fact, I'm counting on it."

CHAPTER SIX

TAYLOR

IT'S RESTFUL, MEANDERING through the streets on Sunday
morning, the houses and their occupants torpid in the heat.
Buddy dawdles, pausing to sniff at every hedge and lamppost,
and I let him set the pace. It isn't as if I'm in any hurry to get
back. I'd walk the city all day, if only it weren't so hot. Sweat
pastes my vest and shorts to my skin, and poor Bud's puffing
like Thomas the Tank Engine.

My sense of peace carries me all the way to the back door,
where it melts faster than an ice cube in a glass of boiling
water. I come up short on the threshold, hand clenched around
Buddy's lead. They're all here, arranged in some warped tableau
of domestic bliss. Mum's checking the oven, letting out the
aroma of sage and onion. She'd rather spontaneously combust
than forego the tradition of Sunday roast, even when it's
thirty degrees outside. My gaze skims over Ben, who's peeling
potatoes like some grown-up version of Horrid Henry's perfect
brother, and takes in the others at the table—Martin inspecting
something Imogen's showing him, Abby chatting to Mum as
she leafs through a copy of *Teen Vogue*.

"I think he sounds lovely," Mum's saying, her voice warm.
"Where's he taking you?"

"To Just Desserts for ice cream." Abby flips a page, tone
nonchalant, though a rosy blush creeps into her cheeks.

Without acknowledging anyone, I unclip Buddy's lead and slip into the utility room to hang it on its hook. The idea of returning to the kitchen and that sickening intimacy has my gut roiling. Instead, I lean against the washing machine, apart from it all, invisible.

"I'm not sure I approve of this young man," Martin says. "He's rather older than you."

"Oh my God, Dad, don't be lame. Three years is nothing. Anyway, most of the boys my age are pathetic."

My stepdad mutters something I don't catch but which earns a tinkling laugh from Mum. "You're such a grumpy old man sometimes. Abby's a sensible girl. She reminds me of myself at fifteen. I had a boyfriend who was older than me, too."

"Really?" Abby sounds intrigued.

Fuck, someone cut off my ears with a rusty hacksaw. I've lost count of how many times Imogen and I have been subjected to this story. When I was younger, it seemed kind of romantic, not that I'd ever have admitted as much. Hearing it now, though, fills me with the desire to kick something.

Impervious to my silent plea, Mum launches into the account of how she met my dad while she was studying for her GCSEs and he was in his second year at Brookminster University. Of course, she doesn't mention Dad by name. Given how that relationship turned out, it would somewhat undermine her point.

Mum also leaves out the fact that her parents' disapproval had less to do with the age gap and more to do with my dad being Turkish. My grandparents are racist like that; it's why we hardly ever see them. Oh, they love Imogen and me in their way, but there's no avoiding the disappointment that clouds their expressions whenever they look at us. Mum can't bear that disappointment, sees it as a reflection on her, so we generally steer clear.

As for Dad's family, they refuse to have anything to do with us. They disowned him when he rebelled, choosing to marry Mum rather than find himself a 'suitable Turkish girl'. So it's mostly been the four of us, Mum and Dad, Imogen and me.

Until now.

I drag in a breath, forcing it through the sudden tightness in my chest. However tempting it might be, I can't skulk in here all day. Mum's come to the end of her epic romance, so I push myself off the washing machine and head back into the kitchen, making a beeline for the fridge. Ben shifts over to give me room, gaze fixed on his mound of potatoes. Since our run the previous morning, he's barely made eye contact with me. No more overtures of friendship. He'll soon realise it's easier this way. No ties. No attachment. Just a clean break at the end of the summer.

"Taylor." Martin greets me with far more enthusiasm than I deserve, given the lukewarm politeness I've displayed towards him since we met. "Look at this. Your sister's mended my old clock. Isn't she clever?"

Abby snorts behind her magazine. "Freak."

"Bitch." I glare razor blades at her, one hand on the open fridge door. I might not like the rapport between her dad and Imogen any more than she does, but no one gets to call my sister names.

If Martin catches the exchange, he pretends otherwise. He turns the clock over in his hands, examining it as though it's performed a tap dance in front of him. "This is incredible.

My great-granddad bought this for my great-nan for their golden wedding anniversary. I've kept it out of sentimentality, but it hasn't worked in years. Well done, Imogen."

She grins, flushing. Something slimy and poisonous claws its way up my throat. I don't understand how she can be so chummy with him. It's like she doesn't care that he was partly responsible for breaking up our family, that his mere existence sent Dad scarpering to London.

In a violent motion, I grab the apple juice from the bottom shelf and swallow a mouthful straight from the carton, because I know it drives Mum berserk.

"Ugh! That's disgusting." Abby's dainty nose wrinkles. "No one else will be able to drink that now. Linda, tell him."

Mum drops the carrot she's skinning and whirls to pluck the carton from my grasp. "Taylor, how many times? I'll have to throw this away now. What a waste. If you've finished gallivanting, you can help with the vegetables."

Is she serious? Anyone would think I've been smoking pot at the bus shelter rather than walking the dog, something no one else has bothered to do. They're all far too busy auditioning for a modern reboot of *The Waltons*. Well, they can deceive themselves all they like. I'm not playing.

The air in the kitchen feels stifling, thick with pretence. Before it can suffocate me, I slope into the hall and up the stairs. In the room that was never truly mine and which is now undeniably Ben's, I flop onto my bed. Staring up at the ceiling, I wish myself anywhere else. Not long now. A couple more months and I'll be at uni. London City is my first choice; they offer a master's in publishing I'd like to take after my degree. It doesn't really matter, though, so long as it's away from here.

I lie there, misery snarling my insides. Sounds drift up from downstairs—Mum clattering saucepans, the trill of the phone in the hall, the soft hum of voices. At some point, I'll be summoned to the dining room to endure the torture of Sunday lunch. I can already picture it, Mum casting me disapproving glances while she gushes over Ben and Abby and how absolutely fucking perfect they are. Christ, kill me now.

Imogen sticks her head around the bedroom door. "Dad's on the phone."

"So?"

"He wants to speak to you."

I turn away from her and glower through the window at the branches of next door's apple tree. Imogen waits a beat, then sighs. Her quiet footsteps retreat along the landing. It's as if a knife pierces my kidneys and twists. When will he get the message that I have nothing to say to him? Not anymore. He'd been my ally, a willing human shield between me and Mum's constant urging to do better, run faster, aim higher. Then he left, scarcely saying goodbye. But for the occasional phone call, he may as well be in Narnia.

Imogen returns a short while later, crossing to perch on the edge of my bed. She doesn't speak, merely studies me with that knowing expression that drives me insane.

I roll to face her. "Stop looking at me like that. You might be able to pretend nothing's happened, but I can't."

My sister fiddles with the duvet cover, pleating it between her fingers. "This isn't Dad's fault."

I huff. We've had this conversation so many times, usually after Dad's sporadic phone calls, and I still don't get how Imogen can defend him. Dad might not have planned for things to turn out the way they have. All the same, if he'd behaved differently, maybe we wouldn't have ended up in this situation. And the worst thing? He didn't even stick around to witness the carnage.

We all suspected something was wrong. During those last months, Dad came home each evening in a foul mood. Gone was the dad I knew, laid-back and full of fun. The dad who would sweep the three of us out to dinner on a week night just because and who teased Mum about her obsessive neatness until even she had to laugh at herself. Though he still asked Imogen and me about school, it was obvious he wasn't really listening, and he snapped at Mum if she dared to so much as enquire how his day was. I suppose it's no wonder she went running to another man. Dad might as well have pushed her into Martin's arms. Hell, he as good as thrust all three of us at him and said, *"Here, they're yours. I can't deal with them anymore."*

We discovered the truth by accident. A friend of Mum's was shopping in Covent Garden and saw Dad seated alone outside a café when he should've been in his Brookminster office. It all came out then—how the graphic design firm he worked for was struggling and had to let him go; how, wanting to spare Mum the worry, he continued to leave the house each morning, only to hop on a train to London where there was less chance of him being spotted. The rest, I pieced together through a series of overheard conversations.

I look at my sister, remembering the nights we sat huddled side by side on the stairs while our parents hurled abuse at each other in the living room. To keep up with the mortgage payments and conceal the fact that anything was wrong, Dad ran up massive bills across numerous credit cards. Then, when the banks all refused to extend his limit any further, he did the only thing he could. He took out a loan against our house.

"It was just to tide us over," Dad told Mum again and again, his voice ragged. "Just until I found another job."

But he hadn't found another job, despite hours spent trawling recruitment websites in internet cafés. The banks were demanding repayment, and since Dad had nothing left, they would collect that repayment in the form of the three-bedroom terrace Mum and Dad bought shortly before I was born.

It went on for weeks—Mum's rage and recriminations, Dad's tears and entreaties. Things finally came to a head when Mum announced she'd fallen in love with her boss. Apparently, she and Martin had fought against their feelings for years, both determined to stay true to their marriages, but these feelings simply couldn't be denied any longer. Now he and his wife had begun the process of separating, Martin had asked Mum to marry him, and she'd said yes. Dad stopped apologising after that. Our house was repossessed, Mum took Imogen and me to live with Martin, and Dad fled to London to share a flat with a mate from his uni days.

Imogen touches my arm, drawing me from my thoughts. "Dad misses you. I can tell."

I scoff. "He has a funny way of showing it."

I could've forgiven Dad a lot of things, for lying to us and for becoming so mired in debt that we lost the only home I'd ever known. The fact remains, though. He abandoned us. He left Imogen and me to pick through the wreckage of his mistakes, and for that, I'll never forgive him.

BEN

BEFORE AUSTRALIA, MEALS were mostly casual bites snatched around the kitchen table. Often, the four of us ate at different times depending on our schedules. My stepmother, however, insists we have a sit-down dinner every day in the dining room.

"It's so important we have this time to connect," she told me that first evening, her face alight with the conviction of a born-again Christian. "Time to talk and really bond as a family."

Not that there's much bonding going on over the roast pork and apple sauce. Taylor picks at his food, radiating hostility like a cloud of sulphurous fumes, while Abby and Imogen each behave as though the other doesn't exist. Linda varnishes right over the awkwardness, smoothing it beneath a gleaming coat of chatter. She seems to think, if she behaves as though everything's fine, no one will notice the tension.

"Marty, I think we should go back and see that house," she says, spearing a roast potato. "The one on Pimlico Drive."

Dad glances up from his plate. "I don't know, Lindy. I'm not sure that's a good idea."

I grimace into my water glass. I'm pleased Dad and Linda are happy, or I'm trying to be, but all the 'Marty this' and 'Lindy that' has me wanting to regurgitate carrots and gravy over Linda's cream tablecloth.

My stepmother dismisses the objection with a wave of her fork. "I know you said we couldn't afford it, but the estate agent did imply they'd be open to offers, and it would be so ideal for us. That walk-in wardrobe...and the terrace overlooking the pool."

"A swimming pool?" Abby, who until now has shown no interest in the conversation, perks up. "Wow, the girls will be so jealous."

Linda smiles, expression dreamy. Bet she really fancies herself draped over a lounger, sipping margaritas while she admires her reflection in the turquoise water.

Dad watches her, his face softening. "I suppose it wouldn't hurt to have another look. I just don't want you getting your hopes up."

Christ, my stepmother has him wrapped around her perfectly manicured finger. Dad would put in an offer on Windsor Castle if she asked him to. I shovel down another forkful of meat, stomach churning.

Linda rewards him with a glowing look, then turns her attention to me. "And where are you off to in September, Ben, darling? Your dad did tell me. Somewhere in London, isn't it?"

Somehow, I cobble together coherent answers to her questions about my uni plans, but my insides are a coiled spring of nerves. I expect my phone to buzz in my pocket at any second, for it to be him. Seb made no secret of his intentions. He wants me back, and what Sebastian Harcourt wants, he usually gets.

The moment she clears her plate, Abby rushes off to meet Carl for ice cream, and Taylor and Imogen escape as soon as dessert's over. Linda goes to answer a call on her mobile and her animated voice carries along the hall from the kitchen. The percolator gurgles away in the background, spewing out the scent of fresh coffee.

I stay seated at the table. It isn't as if I have anywhere else to be. Dad's engrossed in *The Mail on Sunday*, so I pull out my phone to check for messages. Still no word from Seb, thank God, but no word from Raz, either.

Rasiq Ahmed has been my best mate since Mr. Harrison made us lab partners during our first week at Bhelmead. I texted him yesterday, before meeting Dad for lunch, but so far, I've had nothing back. He's probably busy, or else he's mislaid his mobile. We used to wind him up about it, the way Raz was always losing his phone, dropping it behind the sofa cushions or leaving it in someone's car. Damn, I've missed my boys, missed the in-jokes and solidarity built up over eight years of friendship. I shoot off a quick group text.

Hey, what's up?

Then I simply stare at the screen, willing it to light up with a reply. Yet as the minutes crawl by without a single response, I have to face the fact that they're ignoring me.

Linda stalks into the dining room, one hand still clamped around her mobile. She looms over Dad, a purposeful glint in her eye. "Why didn't you tell me?"

Dad's head snaps up. "What's that, love? What should I have told you?"

"About the job. That was Jillian on the phone. You know she's friendly with Diane, Richard's secretary. Well, Di just told her he's retiring."

"That's right. I'm going to miss him. He must be the only person in Accounts who's been there longer than I have."

"And you didn't think to mention it to me?"

"Should I have? I never got the impression you had a lot to do with Richard."

"Don't be obtuse. If Richard's retiring, they'll be looking for a new finance manager, and you're the obvious candidate."

"Oh." Dad sounds taken aback. "I don't know about that."

"And why not? You're one of Harcourts' longest serving employees, and you're more than capable of doing Richard's job."

"That's sweet of you to say, Lindy, but—"

"No buts. This is a wonderful opportunity. You've been stuck in that position far too long. It's high time for a change, and the salary's bound to be more than you're getting now. Just think, we might even be able to afford the Pimlico Drive house."

"I suppose…" Dad runs a hand through his thinning hair, a nervous habit I've inherited. "Perhaps you're right."

"Of course I am." Linda squeezes his shoulder. "At least consider it. I'll get us a coffee. Would you like one, Ben, darling?"

I shake my head, and my stepmother retreats to the kitchen. Reluctantly, I put my phone away. None of my mates are going to answer. Given how I fled the country with barely a goodbye, let alone an explanation, I can't exactly blame them.

Brian Cox's voice drifts from the living room, brimming with enthusiasm as he describes the ice rings of Saturn. I get to my feet, intending to join Imogen in front of the telly, and then my mobile vibrates. Finally. Already grinning, I pull the phone out again and glance at it. But the text isn't from Raz. It's from a number I don't recognise. With a plunging sensation in my gut, I read the three words.

Hi, baby boy.

The blood pounds in my ears. I remember the animal heat of Seb's body, the way my own had reacted when he stepped close. It would be so easy to give in, to slip back into the routine of secrecy and illicit sex. Easier than setting petrol alight, and just as dangerous.

I shove the phone into my pocket. If Sebastian expects an answer, he'll be disappointed. Simple though it would be to pick up our affair, an affair is all it would ever be. Seb broke my heart once; I won't let him do it a second time.

At the door, I hesitate and glance over at Dad. He hasn't returned to his paper, but is fiddling with the edge of the tablecloth, deep grooves furrowing his brow.

Bloody Linda.

"Dad, you don't have to apply for that job."

He looks up at me. "Well, no, obviously I don't have to, but maybe Lindy's right. I have been doing this job for rather a long time."

"Because you enjoy it." I force down my irritation. Why couldn't Linda have kept her mouth shut? If she's as pushy with Taylor as she appears to be with Dad, it's hardly surprising they clash.

"All the same," Dad says, more to himself than to me, "it would be a step up, and if it makes Lindy proud…"

To hell with Linda. If it's more money she wants, why doesn't she go back to work? Before I can say something I'll regret, my mobile buzzes with another text. I shouldn't read it. I should delete the message and put Sebastian Harcourt from my mind. Yet, like drivers who slow down to gawp at an accident, I can't stop myself.

Drink one evening? You know you want to.

Arrogant twat. Had I really once found Seb's self-assurance attractive? Talk about love being blind. I need to get out of this house for a bit, clear my head.

"I'm going to see Mum," I tell Dad and leave him to his dilemma.

I never confided in Mum about Sebastian, not because she wouldn't have understood, but because I knew she'd worry about me getting hurt. Then, when I learned about the baby and everything fell apart, I was too ashamed at having turned out to be such a cliché. Even now, the idea of confessing the whole sordid mess has me wanting to curl up and die. Still, her reassuring presence always makes me feel better.

I reach the front door at the same moment Taylor appears at the foot of the stairs. My stomach tightens, the way it never fails to do at the sight of him. If only he weren't so bloody sexy. Of course, it won't be like this forever. I'm sure to develop an immunity to him after a while. I'll have to, for my own sanity.

Taylor halts, beautiful face unreadable, arms crossed in a defensive gesture. I'm reminded of that morning when he walked in on us all assembled in the kitchen. For an instant, as he observed us from the doorway, he looked almost…lost. I would've felt sorry for him, but what does he expect? If he insists on being as unpleasant as possible, he's bound to get excluded.

Taylor's gaze darts between me and the front door, as though I'm a warden barring the only exit from a prison.

I step back, allowing him to go first. This act of politeness earns me a suspicious glare. Seems I can't do anything right.

I huff out a breath. "Go ahead. I'm just off next door."

"No, you're fine." Taylor sounds angry, far angrier than the situation deserves. He starts edging up the stairs.

Then it hits me.

"Look," I say, treading carefully, "if you were planning to drop in on Mum, I can wait till—"

"No." He flings the word at me as though it's a stone aimed at my skull. "You go. She's your mum, after all."

Before I can protest, he wheels and slinks upstairs. Our bedroom door clicks shut and I'm left standing alone in the hallway.

With a sigh, I slip from the house and into the sluggish heat of the afternoon. I have no reason to feel guilty. She is my mum, like Taylor said, and I'm owed some catching-up time. Still, in the unguarded moment before my stepbrother turned away, I'd glimpsed his expression behind the mask. As I follow the path to the annex, the raw unhappiness I'd seen there remains imprinted on my retinas.

CHAPTER SEVEN

TAYLOR

"IMOGEN!" ABBY'S FEET thunder down the stairs. I lower the book I'm reading and glance at my sister, who shrugs. We're curled at either end of the sofa, me engrossed in *The Lies of Locke Lamora* while Imogen watches David Attenborough. Yet another wild Friday night for the Solomons.

Abby stalks into the living room in her dressing gown, a mini tornado of fury and flying hair. She halts in front of Imogen, hands on hips. "What've you done with it?"

My sister leans around her, attention glued to the telly where a killer whale is hunting a dolphin and her pup. Other than that, she gives no sign she's aware of Abby's presence.

I toss my book onto the sofa cushions with a glare. "Don't make it too clear what you're on about, will you?"

"Shut up, Taylor. She knows what I'm talking about. Don't you?" Abby shifts to block Imogen's view of the screen. "Don't ignore me, you little freak."

I'm on my feet at once, placing my body between them. "Call my sister a freak once more and I'll thump you."

"Go ahead, if you want my boyfriend to kick your head in. Come on, Imogen, stop messing around." Abby dances from foot to foot. "I'm meant to be at the cinema in twenty minutes, and I need that top. The turquoise halterneck with the butterfly on the front. Where is it?"

Brow arched, Imogen glances down at her Infinite Monkey Cage T-shirt and frayed leggings.

I snort. "Yup, definitely sounds like Imogen's style."

"Well, who else would've pinched it? Did you?"

"Oh, yeah, I remember now. I borrowed it the other day to match my new boxers."

"Oh my God, I don't have time for this. Some of us actually have a social life." Abby spins and storms into the hall. "Linda!"

Her complaints drift back to us from the dining room where Mum and Martin have lingered over their after-dinner coffee. Any minute now, Detective Inspector Linda Willoughby will come barging in to investigate the mystery of the missing T-shirt. Christ, sounds like a bad Enid Blyton novel.

"Come on." I reach for Imogen's hand. "Let's get out of this asylum for a bit."

We duck past the doorway to the dining room, collect a delighted Buddy from his bed in the utility and head out into the balmy dusk. Ben's seated on the front steps, hunched over his phone. My shoulders stiffen, just as they do every time I see him. He's only been home three weeks, but already I'm exhausted from the effort of maintaining this barrier between us.

Ben looks up as we edge around him. He offers Imogen a wan smile, his gaze sliding over me as though I'm under an invisibility cloak. It shouldn't sting. Not when this is what I wanted. I have no business feeling all aggrieved.

There are times, though, when I find myself watching him. I watch as he jokes with Abby or debates infinity with Imogen, and I wonder what might have happened if I'd played things differently. What if, rather than shutting him out that first evening, I'd returned his smile of comradeship?

Ah, well, too late now.

Buddy tugs on the lead, eager to say hello to Ben, but I have no desire to hang around. I call him to heel, and we continue towards the street, Imogen a pace behind. I don't slow down until we round the corner onto the Brookminster Road. Here, the tension falls off me like a too-heavy coat on a hot day. I expel a breath I've been holding for what feels like forever.

We walk in easy silence, the space between us filled with the sounds of a summer evening—children playing in unseen back gardens, blackbirds singing from the branches of plane trees. Buddy trots ahead of us, occasionally pausing to snuffle at an interesting scent.

I hand the lead to Imogen and press my knuckles into my sore eyes. Every part of me aches, the constant tiredness dragging at my limbs. I haven't slept properly in months. Not since everything blew up last September. Now, with Ben occupying the bed mere feet away, my nights are an endless cycle of tangled sheets and fitful dreams.

Imogen bumps my shoulder. "OK?"

"Yeah." I let my arms drop and inhale the familiar city smells—petrol fumes mixed with grass and the smoke from a barbecue. "Yeah, I'm fine."

My sister studies me, head on one side, expression sceptical.

"What?" I ask, irritated.

"Just curious. Are you and Ben going to keep this up all summer?"

"Keep what up?"

Imogen raises her eyebrows, mimicking the incredulous gesture she'd used on Abby. I pretend to be fascinated by the elderly man watering his Begonias in the front garden across the road. Of course my sister has noticed. How could she not?

Whenever Ben and I are forced into the same room, tension crackles between us, sparking like a broken telegraph wire.

"Look." Despite the warmth, I hug my arms to my chest. "Mum has her perfect new family to worry about. Even if I wanted to be part of it, which I don't, she doesn't need me screwing things up for her. In seven weeks, I'll be out of here, off to uni. Until then, I'm just going to stay out of it."

"This could be a long seven weeks."

"You can talk. I don't see you being BFFs with Abby."

Imogen's mouth lilts in a sly smile. "Somehow, I don't think that's the same thing."

I'm about to protest, but an excited barking distracts me. I scarcely have time to recognise the black-and-white blur barrelling towards us, to absorb the implications, before the Staffordshire bull terrier is there. He leaps up to rest his paws on my stomach, covering every inch of exposed skin he can reach in ecstatic kisses.

"Pugsey, no!" The dog's owner hurries out of a side street, a lead trailing from his hand, collar still attached. At the sight of me, hot colour floods his face. "Shit. I'm so sorry."

I don't acknowledge him; my focus is entirely on restraining the dog. It's total chaos, a confusion of hands and fur and frantic wagging. At last, I manage to seize the squirming Staffy around the middle so his owner can refasten his collar. With dog and lead reunited, there's no putting it off any longer. I wipe the slobber from my cheek and confront my ex-boyfriend.

In the instant Liam's eyes meet mine, it all rushes back. I remember the countless times these same eyes have looked at me over the years, sparkling with amusement when he teased me about being a grammar nerd, hazy with desire in the dark back seat of his car. Now, as he bends to tighten Pugsey's collar, Liam's expression reveals only shame.

The silence stretches, pulled taut under the weight of our shared history. Imogen has retreated to a safe distance and is observing us with that annoying perceptiveness. Sprawled at her feet, Buddy watches the hyperactive Staffy with mild interest. My sister doesn't know anything about our messy past, no one does, but she'd have to be unconscious to ignore the atmosphere between us.

I met Liam Knowles when he joined the athletics team at the start of Year Ten. He fell into step with me as we walked onto the field for our first training session and offered up a tentative smile. From the moment my gaze snagged his, there was something there—a spark, an awareness. We danced around each other for months, exchanging glances behind our teammates' backs, sitting next to each other on the away coach for the sheer thrill of letting our knees brush.

Finally, when the two of us were alone in the changing room one evening, Liam rested his hand on my leg and left it there. Our eyes locked, connected by a shivering thread of want. Slowly, heart drumming against my ribs, I leaned in and kissed him.

For almost three years, we met in secluded corners of the school and in the park under cover of darkness. When Liam passed his driving test, we used his car. We couldn't get enough. We devoured one another, high on love and sex and the secrecy of it all. Because we had to keep our relationship secret; Liam insisted on that. He wasn't ready to tell people, was sure his mates wouldn't understand.

A gigantic understatement, as it turned out.

Liam finishes adjusting Pugsey's collar and straightens, careful to avoid my eyes this time. "Thanks."

He addresses the pavement, awkwardness in every rigid line of his body. It's impossible to believe we ever shared more than a pencil sharpener. I have nothing to say to him. Even almost a year later, his betrayal burns like an ulcer in my stomach.

He lingers, teeth worrying at his lower lip. For a horrible moment, I'm sure he's about to say more. Apologise, maybe, or attempt to defend himself. In the end, he simply turns and crosses the road, dragging a reluctant Pugsey in his wake.

I refuse to watch him go. Thumbs hooked into the waistband of my jeans, I continue along the street as though there was no interruption. Behind me, Imogen coaxes Buddy off the pavement and hurries to catch up.

"Who was that?"

There are so many possible answers to this question. He was my best friend, the boy I'd loved for two and a half years. He's someone I would've done anything for, even hide our relationship when all I wanted was to go for pizza or to the cinema, to behave like any other teenage couple. Most of all, he's the one who broke my heart and turned my final year of school into a living hell.

I could tell my sister any of these things. Instead, all I say is, "He's no one."

BEN

I'M ON MY way to see Mum when my phone rings. I fish it from my jeans pocket, glancing at the screen, and a smile spreads across my face. After three weeks of unanswered texts, I've pretty much given up on him.

"Benbo!" Raz cries as soon as I hit accept. His words are fuzzy around the edges, and to judge by the noise, he's in the middle of a party. "Sorry I haven't replied to your texts. It's been kind of hectic."

"No worries." All at once, his silence no longer matters. It's enough to hear his voice, to know he isn't mad at me. Raz doesn't sound mad, at least, although he doesn't sound especially apologetic, either. Not that he should. If anyone has a reason to apologise, it's me.

"Been a while," Raz says over the thumping bass. "How was Oz? We all thought you'd gone and got yourself eaten by a great white."

I lower myself onto the front steps. There's no way I can condense an entire year into one phone call. Better to save the details for when he gets back. "Good. Great. And you guys are in Thailand?"

I saw the photos on Instagram. I've never been big on social media, but as days passed with no news from any of my friends, I resorted to going online. And there they were, Raz, Justin and the rest of my crowd. They grinned out at me, their arms around each other, standing on a beach with a sprawling villa in the background. I'd suspected it, that they'd be together having a blast without me, but that didn't stop the jealousy from corroding my insides.

"Seriously, man, you should see this place. It's amazing, on its own private island." Raz breaks off. Perhaps, even through the fog of alcohol, he realises he's being insensitive. "We would've invited you. We just weren't sure when you'd be back, and—"

"It's all right. I get it," I assure him and try not to feel left out.

A cheer rises above the music and someone—Oscar, I think—shouts for Raz to "Get off the bloody phone."

"Oy. I'm trying to talk to Benbo here." Raz moves the microphone away from his mouth to yell back, then reappears on the line. "Gotta go, man. We're about to play this drinking game of Justin's, so you can guess how that'll turn out. Give us a shout in a few weeks when I'm home and we can catch up, yeah?"

"Yeah, sounds good," I say, but he's already hung up.

I stare down at the phone in my hand. Compared with the din on Raz's end, the quiet is almost painful. A pang gnaws at my stomach, loneliness tangled up with regret. Well, what did I expect? That I could jet off to the other side of the world, cut myself off from my friends for an entire year, and come back to find everything as I'd left it? While I'd put my future on hold, Raz and co were getting on with their lives—going to uni, meeting new people, moving on.

It hits me then how hurtful my actions must have been, to Raz in particular. One day we were looking forward to heading off to uni together, excited at the prospect of living away from home; the next, I was on a plane to Australia, too bogged down in my own heartbreak to consider anyone else. What an arse. I'm lucky he called me at all.

No, I have zero right to feel sorry for myself. Still, between my mates going AWOL, the constant stream of potential buyers tramping through the house and the fact that Abby's too absorbed with her new boyfriend to hang out with her big brother, this hasn't been quite the homecoming I'd imagined.

The front door opens behind me, and my stepbrother emerges, Imogen and Buddy at his heels. Imogen returns my feeble attempt at a smile, but Taylor behaves as though I'm one of the potted shrubs. He strolls away down the drive, hips swaying, kicking up gravel with the toes of his trainers. Buddy veers towards me, tail waving, but a word from Taylor has him trotting after my stepbrother. Even my dog doesn't have the time of day to waste on me.

I snort, shaking my head. Could I be any more self-pitying if I tried? Shoving my phone into my pocket, I scramble up and follow the path around the side of the house.

"So, how're things?" Mum asks a short while later.

We're settled on the sofa with mugs of coffee, the telly tuned to some gardening programme, the sound on low. I'm reminded of all the times I've stumbled in after a night out to find Mum waiting up for me, ready with a hot drink and eager to hear the details. The hollowness left over from my phone call eases a fraction.

"Oh, you know. All right. I finally heard from Raz." I fill Mum in on my conversation, trying to conceal how shut out I'd felt.

I must do a poor job because her expression softens. "That's a shame. I know you were hoping to get together with everyone before uni."

"It's my own fault." I grip my mug, the heat stinging my palms. "I feel crappy about it, the way I upped and left. I haven't been much of a mate, have I? Or much of a son."

"Sweetheart, don't say that. I couldn't have asked for a better son."

"But I left. Everything was falling apart here, and I just took off, leaving you to cope."

Mum lays a hand on my knee, squeezing until I meet her gaze. Her eyes are full of love and compassion, no hint of reproach. "You were hurting. I could see that, even if I didn't know why."

A lump forms in my throat. Of course she'd known. I've never been able to hide my feelings from Mum. Not entirely.

"I wasn't the only one hurting," I say, refusing to be let off the hook. "You were going through stuff, too, and I should've been here. It was selfish."

"Give over. Life isn't that simple. Sometimes we have to do what's best for us, and if that means being selfish, so be it." Mum's smile holds a trace of sadness, and it's obvious she isn't only talking about me.

IT'S ALMOST MIDNIGHT when Taylor slouches into our room. I'm sitting up in bed, playing *Toon Blast* on my phone, but glance up when the bedroom door opens.

"Hey," I say automatically. This is the limit of our interaction these days, a brief exchange last thing at night, the only time we're ever alone.

My stepbrother nods, making straight for his own bed. I take in the defeated slump to his shoulders. Where has he been all evening? Imogen and Buddy were in the living room when I got back from Mum's, but Taylor must've gone out again. He does that a lot, disappears for hours without telling anyone where he's going. Yet, if what Abby says is true, he doesn't have any friends.

I'm about to return to my game when Taylor bends to pull off his trainers and I glimpse his expression. In the muted glow from the bedside lamp, his face appears softer, more vulnerable. His usual deadpan mask has slipped, exposing a weary unhappiness.

"You all right?" The question pops out before I can think it through. It isn't as if I expect him to confide in me.

He looks at me then, really looks, and for once there's no hostility. I'm sure he's about to answer, to demolish this wall he's erected between us. I hold my breath, unable to tear my eyes from his.

Taylor shrugs, breaking the connection, and crosses to remove his make-up in front of the mirror. His reflection stares out at me, unreadable as ever. Chest tight with disappointment, I go back to my level, though without really concentrating. For a moment, I'd truly believed my stepbrother was going to let me in. Stupid. He made up his mind about me while I was thousands of miles away, and nothing I say or do will change his opinion.

Still, as Taylor starts to undress, I watch from the corner of my eye. It's wrong of me, I know, but I can't help myself. I watch him peel his T-shirt off over his head, revealing the smooth tautness of his back, muscles rippling beneath skin the colour of treacle toffee. God, he's beautiful.

He unbuttons his jeans, eases them down over his toned thighs. My body—my shallow, traitorous body—reacts as it always does to his nakedness, his blatant sexuality. With an effort, I wrench my gaze from him. He wouldn't appreciate me eyeing him up any more than he appreciated my attempt at friendship.

And yet…

I wait to hear the creak of springs before risking another peep. Taylor has his back to me, knees drawn up to his chest, a quivering ball of tension under the covers. At moments like this, the idea is crazy, laughable. At others, though, I'm sure I feel his eyes on me, burning and intense, sliding away the instant I glance in his direction. Whenever this happens, I'd swear he isn't as immune to me as he pretends.

CHAPTER EIGHT

TAYLOR

WHEN MY PHONE blasts Swedish House Mafia into my ear the following morning, it's all I can do to roll over and check the time. After the encounter with Liam, I dropped Imogen and Buddy back at the house before heading straight out again. If I just kept moving, maybe I wouldn't have to think. Yet, even exhausted from an eternity of aimless wandering, I'd lain awake into the early hours, my thoughts on an endless loop.

Somehow, I find the strength to switch off the alarm and drag myself out of bed. My stepbrother doesn't even stir. He remains curled on his side, a crest of blond hair visible above the duvet, his breathing slow and regular. Christ, I envy him. I'd trade my entire collection of first editions for a single night of uninterrupted sleep.

In a daze, I pull on my work clothes and steal downstairs. With any luck, Mum will be having one of her rare lie-ins. That way, I can grab a thermos of tea and slip out without speaking to anyone.

"Ah, Taylor." Mum swoops on me the moment my foot touches the bottom stair. So much for that. Had she been listening for me, waiting to pounce? She thrusts a carrier bag into my hands. "Remember, I want you straight home after work today."

I peer at the bag's contents. A litre bottle of water and a sandwich box. The stink of tuna hits me, turning my stomach. I push the bag back at her with a grimace. "It's OK. I can buy my own lunch."

"Don't be silly. You'll only waste your money on some greasy burger. Now, did you hear what I said? It's imperative you're here for dinner."

"Why? Are you and Martin getting a divorce already? If so, I want custody of Buddy."

Mum breathes hard through her nose. "It would be nice if you at least pretended to be interested in what goes on in this family. Martin accepted an offer on the house yesterday, and tonight I'm cooking a special meal to celebrate. Jillian and Greg are coming, and Abby's boyfriend. I want everyone to be there, and that includes you."

Seriously? I fix her with the blankest stare I can muster. As if my life isn't enough of a shit show without a Saturday evening spent watching Mum fawn over Abby's poncy boyfriend. I know what he'll be like—some snotty Bhelmead boy with a plum the size of a melon in his mouth and the mistaken belief that the world owes him.

"Don't look at me like that," Mum snaps. "It isn't as if I ask a lot of you. Just make sure you're home by six-thirty at the latest."

"Whatever." Before she can extract any promises from me, I shimmy past her and out through the front door. Let her spend the whole day worrying whether or not I'll decide to show. It'll be character-building for her.

It's an overcast day, the air cool with the threat of rain. I must have lost half the summer pounding these same pavements, but

I particularly love the early mornings when much of the city is asleep. Even when I don't have to be up for work, I've fallen into the habit of going for a run. Sometimes Ben has the same idea, but we always take care to head in opposite directions.

I'm turning into the quiet road that leads to The Inkwell's back entrance when footsteps sound behind me. I barely notice them, not until someone slams me from the side, shoving me into the wall of the optician's.

Pain rips through my shoulder. I swallow a gasp and round on the culprit. "What the fuck?"

"Hi, Tay." CJ smirks at me. "Where've you been hiding?"

"Aw, have you missed me? I'm touched." I glare into his sneering face, furious with myself. I've been so careful these past few weeks, making damned sure to stay off his radar. How could I have let him get the jump on me? At least he's alone this time; I don't think I could've hacked seeing Liam twice in twelve hours.

CJ rams his elbow into my kidneys, and I double up, hissing through my teeth. He leans in close. "Consider that a reminder."

"Of what?" I straighten with an effort. "The fact that you can't keep your hands off me?"

"Fag boy." CJ pushes past, barging me into the wall again, and swaggers on up the road. When he's several metres away, he pauses to glance back. "Just watch your mouth, all right? Breathe a word to anyone and you're dead."

Hours later, his words continue to plague me.

We're getting ready to close for the day, Dean cashing up behind the counter, me shelving the books customers have taken down and not bothered to replace. What the hell had that been about? Not that CJ needs an excuse to harass me, but this had felt deliberate, like he'd been lying in wait. Still, why pick this morning to threaten me? If I hadn't ratted him out over the past year, why is he afraid I might do it now?

"That prick been hassling you lately?" Dean asks, breaking into my thoughts.

I glance up from sorting through a stack of David Walliams'. He's focused on the till and isn't looking at me, but he may as well have read my mind.

"CJ?" Reflexively, my hand goes to the throbbing bruise on my side. "Nah, I can handle him."

He nods, tapping away at the keys, and I go back to my books. Since the afternoon he interrupted CJ and his mates trying it on, Dean's been less wary of me, more inclined to be friendly. It's companionable, the two of us alone with the quiet and that bookshop smell of paper and ink, a light rain pattering against the windows.

"So." Dean checks something on the screen in front of him. "You went to the grammar with CJ?"

"Yup. Lucky me, huh?"

"And has he always given you shit?"

"Only since the start of Year Thirteen." Before that, if CJ registered my existence, it would've been as one of the boffins unworthy of his attention. But for Liam, I doubt he ever would've learned my name.

"How come he's got it in for you?" Dean looks up, expression curious.

Liam's face flashes across my vision, and my mouth fills with the rancid-milk taste of betrayal. But Dean doesn't need to hear about that particular humiliation. Instead, I widen my eyes to maximum effect, fluttering my mascaraed lashes.

"Oh." Dean blushes. "So why do it? I'm not saying you shouldn't, but wouldn't it be easier not to?"

A wry smile pulls at my mouth. "Probably."

"So…?"

"When I came out to my mum, she was all for sweeping it under the carpet, pretending it didn't exist. Since I was pissed off at her, I did the opposite, went out of my way to make sure everyone noticed me. Then I discovered I liked it. The make-up. It felt like I'd unlocked the real me, and I didn't see why I should lock it up again. Not for my mum, and definitely not for an arsehole like CJ."

Dean stares at me with a mixture of incredulity and something that could be admiration. "That's really brave, man."

"I dunno. Maybe it's just stubborn."

"Nah, that takes guts. Not everyone could do it. I couldn't."

"Shame. You'd look totally hot in eyeliner."

"Fuck off." Dean grabs a pen from the counter and lobs it at me. "Get out of here. I'm almost done, anyway."

"You sure? I'm happy to stay." Anything to delay the inevitable.

Dean waves me away. "Yeah, you head off. It's Saturday night. I'm sure you have better things to do."

"Yeah, right. There's an evening of hell I don't want to miss." Reluctant to leave the sanctuary of The Inkwell, I take my time checking my pockets—phone, wallet, keys—before venturing out.

Despite the drizzle, I walk the long way home. I'm tempted to skip the dinner altogether, grab some chips and shelter at a bus stop until it's over. Just not sure it would be worth the fallout. I content myself with taking a roundabout route. All the same, it's an effort to keep my pace casual. I can't help glancing over my shoulder, half expecting CJ to step out of an alleyway. I despise myself for letting him get to me.

When I step through the front door, the scent of lamb and rosemary slaps me in the face. My stomach, already taut with apprehension, clenches into a painful ball. Voices drift into the hall from the kitchen, Mum's laughter rising above the general buzz. My instincts plead with me to retreat, to run while I still can. Resisting the urge, I saunter towards the living room, hands in my pockets. Might as well get this ordeal over with.

I pause on the threshold and scan the group—Imogen squeezed onto the loveseat with her best friend, Toby, their heads bent over a comic; Ben sprawled on the floor next to the open CD cabinet; Abby leaning against the broad shoulder of a young man who must be her boyfriend. As I stand there, absorbing the cosy scene, the fair-haired boy glances over at me and our eyes clash.

Oh, shit.

Shock knees me in the gut, and before I can think them through, the words burst from me. "What the fuck's he doing here?"

BEN

LINDA DROPPED THE news of her little dinner party while I was halfway through my morning cornflakes. "It'll only be a small celebration, just family and close friends, so if there's anyone you'd like to invite…"

I wince, remembering that last remark. She meant well, I know that, but the words still stung. After all, the one person I'd have wanted to be here is currently living it up in Thailand. I wish I'd had the guts to duck out, to lie and say I had other plans tonight, but I didn't. It's tedious, always being the good boy.

So here I am, the self-appointed DJ, flipping through Mum and Dad's CD collection in search of something released this side of the millennium. Anything to keep me occupied and hide how much I hate this whole charade. Not that the others seem aware of my mood. Abby's absorbed in Carl, giggling at something he's saying in her ear, while Toby reads aloud to Imogen from an X-Men comic.

Linda sweeps into the room in full-on hostess mode. "Can I get anyone another drink? Some more raspberry lemonade, Carl darling?"

"Uh, that'd be great. Thanks." Actually, the poor guy looks like he could use a beer. Beneath the charming smile, he seems on edge, constantly shifting against the sofa cushions as though unable to get comfortable. It must be daunting, meeting his girlfriend's family.

"You're welcome." Linda takes his empty glass, beaming, and nudges a plate of cheese straws towards him across the coffee table. "And do help yourself to some more hors d'oeuvres."

Hors…what? Toby raises his eyebrows at Imogen, who smothers a laugh behind her hand.

Carl takes one, although he's already polished off half a plateful. "Did you make these? They're amazing."

"I did. I'm glad you like them." Flushing with obvious pleasure, Linda turns to me. "Need a top-up, darling?"

"I'm good, thanks." I can't bring myself to look at her. It's all I can do to keep my tone civil.

My stepmother sails from the room to refill Carl's glass, and I let my head rest against the closest shelf. She's so wrapped up in her vision for the future, her and Dad starting afresh in their new house, she's completely forgotten this has been my home for most of my life. It isn't just a pile of bricks and mortar she's selling out from beneath me; it's all the memories of growing up—the birthdays and Christmases, sleepovers and barbecues. It's summer days hopping in and out of the paddling pool, and rainy afternoons watching films under a duvet. It's wading through GCSE coursework at the kitchen table, boisterous games of Jenga and Monopoly, and licking out the mixing bowl on the rare occasions Mum tried her hand at baking. It's all these things, the little mementos that make up the scrapbook of my childhood, but Linda's behaving as though they mean nothing.

I knew, of course, that I'd be leaving for uni in September. Still, even after Mum and Dad separated, I believed this house would always be here, believed my home and everything in it would stay the same, waiting for me to come back.

Stupid, really.

Unlike me, my sister isn't wasting her energy clinging to the past. She's completely grounded in the present, nuzzling against Carl the way she used to with Horace, the enormous teddy bear she insisted on squeezing into bed with her when she was little. I watch the two of them, my fingers trailing over the spines of the CDs. It's easy to see why Abby's so besotted. With his Liam Hemsworth sexiness, Carl is any straight fifteen-year-old girl's dream.

Perhaps sensing my scrutiny, he glances over, his smile friendly. "Abby said you've just come back from Oz. Bet that was awesome."

"Yeah." With an effort, I drag myself from the mire of resentment. "I mean, it was hard work and everything, I had to pay my way, but it was fun, too. I'd definitely recommend it."

"Hey," Abby says, indignant. "Carl and me have only just found each other and now you're trying to send him to the other side of the planet."

Carl laughs, pressing her into his side. "Maybe we can go together one day, travel the world, just the two of us."

Colour blooms in Abby's cheeks, and she gazes at him with pure adoration. Unease coils itself around my stomach. The age gap between them might not matter now. In a couple of months, though, Carl will be exploring his newfound freedom at uni, while Abby continues to lead her sheltered life of school and home-cooked meals. They'll inhabit far more than different cities, but different worlds. I have a horrible feeling their romance is as doomed to fail as mine had been, and I won't even be here to help piece my sister's heart back together.

Linda returns, handing Carl his drink. "Dinner won't be long. I'm just waiting for the vegetables." She frowns at her watch. "Where's Taylor got to?"

"I doubt he'll come," Toby pipes up from behind his comic. "Taylor hates this sort of thing."

"Don't be silly, Toby. Of course he'll be here." Linda's breezy tone doesn't entirely disguise her annoyance.

I conceal my grin in the nearest shelf of CDs. It's the first time I've smiled properly all day. Toby has this knack for saying exactly what he thinks, eyes earnest and guileless behind his thick glasses. I get the feeling Linda only tolerates him out of a sense of duty. His mum died when he was young, Imogen told me, and his dad works long hours as a police officer, so Toby stays over a lot. I've grown used to having him around these past few weeks. Often, I'll walk into the living room to find him and my stepsister watching Brian Cox or poring over the intestines of some electrical appliance they've dismantled.

"Well, I hope Taylor doesn't come," Abby says. "He'll only spoil everything."

The glare Imogen hurls her way is ferocious enough to blow the coffee table and its plate of nibbles to shrapnel. Abby does have a point, though; my stepbrother's silent antagonism is enough to wear anyone down.

"Don't worry, darling. Taylor knows to be on his best behaviour," Linda assures her with a brittle confidence. "We'll give him another quarter of an hour. If he isn't home by then, we'll eat without him. The meat will be ruined otherwise."

She leaves to re-join her own friends in the kitchen, her practised chatter carrying over the chink of glass and china.

"Hey, Mr. DJ," Abby calls over to me, "what's happened to the music?"

"Right, sorry." I go back to perusing the CDs.

Apart from her favourite Beatles albums, Mum doesn't appear to have taken many with her. There's no order to the collection, no organisation by alphabet or genre. Stevie Wonder's *Hotter than July* sits next to Alanis Morissette's *Jagged*

Little Pill, which in turn jostles for space with Andrea Bocelli's *Love in Portofino*.

So many of these songs are intertwined with our lives before the divorce. I remember Mum singing along to 'Wonder Wall' as she threw together a makeshift dinner; the strains of *Tosca* drifting from Dad's study while he worked late; our parents dancing to 'Rockin' Around the Christmas Tree' one New Year's Eve when they'd drunk too much Prosecco. I stare at all the CDs, each with its own track list of memories, and sadness clutches at my heart.

Abby sighs. "Forget it. I'll find something on the telly. Pass the remote, Imogen."

My stepsister flips a page of the comic, acting as though she hasn't heard.

"Imogen, I said—"

"You know," Toby cuts in, his tone conversational, "you could try saying 'please'. I usually find that helps."

"Funny, but I don't actually remember asking for your opinion."

"No, well, you're not very good at asking, are you? That's kind of the point."

Abby jerks upright, eyes flashing, but Carl lays a hand on her back. "It's OK, babe. I'll get it."

He crosses to snag the remote from the arm of the loveseat, and I subside onto the carpet. I'd been about to fetch the damned thing myself; anything to avert another row. While Abby flicks through music channels, I close the cabinet door and sag against it.

If I'm honest, Taylor isn't solely to blame for the bad feeling in the house. Between Linda's impatience with her children, Abby and Imogen rubbing each other the wrong way and my stepbrother's anger towards the entire universe, it can't be the harmonious family life Dad must have imagined when he asked my stepmother to marry him.

"So, you guys go to the grammar?" Carl smiles at Imogen and Toby, an obvious attempt to ease the tension. "I just left this year."

Toby regards him with his level gaze. "Yes, we know."

"Oh." Carl looks pleased. "You saw me play rugby?"

"No. Sport isn't really our thing."

"Fair enough. So where—"

"You weren't very nice to Taylor."

This hooks my interest. I raise my head in time to catch Carl's smile falter.

"Well, no," he admits. "We didn't exactly get on, that's true."

Abby slips her hand into his. "Shut up, Toby. You don't know what you're talking about."

"I know more than you, clearly." Toby spares her a pitying look, then returns his attention to Carl. "I was late for science club one lunchtime, and I saw you. I saw…"

The front door clicks shut. Toby hesitates, exchanging a meaningful glance with Imogen.

A moment later, Taylor appears in the doorway. He leans against the frame, emanating defiance, and takes us all in. When his gaze lands on Carl, his whole body stiffens. Emotion flashes across his face, vanishing before I can put a name to it. Then his expression goes utterly blank. "What the fuck's he doing here?"

CHAPTER NINE

TAYLOR

MY WORDS EXPLODE like a stink bomb over the gathering. On the telly, Pharrell Williams sings about happiness, the upbeat music at odds with the tension. This can't be real. I've walked into a nightmare, my Room 101. I stare at CJ, seated on the sofa with his arm around my stepsister as though he belongs there, and bile rises in my throat. His threat makes perfect sense now. He knew he'd be coming here this evening and didn't want me exposing him for the arsehole he is in front of his new girlfriend.

CJ recovers first, flashing me the charming smile that made him such a favourite among teachers and students alike. His stare, though, carries the promise of danger. "Hey, man, been a while. How's it going?"

"Get out."

"I… What?"

"I said get out." The venom in my voice shocks even me. I'm surprised it doesn't burn a hole through my tongue.

"Taylor…" Ben scrambles to his feet, one hand outstretched as though to…what? Placate me? Ward me off?

"No, you get out." Abby talks over him, glaring at me with pure hatred. "At least Carl's actually welcome here, which is more than I can say for you."

"Speak for yourself," Toby mutters, while my normally placid sister looks ready to scratch someone's eyes out. If I weren't so off balance, I'd hug the pair of them.

"Guys, come on." Ben runs a hand through his hair, something I've noticed he does when he's stressed.

"What?" Abby shoots back. "I don't care what Dad says. This isn't Taylor's house. He can't just barge in here and tell my boyfriend to leave."

"Watch me." Fists clenched, I practically spit the words at her.

"All right." Ben moves to stand between us. "Everyone calm down. Taylor, you need to apologise."

I stab him with a look. That's right, suck up to CJ—sorry, Carl—like everyone else. If it were up to my stepbrother, we'd kiss and make up, then gaze dreamily at one another across the dinner table in a shower of glitter and heart-shaped confetti. The thought would be funny if I weren't so fucking mad.

"No, it's fine." CJ rubs his jaw, doing a credible job of looking upset. "Really. Maybe I shouldn't have come."

I force myself to meet his eyes. "Too damned right you shouldn't. Best do a runner before I make things awkward for you."

"Carl isn't going anywhere." Abby hangs off his arm, her narrowed gaze fixed on me. "And if you don't like it, you can leave."

I open my mouth to retort. For an insane moment, I teeter on the brink of blurting it all out—the taunts, the shoves into walls and lockers—but what would be the point? While Imogen and Toby might believe me, no one else would. CJ's clearly already charmed Ben. Mum and Martin, too, probably.

He could always sweet talk his way out of trouble whenever he was late for lessons or handing in his homework. Why should this be any different?

I turn my back on the lot of them, disgusted as much with myself as with CJ, and come face-to-face with Mum.

"About time." Her expression dithers between irritation and relief. "I'm about to dish up. Tell the others to come and sit... Where are you going?"

"Out." I angle my body in an attempt to sidle past her.

She's too quick for me, though, and flings out an arm to bar my escape. "Don't be ridiculous. Go and sit at the table this minute."

"Not until you tell that prick to leave." I jerk a thumb over my shoulder, not bothering to lower my voice.

Scarlet patches flame in Mum's cheeks. "How dare you. Go straight back in there and apologise."

I ignore her, ducking under her arm, and head for the front door. Even through my anger, I can appreciate what this is doing to her, the embarrassment it will cause. The thought gives me a surge of sadistic satisfaction.

"Taylor Solomon." The command cracks like a palm against bare flesh. "Come here at once, or I'll—"

Whatever punishment my mother might have in store for me, I don't wait to find out. I slip through the front door and slam it behind me, cutting myself off from her tirade. Then I walk. I walk fast, head down, no idea where I'm going. It doesn't matter, so long as I'm out of there, away from CJ's smugness and poisonous smile.

My hands are shaking. I jam them into my sweatshirt pockets, detesting myself for reacting, for allowing him this power over me. Will I ever be free of him? It's bad enough that he's able to ambush me in the street, without turning up at the house as well. Is that why he's going out with Abby? He discovered she's my stepsister and decided to use her as another means of getting to me? I wouldn't put it past him.

The rain has stopped, but the evening is still cloudy and cool. Despite the dismal weather, the city bursts with activity—cars speeding by on the main road, fragments of music and conversation spilling from pub doorways. I feel detached from it. Everything seems too loud, unreal, a drama being played out on a TV screen. A well-aimed brick could shatter the scene in a shower of sparks and broken glass.

I veer away from the busier streets, seeking refuge in the quieter residential estates, and eventually wind up at the park. It's deserted except for a group of teenagers. They look to be around fourteen or fifteen, too old to be persuaded to stay in, too young to go to the pub. They're clustered around the swings, knocking back cans of Stella and sharing a joint. Fuck, I need a drink.

I amble over and nudge the nearest six-pack with my foot. "OK if I pinch one?"

"Sure, man." A boy with a skull earring gestures for me to help myself.

I thank them before retreating to a bench on the far side of the park. With my sweatshirt folded under me to soak up the rainwater, I sit and crack open my beer. Dusk settles around me. The temperature drops. Still I sit there, the lukewarm Stella doing nothing to ward off the chill, putting off the inevitable moment when I'll have to go back.

BEN

"THAT WAS AWFUL." Abby throws herself onto her bed, burying her face in the pillow. "An absolute disaster."

I sit next to her and rub her back. It's all I can think to do. As far as the past couple of hours are concerned, 'absolute disaster' might be an exaggeration, but not by much.

A subdued hush hovers over the house. The soft clink of china drifts up the stairs as Linda clears away the remnants of the night, while the murmur of the TV filters through the floor from the living room where Dad's watching National Geographic with Imogen and Toby.

Taylor still isn't home. A sliver of anxiety pierces the anger that's been simmering inside me all evening. I picture him walking the streets in the dark, furious and resentful, refusing to return until he's sure Carl has left. My stepbrother's usually so deadpan, so contained. What could've happened between him and Carl to set off such a strong reaction? My anger resurges, drowning the concern. Whatever it was, nothing excuses the way he behaved.

After Taylor stormed out, Carl wondered if it would be better if he went. It took the combined efforts of Abby and my stepmother to convince him to stay. Abby clung to him, almost in tears, while Linda apologised profusely for her son's rudeness and insisted he shouldn't be allowed to spoil the celebratory dinner.

But despite everyone's best efforts, Taylor had spoilt it. His absence haunted the table like a malignant ghost, chilling the atmosphere and making the food taste sour. His voice plagued me, raw and jagged with hostility. I couldn't get it out of my mind, and to judge from the falsely bright conversation, neither could anyone else.

The rotten cherry on top of the already inedible cake was Toby turning to Carl as we headed into the dining room and saying, "Well, you can't really have expected anything else, can you?"

"Oh, God." Abby rolls her head on the pillow to look at me, her eyes glistening with tears. "Poor Carl was so upset. I invite him here specially to meet my family, and look what happens. No wonder he couldn't get away fast enough."

"That's not true." It's a lie and we both know it. Carl might have put on a brave performance throughout the meal, but he was clearly uncomfortable. I'm pretty sure only my stepmother plying him with second helpings of everything and urging him to stay for coffee prevented him from bolting.

"It is true. He obviously couldn't wait to leave." A sob catches in Abby's throat and she swipes at her cheeks.

"Hey." Heart aching for her, I hold out my arms.

She crawls into them, the way she used to when she was little, and rests her head on my shoulder. "I really like him, Ben. Really, really like him."

"I know."

"And now he probably hates me."

"Don't be silly. He's crazy about you. Any idiot can see that."

"You think so?"

"Definitely."

Abby sniffs and sits back on her heels, wiping her face on her sleeve. "Did you like him?"

"Carl?"

"Yes. Did you?"

I hesitate, unsure how to answer. Carl had seemed nice enough—friendly, polite, very affectionate with Abby. Yet I can't get Toby's words out of my mind or forget Taylor's expression when he walked into the living room to find Carl sitting there.

The click of the front door and the quiet tread of feet on the stairs save me from conjuring up a tactful reply. Abby and I exchange a look, then turn as one to peer out at the landing. Taylor saunters past, thumbs hooked into the belt loops of his jeans. His nonchalance, so at odds with Abby's unhappiness, has me seething. Does he seriously think he can hurt my sister like this and get away with it?

"Where're you going?" Abby asks when I push myself to my feet.

"There's something I need to do. Will you be all right?"

"Think so. I'm going to text Carl, make sure he got home safely. If he's even speaking to me."

Abby's already reaching for her phone, so I leave her to it and pursue Taylor along the landing. In our bedroom, I shut the door behind me and lean against it, arms folded. My stepbrother glances over from his spot in front of the mirror. He looks exhausted, eyes shadowed in his drawn face, eyeliner bleeding into the dark rings around them.

The stab of pity catches me off guard. Then I remember Abby's tears and glare at him. "Hope you're pleased with yourself."

He turns away without a word. Fishing a cleansing wipe from the pack on the chest of drawers, he starts removing his make-up.

"Well, are you?" I advance a few paces into the room. "You throw a tantrum, upset my sister, and then leave everyone else to pick up the pieces."

Taylor continues to ignore me, tossing the used wipe into the bin and extracting another. His indifference makes me want to shake him, to seize him by the shoulders and force him to listen.

"Look, the rest of us are trying here. We're doing our best to make this work, and all you can do is sulk and cause trouble. What's your problem?"

Taylor leans in to the mirror, apparently engrossed in rubbing a persistent smudge from the corner of his eye. His gaze, reflected in the glass, slides past me without recognition. It's as though I'm invisible.

My temper boils over. "For Christ's sake, what's the matter with you? I get that you don't like the way things have turned out. I'm not exactly thrilled about it either, but you don't see me acting like a spoilt brat. So you and Carl weren't best mates at school. Big deal. You had no right behaving like a—"

"Shut up." Taylor whips around, and his ferocity traps the words in my throat. He takes a step towards me, balling the wipe in his fist. "Just shut the fuck up, all right? You don't know what you're talking about."

In a violent gesture, he hurls the crumpled wipe towards the bin. It bounces off the rim and falls to the carpet. Cursing, Taylor goes to retrieve it. As he stoops, his T-shirt rides up a couple of inches, exposing the skin above the waistband of his jeans.

I stare, riveted. "What's that?"

"What's what?"

"That. On your side."

"It's nothing." Taylor straightens, tugging down his T-shirt.

His defensiveness stokes my suspicion. "Doesn't look like nothing to me. Let me see."

Before he can protest, I'm beside him, lifting the hem of his top to reveal the bruise. It stands out above his hipbone, a livid, purple stain about the size of my palm. I wince just looking at it.

Taylor has gone oddly still. All at once, I'm aware how close we are—so close I can feel the tension emanating from him, feel the heat from his body, his breath grazing my neck.

"Who did this to you?" My voice comes out hoarse, drained of anger. Without pausing to think, I reach out and trace the bruise. His skin is smooth and warm, stretched taut over hard muscles. Electricity flares at the contact, zinging up my arm. Taylor gasps, flinches as though my touch burns.

"Taylor, who—"

"No one." He backs away, hands raised to hold me off. "It was an accident, that's all. Just an accident."

Then he's gone, disappearing onto the landing. A second later, the bathroom door closes and the lock clunks into place.

I sink onto my bed and drop my head in my hands. My pulse is racing, skin prickling as though I've walked through a hot shower. What just happened? One minute I'd been mad enough to shake my stepbrother until he got whiplash, and the next...

The next I'd wanted to crush my mouth on his, kiss all that belligerence out of him until neither of us knew where we were. And the instant before he pulled away, I could have sworn Taylor wanted it every bit as much as I did.

CHAPTER TEN

T HE LAST PLACE in the galaxy I want to be when I haul myself out of bed next morning is my stepsister's room. A persistent ache throbs at my temples and my eyelids are scratchy from too little sleep. All I want to do is crawl back under the covers and pretend the previous evening never happened. Yet, here I am, tapping on Abby's door like the model stepbrother, because she should know the sort of scum she's going out with. She might be a pain in my arse, but no one deserves CJ Farmer.

I've barely poked my head around the door when a pillow sails towards me. I pluck it out of the air and lob it into a far corner. "Good morning to you, too."

"Get out of my room." Abby shoots up in bed, cheeks flushed with sleep and indignation. "Go on, get out."

"I want to talk to you."

"Well, I don't want to talk to you. God, I don't even want to look at you after last night. Go away and leave me alone."

I ignore her, stepping farther into the room. I lean against the nearest wall, arms folded, and rest my head against it. Late morning sunshine pierces through a gap in the curtains, jabbing at my eyes. The pounding in my skull intensifies. My brain feels foggy and slow, the result of lying awake till dawn. I'd replayed everything over and over in my mind, more conscious than ever of Ben asleep mere feet away.

"Taylor," Abby's voice takes on a shrill edge, "if you don't get out right now, I'll—"

"It's about CJ. Carl."

Abby's mouth drops open. "Seriously? You think you have anything to say about my boyfriend I'd want to hear?"

"You need to hear this."

"Trust me, I really don't."

"For fuck's sake. Shut up and listen, will you?" My head gives a particularly aggressive twinge. The smell of sausages wafts up the stairs, reminding me I haven't eaten since the few bites of tuna sandwich I forced down yesterday lunchtime.

Abby glares at me, fingers clenched on the duvet, but she falls quiet.

"Look." I keep my tone level with an effort. "I know Carl, all right? I know he comes across as this great guy, but he isn't. You have no idea what he's like."

"Whereas you do, I suppose." A sneer pulls at her lips, twisting them out of shape.

I disregard her scepticism. "I went to school with him. I've seen how he treats anyone who doesn't fit in. Anyone different. He's a bully, Abby. A bully and a creep. He's made my life hell this past year."

"Oh, give it up." Abby swings her legs in their pink-striped pyjama shorts out of bed and leans towards me, gaze hard. "You think I don't know what this is about?"

"I'm sorry?"

"What? You thought Carl wouldn't tell me? I know all about you, Taylor Solomon, about what you did. I know how you're so sad and desperate that you—"

"Shut your mouth." So much for staying calm. I push myself off the wall and loom over her, hands balled into fists.

She doesn't flinch. "Why? Can't handle the truth?"

"The truth?" My laugh comes out bitter and ugly. "Like you give a damn about the truth. All you care about is swallowing the lies that prick feeds you like the good little sheep you are."

"Don't call Carl a—"

"Hey." Ben appears in the doorway. "What's going on?"

At the sight of him, my stomach tightens in a way that has nothing to do with the anger coursing through me. My eyes linger, taking in his hair, damp and dishevelled from the shower, the shorts hugging muscular thighs. He glances between us, fingers tapping against the doorframe. Those same fingers that had sketched the bruise on my side and set my skin on fire. He'd been so close, his lips centimetres from mine, stealing the breath from my lungs. Our gazes snag, and the intensity in Ben's expression tells me he's remembering, too.

"Make Taylor get out," Abby demands, breaking the spell.

I look away, confused, my face hot. As I tossed and turned into the early hours, I convinced myself my reaction to Ben was an anomaly, brought on by physical and emotional exhaustion. Who was I kidding? My stepbrother might irritate the hell out of me, but I want him. I've wanted him from that first evening when he caught me watching him on the driveway.

"Taylor?" Ben sounds unsure of himself.

"It's fine," I tell him. "I'm going. Was only trying to help, but I shouldn't have bothered."

"If help means spreading lies about my boyfriend, you can keep it to yourself," Abby says.

I snort. "You wouldn't recognise a lie if it did a striptease on the end of your bed, but you'll find out soon enough."

I make to squeeze by Ben in the doorway, but he puts out an arm to block me. "Whoa. What's this about Carl?"

"It's nothing," Abby says. "Taylor's got it in for him because Carl knows how pathetic he really—"

The doorbell chimes. I normally avoid answering the front door in case I get trapped into making small talk with one of Mum's revolting charity work friends, but anything's better than staying to listen while Abby spouts CJ's poison.

"I've got it." Without looking at either of them, I slip past Ben and down the stairs.

Poppy stands on the front steps, hands twisting together, a crease between her eyebrows. Still, she smiles when she sees me. "Hey. Where've you been hiding? I haven't seen you in ages."

"Oh." I shift from foot to foot. Truth is, I've avoided the annex since Ben and I bumped into each other on our way to see his mum. Seeking refuge at Poppy's no longer seems right. Not now she has her own son home. Yet confronted with her obvious pleasure to see me, I realise I've been an idiot.

Poppy touches my shoulder. "Don't be a stranger, OK? I've missed our chats."

"OK. Sorry." I take in her agitation. "Something up?"

"It's the computer." Poppy runs her fingers through her curls, which are even wilder than usual. "I went to turn it on this morning and…nothing. I hate to bother her, but could you ask Imogen if she minds taking a look?"

"Imogen doesn't." My sister emerges from the living room, Toby close behind. She joins me in the doorway. "Computer trouble?"

Poppy nods. "You could say that. It's completely dead. Everything seems to be connected properly, but you know how useless I am with these things. I haven't got a clue what to do."

"We're on it." Imogen pats Poppy's arm. She beckons to Toby, then leads the way around the side of the house.

I'm tempted to follow, but my stomach lets out a plaintive growl. Well, I'll have to face the executioner sooner or later. I shut the front door and slink into the kitchen where Martin's tucking into a fried breakfast. Mum's seated across from him, sipping coffee over the Sunday supplements, but she looks up to frown at me when I come in.

"I see you've finally dared to show your face," she says by way of a good morning. "I think you and I need to have a little chat later, don't you?"

I shrug. I knew walking out last night would have its repercussions, but what choice did I have? Sit at the dinner table with CJ and behave as though he hasn't spent the past year laying into me?

Yeah, right.

"I mean it, Taylor. This isn't over."

"Chill, Mum, I get it." I help myself to a slice of toast from the rack and begin slathering it with apricot jam. Should I bother telling Mum about CJ, explain our history? I snort under my breath. Like she'd listen. Last night, Mum hadn't stopped for a moment to wonder at my reaction to CJ being there. She'd simply assumed I was the one in the wrong. As far as she's concerned, I always am. No point trying to excuse myself to her.

"Sit down if you're going to eat that," Mum snaps. "Was that Poppy I heard just now?"

"Yup."

"What did she want?"

"Imogen."

"Imogen?" Mum sniffs, clearly unable to fathom what use anyone could have for her daughter. She turns to Martin. "I wish your ex-wife wouldn't do this, barge in on us on a Sunday morning."

I tune her out, my attention on heaping another piece of toast with jam. Upstairs, Abby will be filling Ben in on the so-called truth about me. And he'll believe it. Why wouldn't he? Everyone else does. I remember the tentative brush of Ben's gaze, the fragile beginnings of…something. Whatever connection had kindled between us will have sputtered and died. A weight drags at my gut. Sometimes it feels as though I'll never be free of the lies.

BEN

I'M HALFWAY DOWN the stairs when my stepmother's voice carries from the kitchen. She's clearly in the midst of a rant, so I pause to listen.

"I mean it, Marty, if we hadn't got the offer on the house, I'm not sure what I'd have done."

"I know, Lindy. You've been very patient."

"Yes, well, I've tried to be accommodating. There aren't many women who'd put up with their husband's ex-wife living practically under the same roof."

"This has all been extremely hard on you, I realise that, but it won't be for much longer."

"Let's hope not. Apart from anything else, it reflects badly on me. People will think you haven't made up your mind."

Anger burns the back of my throat. How dare she? Linda's talking as if Mum living here is some kind of imposition on her, an embarrassment. Yet, if it hadn't been for Mum's kindness, allowing my stepmother and her kids to move into the house she still part owns, they'd be slumming it in some grotty council flat on the Brickwell Estate.

When I enter the kitchen, Linda stops talking abruptly. She forces a smile. "Morning, darling. Sleep well?"

"Fine." I can barely bring myself to answer, let alone be polite.

Taylor, standing with his hip propped against the table, grimaces and offers me a piece of toast. The gesture, so unexpected, has a tendril of warmth unfurling in my stomach. I accept it gratefully.

"Actually," Dad says, reaching out to touch Linda's hand, "I have a bit of good news."

Her eyes spark with triumph. "Don't tell me. You've got an interview for the finance manager job."

"Yep, on Tuesday. The email came through last night."

The toast turns to grit in my mouth. I didn't even know he'd applied. Still, I should've guessed he'd cave under the pressure. At this rate, Mum'll be homeless by the end of the day.

Linda beams. "But that's wonderful! I knew you would. I'm so proud of you. We must go out and celeb… Marty?"

Dad winces, putting a hand to his chest. "It's nothing. Just indigestion."

"You poor love." Linda's on her feet at once, rummaging in the cupboard. "Go through to the living room and I'll bring you a nice cup of tea and some Gaviscon."

Dad does as he's told, the pain evident in his expression as he pushes his chair back and shuffles into the hall. Taylor raises an eyebrow at me, his gaze flitting towards the back door. Anxious to avoid speaking to Linda, I nod and follow him outside.

At the gate, Taylor pauses with his hand on the latch. "I, uh, thought I'd go and see your mum. She was having computer trouble."

"Uh-oh." Beyond the basics—word processing, checking emails, browsing the web—technology has always intimidated Mum, and she flies into a panic whenever anything goes wrong. "I'll come with you."

We wander around the side of the house, munching our toast. The hedge throws a constellation of sunlight and shade across the path. It's more companionable than I could've imagined only twenty-four hours ago.

"Sorry about my mother." Taylor shoots me a sidelong glance. He's keeping a respectable distance between us, but his tone holds none of its former hostility. "She can be a bitch."

I bite off another chunk of toast. "Not your fault. We don't get to choose our parents."

"More's the pity."

I have the sense he isn't just talking about Linda. Come to think of it, I haven't seen any sign of his and Imogen's dad since I got home. Abby said something about him crashing with a mate in London, but surely there's nothing to stop him visiting his kids. Still, the wary set to Taylor's jaw warns me against broaching the subject.

"Have you and your mum never got on?" I ask instead.

"Nope. You've seen how she is. Mum's always been obsessed with what other people think, and Imogen and me...we don't give a shit."

"I've gathered." A grin teases the corner of my mouth. My mind goes to what Abby told me up in her room after Taylor left, the alleged reason for the animosity between him and Carl. Again, I refuse to accept it.

In the annex, we find Imogen and Toby kneeling on the floor, the computer tower disgorging its innards over the carpet. Mum looks on, teeth gnawing at her lower lip.

"I just don't understand. It was working fine when I switched it off last night. Hey, sweethearts." She manages a smile when we join them. "We're having a bit of a crisis. Let me get you both a coffee."

"S'all right, I'll make it." Taylor touches her on the shoulder. "You sit down."

She squeezes his arm as he steps around her. This is the first time I've seen them together, but the affection they share is obvious. How often has Taylor dropped in on Mum since I've been home? Not very, so far as I've noticed. I have a horrible feeling I'm partly responsible for that.

Mum lowers herself onto the sofa as though it's made of polystyrene. In the kitchen area, Taylor's bending to retrieve the milk from the fridge, skintight denim clinging to runner's thighs. I tear my gaze from him and sit beside her.

"You OK?" I ask.

"I was, until I tried to turn on the computer this morning. My editor's expecting a first draft by tomorrow and I still need to do a final read-through."

"You have everything backed up, though, right?"

Mum starts to reply, her expression agonised, when Toby pipes up. "Panic over. At least, it is if we're right, and I'm ninety-eight point six per cent sure we are."

"As sure as that?" Amusement filters through Mum's anxiety.

Imogen nods and waves at Toby, who explains, "All evidence points to your power supply being the culprit."

"Ah, right…" Mum's face remains uncomprehending.

My attention drifts to Taylor, now pouring boiling water into mugs. His T-shirt has risen to show a slice of skin above his waistband, and I flush, recalling the electric heat of it under my fingers. Then I remember the bruise, how Taylor's defences slammed into place when I asked about it. Who had done that to him? He claimed it was an accident, and maybe that's all it was, but I can't entirely shake my unease.

Taylor turns from the worktop, a mug in each hand. I glance away before he clocks me staring. All the same, I continue to watch him from beneath my lashes, his fluid grace at odds with the belligerence that never seems far from the surface.

As he passes Mum and me our coffee, Toby's saying, "So, provided we're correct and your hard drive hasn't snuffed it—which we're positive it hasn't," he adds at a reproachful look from Imogen, "your data won't be affected. Replace the power supply, and you'll be straight back to writing steamy bedroom action."

I almost spit out my mouthful of coffee. Taylor has retreated to the kitchen for his own drink, but he tosses me a smirk over his shoulder. Imogen arches a brow at her friend, but Toby merely shrugs, unembarrassed.

Mum's lips twitch. "Well, that's a relief. I don't suppose I can get it up and running today, though. I'll have to call Shelly and explain."

Tyres crunch on the driveway, and Toby exchanges a pointed look with Imogen.

"There might be a way," he says, scrambling to his feet, and hurries from the annex.

I watch him vanish from view. "What's he up to?"

"With Toby, you never can tell." Taylor sits on Mum's other side, nudging her with his elbow. "Don't worry about it. Your editor will understand."

"Yeah." Even as the word forms on my tongue, it strikes me how weird it is to be agreeing with my stepbrother. "Computers go wrong all the time."

Mum smiles at us. Before she can reply, footsteps and the murmur of voices announce Toby's return. He reappears in the doorway, accompanied by a man in his mid-thirties. The newcomer has on faded jeans and a T-shirt covered in what looks to be duck-egg blue paint. With his sandy hair and earnest face, he's an older version of Toby.

"Hey." He pauses on the threshold, adjusting his glasses. "Sorry to gatecrash. I'm Jon, Toby's dad."

"Oh." Mum jumps up. Her hands go to her hair, pushing the tangle behind her ears. "Lovely to meet you. I'm Poppy." She hesitates, perhaps considering how best to introduce herself, then evidently decides to leave it at that. "Can I get you a drink? Tea? Coffee?"

"Coffee would be great, cheers. Tobes tells me your PC's misbehaving."

"Dad builds computers in his spare time," Toby puts in. "Our flat's full of parts. I thought he might have a power supply lying around."

"Gosh, how clever! Blast it." Mum goes to refill the kettle, turning the tap on too far and spraying herself with water. "This is really kind of you, Jon, but I don't want to put you out."

"It's no trouble. Tobes is right. I have whole boxes of motherboards and wires and stuff. I'll take a quick look and see what I can do." Jon flashes her a smile. It's a nice smile, open and reassuring, but the lines around his eyes and mouth suggest a certain toughness.

"You're a lifesaver." Mum puts the kettle on to boil, her own smile sheepish as she dabs the front of her dress with a tea towel.

"No probs. Hey, kiddo." Jon ruffles Imogen's hair and settles next to her on the floor. "What've we got here?"

Mum brings him his coffee, and while he examines what I take to be the power supply, they fall into an easy conversation about computers and books. Behind their backs, Imogen and Toby swap another significant glance, and I have the sneaking suspicion they're up to something.

CHAPTER ELEVEN

TAYLOR

"And you're sure you'll be OK?" my stepdad asks for what has to be the fifth time in as many minutes.

I huff, leaning against the kitchen counter. "No, Martin. We'll starve to death, leave the gas on and burn the house down around our emaciated skeletons."

Imogen frowns at me over her cornflakes, but Martin merely chuckles. "Point taken. I know you and Ben are more than capable of looking after yourselves and the girls. So long as you don't feel we're abandoning you."

The previous evening, Martin came home from work armed with an enormous bouquet of Mum's favourite lilies and the news that the two of them were off on holiday. Apparently, a colleague was all set to fly out to his villa in Marbella with his wife and some friends of theirs. However, these friends had cancelled at the last minute—something to do with their daughter being rushed to hospital—and so Martin and Mum had been invited to go in their place.

Mum refused at first. "I can't possibly go away at such short notice. There's so much to organise. And who will keep an eye on Abby and Imogen? Poppy can hardly be considered responsible. She's in her own little world half the time."

Eventually, though, we convinced her the break would do her good. I think Ben's calm reassurances did more to persuade her than my impatience, but the result was the same—a whole seven days without Mum treating me like a scrounging relative who has long outstayed his welcome.

Before I can dismiss my stepdad's concerns yet again, a shriek echoes down the stairs, shattering what till now has been a peaceful Thursday morning.

"Good God." The newspaper slips from Martin's grasp, plopping onto his plate of toast and marmalade. He scrapes his chair back, face full of alarm.

I wave him off, sharing a knowing look with Imogen. "It's all right. I'll go."

I swallow the dregs of my coffee, dump the mug in the sink and head into the hall. If Mum's being devoured by a wardrobe-dwelling monster, I don't want to miss the fun.

Upstairs, I almost collide with Abby as she emerges from the bathroom in her dressing gown, hair wrapped in a towel. She gapes at me, eyes wide. I ignore her, slipping past to reach the end of the landing just as Mum yanks a sheepish-looking Buddy from the master bedroom by his collar.

"Out! Go on, shoo, you filthy, revolting animal." Catching sight of me, she thrusts the unfortunate dog in my direction. "Taylor, take him away."

"What's up?" I peer over Mum's shoulder. A suitcase lies open on the bed, and beside it, crumpled and dusted with dog hair, is what I assume had been a pile of neatly folded clothes.

Mum glowers at me. "Just get him out of my sight. I've had about as much as I can take. I'm warning you now. If I catch this brute within ten feet of my bed again, I'll drag him straight to the nearest rescue centre."

As though in understanding, Buddy's ears droop. He gazes up at Mum with eyes full of entreaty.

"Like hell you will." I skewer Mum with a glare of pure loathing and scratch Buddy behind his ears. "Don't listen to the old witch. I won't let anything happen to you. Come on, let's go for a walk."

At the mention of the W-word—walk, not witch—Buddy's head snaps up. I turn my back on Mum and stalk away with Buddy trotting beside me, tail wagging.

My stepsister, never one to miss an opportunity to suck up, rushes to Mum's side. "I'm so sorry, Linda. Can I help?"

I suppress the urge to gag. As I start downstairs, Mum's saying, "I don't think so, darling. Oh, why did I let your dad talk me into this? I should be at the hairdresser's in half an hour. Then I need to get my nails done, have my legs waxed, and finish packing. And now I'll have to wash and iron these clothes all over again."

"It's OK. See? They're really not that bad. I'll find the clothes brush."

I roll my eyes and fetch Buddy's lead from the utility room. On my way back through the kitchen, Martin looks up at me, expression quizzical.

"It's fine," I tell him. "No axe-wielding maniac, more's the pity."

My stepdad opens his mouth, no doubt to reprove me, but I make myself scarce. I have the front door open when Ben sprints down the stairs.

"All right if I come with you?" He casts a nervous glance behind him at the landing.

"Sure." I shrug. "Let's get out of here."

We step out onto the driveway, Buddy at our heels. As soon as I pull the door shut, trapping the fraught atmosphere inside,

I release a breath. Beside me, Ben's shoulders relax. He catches my eye, and a current of solidarity hums between us.

Despite the early morning freshness, the sun is already hot against my skin. We stick to the shade of the plane trees, Buddy insisting we let him sniff at every trunk.

"Is your mum always like this before she goes on holiday?" Ben asks. "So…manic?"

"Always. My da—" I choke back the words. I'd been about to let it all spill out—how the day before the annual family holiday, Dad would take the extra time off work to spend with Imogen and me. While Mum whipped herself into a frenzy over mountains of ironing and passports that had inexplicably vanished, Dad took us on magical mystery tours to theme parks, the science museum or the zoo. If I'm honest, I looked forward to these outings far more than the actual holiday.

Ben breaks into my thoughts, tone hesitant. "You never talk about him. Your dad."

"Would you talk about yours if he dropped you in the shit and didn't even hang around to watch you drown?"

"Fair enough."

Silence settles over us, a pensive sort of silence that holds no awkwardness. We walk side by side, closer than we might've done a week ago, although still with a careful foot of space between us.

Things haven't been entirely easy since the night I came home to find CJ in our living room. The awareness of my stepbrother, the one that has chafed like a stone in my shoe from the moment we met, is still there. It's stronger, if anything, and yet softer somehow, a constant buzz of anticipation in my belly. Every so often, his eyes will brush mine, his expression half shy, half intrigued, and I know he feels it, too, whatever this is.

When we reach the park, I lead Ben over to the same bench I'd sought refuge on the previous Saturday, drinking cheap beer in the dark, and let Buddy off. Ben flops onto the seat beside me, and for a while we watch Buddy lumber around in a half-hearted show of exercise before he collapses, panting, at our feet.

"Lazy dog." I stoop to pat him. At once, he rolls onto his back with his tongue lolling.

Ben smiles at me, tickling Buddy under the chin. "You're really good with him."

"Buddy's great. He's so…"

"Uncomplicated?"

"Yeah." That's it exactly. Amidst all the weirdness of these past months, Buddy has been a steady source of comfort. Even my friendship with Poppy is tangled up with feelings of guilt, no matter how often she assures me they're misplaced. I look down at the hulking mass of fur sprawled on the grass. "I'm going to miss him."

"Where're you headed in September?"

"City. They offer this MA in publishing. I'd really like to take it once I've finished my English degree."

"Is that what you want to get into after uni? Publishing?"

"That's the dream. I've always loved books. It's fascinating, all the work that goes into putting them together. I want to be a part of that."

"Good for you."

The respect in Ben's voice has me blushing, and I glance away. This is the first time I've shared my ambition with anyone other than Poppy since Dad left.

"No, seriously," Ben says. "It must be great to know what you want to do with your life. I haven't got a clue. I'm into science, so I applied to study biology, but beyond that..." He trails off, shaking his head.

I bump his arm with my knuckles, the contact sending sparks along my nerves. "Don't worry about it. You have three years to figure things out. Which uni are you going to?"

"Kings." Ben's gaze searches mine. "So we'll be neighbours in September."

Less than a week ago, the prospect of Ben and me attending universities within a hundred miles of one another would've had me buying a one-way ticket to Hong Kong. Now, though, my body floods with warmth that has nothing to do with the summer day.

BEN

"OK, MY TURN." I prod the contents of the saucepan with a wooden spoon and cast a sideways look at Taylor.

He leans in to pour stock over the meat, which spits and sizzles in a satisfying way. "Go for it."

When he draws back, his arm brushes mine. The contact burns, as though a drop of fat has splashed onto my skin. I concentrate on stirring the mixture, filling the kitchen with the smell of mince and spices, and consider my next question.

A nervous exhilaration fizzes inside me, frothing like the can of beer at my elbow. We're only making dinner, and yet it feels as if we're doing something illicit, forbidden. Stupid, really. Linda didn't say we couldn't cook while they were away, not in so many words. All the same, I can't help imagining her horrified expression if she could see the state of her normally sparkling surfaces, the carrot peel and pepper seeds strewn amidst splatters of tomato puree. The thought has me hiding a grin. You'd think my stepmother were Gordon Ramsay the way she guards her domain, pouncing on anyone who dares to so much as boil the kettle.

The moment Dad and Linda left for the airport that afternoon, all the tension seemed to drain from the house. It was as if the bricks themselves realised they no longer had to stand to attention and sagged in relief. I had the powerful urge to charge from room to room like a little kid, jumping on the beds and using the bannisters as a slide. Instead, I followed Taylor into the kitchen to inspect the contents of the freezer.

My stepbrother drew out the container labelled 'Fish pie, Friday dinner' in Linda's precise handwriting and grimaced. "Fuck that. Let's make a chilli."

"Suits me," I said and dug out my phone to google recipes.

It began during the drive to the supermarket. We were chatting about films—the ones that didn't live up to the hype and the favourites we could watch over and over. As I pulled Esmerelda into the car park, Taylor asked, "What was the first film you ever saw at the cinema?"

"*Ratatouille*." I didn't even have to think. It was the first time Mum and I went out, just the two of us, after Abby was born. We shared a giant bucket of popcorn and stopped off at McDonald's on the way home.

Taylor's mouth quirked. "Good choice. Mine was *WALL-E*, but all I really remember is that Dad cried his eyes out."

"God, me too."

"Really? How old were you?"

"Fifteen." Taylor snorted, and I punched him lightly on the arm. "All right, what was the first album you ever bought?"

The game continued for the rest of that afternoon. As we browsed the aisles of Pardo's for ingredients and bore them back to the house, as we measured spices and chopped vegetables, the two of us volleyed questions back and forth. Rather than satisfying my curiosity, the more Taylor revealed, the more I wanted to know. After weeks of him shutting me out, he was finally allowing me a glimpse through the shutters, and I liked what I saw. I liked it way more than I should.

Now, with the saucepan bubbling on the hob, I turn to Taylor. "OK, here's one. Supposing you were exiled to a desert island—"

"Christ, don't say that in front of Mum. You'll give her ideas." He smirks, propping himself against the worktop beside me.

I nudge his foot with mine. "Shut up. This is a serious question. So, you're about to be shipped off and you're told you can only take one book with you. What would it be?"

"Wow, that *is* serious." Taylor picks up the potato peeler, toying with it as he ponders.

I fight a grin. I love watching him think, the way he stares off into space, eyes intense and faraway. It's as though he's peering through a window into a world only he can see.

At last, Taylor drops the peeler to the counter and shakes his head. "Nope, can't do it."

"Seriously? I thought that would be a no-brainer. You must have a favourite book."

"I have about a hundred. Making me pick one would be like…I dunno. Like asking you to choose a favourite finger."

"That's easy." I let the wooden spoon clatter onto the rim of the saucepan and show Taylor my right index finger. "My war wound."

He examines it. His eyes widen when they settle on the small chunk missing from the tip. "I've never noticed that before. How'd you do it?"

"Caught it in the garage door when I was three. Bled everywhere, apparently. Lucky for me, Mum trained as a nurse so knew what to do."

Taylor winces. Perhaps he's picturing a fair-haired toddler, his tiny finger crushed beneath the weight of metal. He makes a sudden movement, and for a moment I'm sure he's about to take my hand. I hold my breath, skin already tingling. Then my stepbrother reaches past me.

"Careful. Meat's burning," he says, and reduces the heat under the pan.

I'm ladling the results of our labours into bowls when the front door slams. Abby marches into the kitchen and peers at the contents of the saucepan, nose wrinkled. "What's that? Looks like cow dung."

"Charming." I swat her with the tea towel. "I'm guessing you don't want any dinner then."

"God, no." She swipes our Doritos from the worktop, along with the tub of sour cream, and stalks out again. A few moments later, her bedroom door bangs shut.

Taylor arches an eyebrow. "What's up with her?"

"No idea. Maybe she and Lauren fell out. Feeling brave enough to try some of this cow dung?"

"I'm up for it if you are. I'll tell Imogen it's ready."

Taylor retreats into the hallway to call his sister downstairs while I unearth a half-empty bag of tortilla chips from the back of a cupboard. Once Imogen joins us, we carry our chilli through to the living room, where we eat it in front of the telly. The first mouthful of spices and tingling heat explodes on my tongue. Abby can turn her nose up all she likes, but it tastes pretty all right to me. Picturing my stepmother's panic at the thought of tomato stains on her cream leather makes me savour it even more.

"Not bad, huh?" I grin over at Taylor, who's occupying the other end of the sofa. "Maybe we won't actually starve at uni."

Mouth full, he gives me the thumbs up. Beneath their mascaraed lashes, his eyes gleam with amusement...and something warmer. Something that has my entire body flushing.

After we've all demolished seconds, I get up to collect our empty bowls. "You guys want to watch a film?"

"Sure. Not like I have a hot date lined up." Taylor passes me his bowl, the corner of his mouth lifting in a crooked smirk.

Is he flirting with me? My throat goes dry, and I have to swallow before getting the words out. "OK. You, uh, pick something out and I'll see if Abs wants to come down."

Taylor and Imogen exchange a grimace at this, but I pretend not to notice. If the three of them would just give each other a chance... In the kitchen, I dump our dirty dishes on the draining board, something else that would've sent Linda into a frenzy, and head upstairs.

I'm about to tap on Abby's bedroom door when I hear her speaking to someone. "What? ... No, of course I want to! ... How can you even think that? ... Please, don't be like— Carl, are you still there? Carl?"

Silence.

I wait a beat to make sure she's finished her conversation, then poke my head into the room. My sister's lying on her bed, staring blankly at the phone in her hand.

"You OK?" I ask.

"Yeah." She averts her face, although not before I see the tears on her lashes. "Fine."

Protectiveness swells inside me, and I cross to sit beside her. "Has Carl upset you?"

"It isn't his fault. It's Dad's stupid rule about me not going to parties while he's away. Now Carl thinks I'm avoiding him."

"Why would he think that?"

"Because of Taylor, obviously. I told Carl what he's been saying, and now he's got it into his head I actually believe that crap."

I hesitate, biting my lip, but I have to at least put it out there. "You don't think there might be some truth to what Taylor said."

"Oh, I get it." Abby glares at me, dashing a hand across her eyes. "Just because you and our stepbrother are BFFs now, Carl's suddenly the bad guy."

"I didn't say that."

"Whatever, but I know Carl, all right? He isn't capable of bullying anyone."

"No, well." I massage the bridge of my nose. "Still, if he wants to see you that badly, he can always come here."

Abby snorts. "Yeah, like he'd risk that after the way he was treated last time. Anyway, Carl's eighteen. He doesn't want to be stuck in on a Friday night."

"Carl may be eighteen, but you're not. He needs to remember that."

"You don't like him, do you?"

"I don't like him upsetting my sister, no." I rub her shoulder. "Forget about Carl. We're going to watch a film. Come and sit with us."

"I'd rather shave my armpits with a cheese grater." She shrugs me off, rolling away onto her side. "Just leave me alone."

I sigh and get to my feet. Bloody Carl. The sooner that relationship ends, the better. Whatever may or may not have gone on between him and Taylor, the fact that he made my sister cry is a black mark against him.

As I enter the living room, wheels crunch on the driveway outside. I cross to peer through the open window in time to see a familiar Vauxhall Astra pull up. I automatically look for Toby, although Imogen hadn't mentioned he was coming over. Only his dad gets out, though. Dressed in dark jeans and a pale-blue shirt, Jon looks much smarter than the last time I saw him.

He spies me watching him and waves before disappearing around the side of the house.

Hmmm.

I turn to the others. "Toby's dad's here. He's gone to see Mum."

Taylor, sprawled full-length on the sofa, merely shrugs. I glance at Imogen, who's kneeling in front of the telly. I expect some curiosity over what her best friend's dad might be up to. Instead, she continues scrolling through Netflix with studied concentration. Her lack of reaction strikes me as suspicious.

I crouch next to her. "Did you know he was coming?"

Imogen shakes her head, but one side of her mouth curves in a secretive smile.

"You did!" I cuff her playfully on the shoulder. "Didn't you?"

"I didn't. Not really. We just—"

"Who's we?"

"Toby and me. When he asked his dad to have a look at your mum's computer the other day, we kind of hoped once we introduced them…" She trails off, expression anxious.

I laugh. "Knew you were up to something."

"You don't mind?"

"'Course not. Mum deserves some happiness, and Jon seems like a decent guy."

"He's the best," Imogen assures me, her certainty that of a chemist reciting the formula for common salt.

I smile at her, then get up to nudge Taylor's legs off my end of the sofa. "So, what're we watching?"

THE FILM IS laughably bad, some futuristic action flick about a bank heist gone wrong. I scarcely register the increasingly implausible events unfolding on screen; I'm too aware of Taylor stretched out beside me, arms hooked behind his head. He has his knees drawn up, bare feet millimetres from my leg, and every so often his toes brush my thigh through the denim. It could be accidental, an unconscious flexing of muscles. Still, every touch sends a flood of sensation to my groin.

Oh, God. His toes graze my thigh again, igniting a firework display along my nerves. If he keeps this up, I'm going to bust my flies. I shift against the cushions. With any luck, it'll appear as though I'm searching for a more comfortable position. Does he have any idea of the havoc he's wreaking on my body? I glance sideways at him, but he's intent on the TV and his deadpan expression gives nothing away.

As soon as the film comes to a farcical end, I offer to put the kettle on and practically run from the room. In the kitchen, I slump against the worktop and take several calming breaths. I can't suppress my grin. I'm giddy, my heart racing. It feels as though Taylor and I are facing each other across a yawning chasm. We stand at either end of the only bridge, a delicate mesh of shared glances and almost touches, both waiting to see which of us will be the first to cross.

My phone vibrates in my pocket. I pull it out, my mind still on Taylor. It'll be Dad letting me know they've arrived safely. I glance at the screen, and the words hit me like a slug to the gut.

Missed me, baby boy?

The happiness drains out of me. Bile burns the back of my throat. It's been weeks since I last heard from Seb, long enough that I'd started to hope he'd given up on me. Who was I kidding? Sebastian Harcourt never gives up on anything he truly wants.

Before I can shove the phone back in my pocket, it buzzes with a second text.

How about dinner tomorrow? Assaggiare. My treat.

I glare at the message. My fist clenches so tightly it's a miracle the phone doesn't shatter. And I'd thought I was in love with him. The idea turns my stomach now. Does he really think the lure of a romantic meal at my favourite Italian restaurant will erase all the hurt he caused?

Apparently not.

After several minutes have passed with no reply from me, another text appears. The tone has changed, becoming brisk and business like.

It's about the job. Promise it'll be worth your while.

What job? The one Dad went for? I frown, rereading the message. Why would Sebastian care about Dad applying to be the new finance manager? Seb might be head of HR, but only in name. In practice, he leaves the day-to-day stuff to his underlings.

A movement catches my attention. I look up to find Taylor lounging in the doorway. He regards me, his gaze amused. "Thought you'd got lost on your way to the kettle."

"Oh, the coffee." I shake my head, trying to clear it of Sebastian Harcourt and whatever game he's playing. "Sorry, I'll... I'm right on it."

Taylor examines me more closely and his amusement melds into concern. "You OK?"

"Yeah." I try to smile, but my stepbrother's raised eyebrow tells me he doesn't buy it. My breath leaves me in a sigh. "Just my ex."

"Ah." That single syllable contains a universe of understanding.

What has he been through? I hover on the brink of asking about what Abby heard from Carl, curious to know the truth behind it, but I step away from the temptation. This bridge connecting us is still so fragile; one false move could have the whole structure disintegrating beneath our feet.

Perhaps Taylor feels it too, because he merely crosses to the cupboard above the kettle and grabs a handful of mugs. "I'll make that coffee, shall I?"

I'm about to protest when my phone shudders against my palm. Sebastian hadn't waited for me to respond; he knew bringing Dad into the equation would draw me in as surely as a dolphin in a net. His text reads more like a summons.

The Magnolia. Five-thirty. Be there.

CHAPTER TWELVE

A MUFFLED CURSE COMES from the front of the shop. Brows raised, I duck out from the biography section in time to watch Dean slam a book onto the display table. The whole thing shudders, and then...*thud...thud...thud*. The collective works of a local thriller writer, which Dean has spent the past ten minutes arranging, spill in a landslide to the floor.

"Fuck." He kicks the nearest table leg as though the unsuspecting lump of wood is somehow responsible and bends to gather up the scattered hardbacks.

Rolling my eyes, I cross to kneel beside him. "I'll do that. You go and cash up."

Dean nods, the only response he seems capable of, and retreats behind the counter. I sigh. He's been in a rotten temper all day, although he denied it when I asked what was up. I've done my best to steer clear of him and made sure the customers did the same. Business is slow enough without frightening off potential buyers.

I begin sorting through the jumble of books, periodically checking the time on my phone. Not long now before I can clock off, escape Dean's black mood and walk along the high street with Ben to Bar Basco. Is it a date? I remember the shy way my stepbrother called out to me as I was leaving that morning, the hope in his expression when he asked if I'd like to have a drink with him after work.

Dean clears his throat. The sound shatters the quiet with the abruptness of a bottle lobbed through a window. "So, I have a question."

"OK." The accusation in his tone puts me on my guard. "Go for it."

Dean leans his elbows on the counter, eyes narrowed in a glare, although I don't think it's directed at me. "When did you figure out you were...? You know."

Another day I might've wound him up a bit, pretended not to understand what he was asking. In his current frame of mind, though, I wouldn't put it past him to hurl the heavy till at my head.

I return to stacking the books, considering. "Not sure, really. There wasn't this lightning flash moment. Not for me. It's just something I always knew, deep down."

"And that's the same for most, uh..."

"Gay guys?"

Dean nods, cringing. For whatever reason, he's more sensitive than usual to the dreaded G-word today.

I snort. "Hardly. Some go through years of confusion over their sexuality, and others never stop hiding who they are." Liam's face floats into my mind and I thrust it away.

"All right." Dean sounds sceptical. "But you can't go your whole life thinking you're straight, then meet some guy and... bang! You're gay. It doesn't work like that."

I shrug. "Not for me, maybe, but I can't speak for anyone else. We're all different."

Dean lapses into silence. I pick up one of the thrillers and leaf through its pages. What's with all the questions? If not for the number of times I've overheard him talking mush on the phone to his girlfriend, I'd assume Dean's having doubts about his own sexuality.

Rattle…snap. He opens the drawer of the till, then slams it shut again. "Ever thought you knew someone, really knew them, only to realise you didn't know them at all?"

My laugh catches, tasting bitter on my tongue. I stare down at the book in my hands, but the image of Liam is back, and it obscures the print. His eyes plead with me, just as they had on that last terrible afternoon. Somehow, though, I doubt Dean wants to hear about my fucked-up love life. I blink, and another face surfaces to blot out the first.

I meet Dean's gaze. "Yeah."

He waits, expectant.

"My dad. He just got me, you know? More than my mum ever has. I took it for granted he'd always be there. Then my parents' marriage went to hell and he pissed off to London, left my sister and me to pick up the pieces."

"Wow, that's tough. Sorry, man."

"Thanks. Maybe we never really know anyone. Not when it comes down to it."

Dean falls quiet again. It's obvious he feels let down by someone, and I know how painful that can be to swallow. He's unlikely to open up to me, however, so I go back to arranging the thrillers.

I'm putting the finishing touches to the display when Dean glances beyond me at the door. "Um, you know that guy?"

My heart jolts and the final book slips from my grasp onto the table. I twist to follow Dean's gaze, expecting to see my stepbrother. It isn't Ben, though. I frown, surprise warring with my disappointment. Peering through the glass door above the 'closed' sign, as though my thoughts have drawn him there, is Liam.

"What do you want?" I ask when I join him outside a few moments later.

Liam flinches at my coldness, but what else did he expect? He isn't deluded enough to think I'd actually be pleased to see him. Christ, he can't even bring himself to look at me.

"I have to talk to you," Liam says, addressing the pavement.

I scoff. All these months acting as though I don't exist, and now he wants to talk?

"No, really." Liam locks his fingers together, crushing hard enough it's a wonder he doesn't fracture a bone. "Just hear me out. Please, Tay."

His voice cracks on my name. Is he remembering the countless times he uttered it while we were together—how he breathed it into my mouth, delirious with pleasure, or almost choked on it when I said something that had him convulsing with laughter?

I stomp on the memory and fold my arms over my chest. "I'm listening."

"Not here." Liam drops his voice to a whisper, still looking anywhere but at me. "I… There's somewhere we can talk. It'll only take a minute. Please."

I could refuse. It isn't as if I owe him anything. Liam forfeited any right to ask favours of me the instant he threw me to CJ and his minions. Yet, even after everything he's done, his obvious agitation kindles a tiny spark of concern in me. It can't hurt to hear him out.

I sigh. "All right, but it'll have to be quick."

Liam nods, although his posture remains tense, as he leads me along the high street, busy with students and young professionals eager to kickstart their Saturday night. He darts furtive glances at everyone we pass, clearly anxious not to be seen with me. It must be exhausting being him, living in constant fear someone will discover his secret. I might've pitied him, except that his betrayal overshadows everything else.

WE'D BECOME CARELESS, the two of us high on secrecy and love, giddy with the thrill of getting away with it for so long. It was our first day back after the summer break, the start of our final year of sixth form. Liam had returned from a family holiday to Tenerife, tanned and gorgeous and greedy for me after two weeks apart. I was reeling from my parents' break-up and hungry for comfort.

That Monday lunchtime, we hustled into the first empty classroom we could find and fell on each other. I had Liam pushed up against the wall, my mouth on his neck, his hands inside my shirt, when he went still.

Before my brain could register something was wrong, he shoved me so hard I stumbled into the desk behind me. "Get off me, you perv."

"Li...?" I reached out to steady myself, head spinning. What just happened? I'd never heard Liam speak with such venom, never imagined he had it in him. His words sank deep, hooking barbed claws into my heart.

"What the fuck?" Liam's eyes were wild, the pupils dilated. "You're sick in the head. Sick!"

He began edging away from me, hands extended as if to ward me off, but his attention was on the door. Dread slid, icy and viscous, into my gut. I turned, wincing at the bruise already forming on my lower back. And there he was, Carl James Farmer, the reason Liam had been so insistent we keep our relationship a secret.

"So sorry." CJ stared at Liam, his expression slowly morphing from shock to disgust. "Didn't mean to interrupt your fun."

"It was him." Liam almost tripped over his own feet in his haste to distance himself from me. "That…that poof. He just came at me."

The words tumbled out of him, piling lie upon lie—how I'd cornered him in the classroom, offering him money for the privilege of sucking him off; how, when he'd told me where to go, I'd forced myself on him. CJ listened, a smirk tugging at his mouth, until Liam stuttered to a halt. Then he rounded on me, face alight with malice.

"Well, well, well. Sounds like somebody's been a naughty boy," he said, and in that moment, I knew I was doomed.

"Down here," Liam says, gesturing to our right.

Nestled between Wilde Land Records and Cafe Ole, is the entrance to a narrow alleyway. I huff but let him usher me ahead of him. The sooner we get this over with, the sooner I can meet Ben.

When we reach the midpoint of the alley, Liam rests a hand on my arm to bring me to a stop. I shrug him off and lean against the rough brick wall, arms folded. It's surprisingly dark here, the buildings looming on either side to block out the golden evening light. Though we can't be more than seven metres from the street, the noise of the city feels strangely far away.

Liam faces me and takes a deep breath. "I'm so sorry, Tay."

For the first time since we broke up, he looks at me head on. His eyes appear shadowed in the dimness, more grey than blue, and full of regret. Before I can respond, a movement at the edge of my vision has me peering back the way we came. Pete ambles towards us, Syed at his shoulder. Their combined bulk stretches from wall to unscalable wall.

I glance at Liam, but he shows no hint of surprise. He holds my gaze for an instant, expression racked with misery, before staring down at the concrete. Numb realisation settles over me. So much for him wanting to talk. This whole thing has been a set-up, and like the idiot I am, I walked straight into it. I spin, intending to make a dash for the other end of the alley, only to come face-to-face with CJ.

"Taylor Solomon." The weight of his smile drops like a medicine ball onto my chest. "Fancy meeting you here."

I square up to him, refusing to let him see my fear. "Funny how you keep showing up like this. Anyone would think you're stalking me."

He crowds in on me, features twisted. "Filthy queer. My girlfriend says you've been spreading lies about me."

"Really?" I stand my ground, raising an eyebrow. "Wait till she hears you're so desperate to have me to yourself, you get one of your mates to lure me down an alley."

CJ shoves me so hard I stumble against the wall. "I warned you, faggot. I warned you to keep your fucking mouth shut."

Then his fist slams into my cheekbone. My head cracks against the brickwork behind me, and my world fractures, splintering into an explosion of tiny stars.

BEN

"THIS IS COSY." Sebastian smiles across the table at me, his charm oozing like treacle over my skin. "Just like old times."

"Hardly." I rebuff his smile, granite-faced.

Still, I can't entirely shake my sense of déjà vu. So much about this reminds me of our past encounters—same swanky hotel bar, same corner table screened behind a curtain of foliage, same air of secrecy. Seb preferred to drive out of town where nobody knew us, but when we did get together in the city, he always insisted we meet at The Magnolia. The majority of its guests are wealthy tourists and visiting business people, so there was far less risk of us being recognised.

Yeah, everything is exactly as it was more than a year ago. I'm the one who's changed. Back then, I was utterly wrapped up in Seb, the teasing brush of his hand on my leg, his hungry expression promising what he would do to me once he had me alone. I scarcely registered the opulence of our surroundings. Now, all I want is to be with Taylor, to sink into his wry humour and beautiful eyes and forget I ever knew Sebastian Harcourt.

He shakes his head at my curtness, as though admonishing a petulant child. "Don't be like that, baby boy."

Seb reaches across the table to caress my knuckles where they lie clenched beside my untouched drink. I snatch my hand away.

"Don't touch me." The contempt in my voice startles even me. "And I told you not to call me that."

He raises his palms in a placating gesture. "Calm down, babe...Ben. I just want to talk."

Calm down? I'm not sure I could be less calm if I tried. The urge to run has my leg bouncing and my heart skittering as if I've downed too many espressos. He's right, though; I do need to get it together. Not to please him, but because it's vital I keep my wits about me.

More than anything, I wish I hadn't come, but there's no way I could've ignored Sebastian's text; he'd known that only too well. I have to find out the nature of this game he's playing so I can anticipate his next move. That doesn't mean I'm going to let him string it out.

"Fine." I swallow some sparkling water—the last thing I want is to meet Taylor reeking of booze—and set my glass down with a thunk. "Let's talk. What the hell was that text about?"

Seb smirks. "Somebody found a backbone while they were away. I like it."

I merely glare at him, arms folded, until his smile falters.

"Look." His tone is coaxing, lined with velvet. "Forget about the text. It isn't important. Let's just have a drink and catch up, get to know each other again. What do you say?"

"I say thanks for the offer, but I have better things to do." I push my chair back, ready to bolt.

"Not so fast." Seb's fingers snap like a steel cuff around my wrist. I flinch at the contact, try to pull away, but his grip tightens. "Hear me out. We were good together, you and me, you know we were. I hurt you, I realise that, but I can make it up to you…if you'll let me."

He imprisons me with eyes as rich and deep as his favourite Swiss dark chocolate. They're mesmerising, brimming with regret. It's no wonder my naïve, seventeen-year-old self fell for him and his lies. However, that boy is long gone.

I yank my arm from his grasp and stand. "You can save your breath. We're done. We were done the moment I stepped on that plane."

Sebastian's face hardens. His lip curls, a cat about to torture his prey. It's like looking at a stranger.

"Have it your own way." His voice turns cold, lethal as the paper-thin ice on the surface of a lake. "Let's move on to your dad's application."

"What about it?" A man and woman at the bar, both in sharp business suits, cast curious glances in our direction. I lower myself back into my chair, grateful for the shield of greenery, and frown at my ex.

He shrugs. "As you know, I don't normally get involved in the day-to-day running of Harcourts. I have far more pleasurable ways to spend my time. That said, being head of HR does give me a certain influence, should I choose to use it."

He pauses, perhaps expecting a response. Either that, or he's enjoying keeping me in suspense. I simply stare at him, wait for him to get to the point. A thread of unease unravels in the pit of my stomach. Wherever he's going with this, I'm positive I won't like it.

"For instance," Sebastian drops his voice to a confidential murmur, "if I felt a particular candidate to be unsuitable, it would be within my power to see that the job went to, shall we say, a worthier applicant."

It's as though the ice under my feet has cracked, plunging me into the freezing waters below. I grip the edge of the table. "What're you talking about?"

Seb's eyes glitter. "I think you know, clever boy that you are, but I'll put it another way. Consensus is that your dad pretty much has the job in the bag. He's the obvious choice, given his record with the company, but there are a couple of other people under consideration. If I so desired, I could see the position went to one of them instead."

He delivers the threat with a nonchalance verging on boredom. All the same, the force of it punches the air from my lungs. I inhale, trying to steady my breathing. "That's blackmail."

"Such a sordid word. I'm only trying to help you see sense. Come back to me like I know you want to, and everyone will be happy."

"And if I refuse, you'll cheat my dad out of a job we both know he deserves?"

"I don't want to do it, but I will…if you push me. Your dad's career is in your hands, baby boy. Imagine how humiliating it would be for him, all his colleagues knowing he wasn't good enough. I'm sure I can rely on you to do the right thing."

I shove my chair away from the table so violently I almost tip backwards onto the plush carpet. If I have to swallow another drop of Sebastian's poison, I'll vomit into his gin and tonic. Before he can stop me, I'm on my feet, stumbling from the bar and through the hotel foyer onto the pavement.

After the low-lit intimacy of The Magnolia, the evening sun dazzles me. I squint, reorientating myself, then wobble my way through the leafy residential roads towards the high street. I walk fast, despite my shaking legs, determined to put as much distance between myself and Sebastian as possible.

As I near the city centre, the streets grow crowded with people heading for the bars and restaurants or to see whatever's on at the theatre. Snippets of conversation eddy around me, jumbled up with laughter and the clip-clop of heels—the sounds of people looking forward to a normal Saturday night. That should have been me. It would've been if not for Sebastian.

I replay his words in my mind, grappling for understanding. Had he been serious, or was this simply part of the game, a bluff to force me into doing what he wants? I'd known Seb was arrogant, even ruthless, but blackmail? I shake my head. It makes no sense. He'd been my world for eleven months. Is he really capable of something like this? How could I not have known?

I've lost track of how much time has passed since I joined Sebastian at the bar. Taylor could be waiting for me even now, wondering why I'm late. God, Taylor. Dread tangles my stomach in knots. How can I face him in the state I'm in? How can I take him for a drink, sit across from him as I had with Sebastian, and pretend everything's fine? Perhaps I should confide in him, ask for his advice. Wow, what a spectacular first date that would be. Whatever promise the evening might have held, it's in ruins now.

I arrive at The Inkwell to find the windows shuttered and the door displaying its 'closed' sign, but no Taylor. He must be finishing up inside. At least that gives me a few minutes to compose myself, work out how to play this. Maybe I should cry off, say I'm ill. The way my gut's churning, it wouldn't be a lie.

The pound of feet on the pavement cuts through the general bustle. My heart lurches. I look up, half expectant, half apprehensive, but it isn't my stepbrother. A boy, dark-haired and lanky, is dodging through the throng towards the bookshop. His eyes are wild, terrified, and when he catches sight of me, he hurries over.

"You have to help me." He seizes my arm, practically sobbing. "Please. I think they're going to kill him."

CHAPTER THIRTEEN

TAYLOR

"I DON'T NEED TO go to the hospit—" My denial morphs into a gasp, somewhat ruining the effect. I wince, putting a hand to my ribs.

Anger pulses in sync with the pain—anger at Liam for being a double-crossing arsehole, and at Ben for seeing me like this, a bruised and bloody mess on the concrete. Most of all, I'm furious at myself for walking so blindly into CJ's trap.

Ben runs fingers through his hair, strain evident in his expression. "You should probably get checked out. Something could be broken."

"No." I start to shake my head, but even that movement sends daggers through my skull. "I just want to go home."

Ben and Liam exchange an exasperated look. How come they're so friendly all of a sudden? From what I can gather, Liam legged it while CJ and his mates were laying into me. He headed straight for the bookshop, hoping the guy I work with might still be there, and bumped into Ben instead. The moment the two of them pelted into the alley, CJ and his crew ran for it. I suppose I should be grateful; if Liam hadn't gone for help, I'm not sure what state I'd be in. As it is, they only got in a few solid hits. Then again, he was also the one who lured me down here in the first place, so forgive me if I don't thank him on bended knees.

Ben and my ex confer in low voices, but I'm too exhausted to listen. I let my head loll against the wall and close my eyes. Warm blood trickles down my arms and seeps through the rips in my jeans. Everything hurts. Even the simple act of inhaling earns me a knife to the side. Still, it could've been so much worse.

Behind my closed eyelids, I see again the loathing in CJ's expression as he knocked me to the ground, hear the hate-filled words he spewed with every vicious kick. I'd tried to save myself, had managed to scramble to my feet, but before I could make a dash for it, Pete and Syed shoved me back down.

"Fucking poofter." CJ towered over me, his foot crushing my chest. "This'll teach you to bad-mouth me to my girlfriend."

"Fuck you," I spat with all the venom I could summon, given that I could scarcely breathe.

CJ's trainer collided with my cheekbone, smacking my head against the pavement. Ears ringing, vision blurred, I'd looked up into his snarling face and been certain I was about to die.

Footsteps retreat along the alley, pulling me from the memory. When a firm hand rests on my thigh, I open my eyes to find Ben crouched beside me, brow creased with worry.

"Liam's gone to get his car," he says. "He'll give us a lift home."

Despite the pain, I'm acutely aware of Ben's touch, gentle and reassuring. I have the overwhelming urge to sag against him, to burrow into his solid strength and let him hold me.

I scowl at my grazed palms. "I don't want anything from him."

Ben studies me, clearly curious, but asks no questions. He merely squeezes my leg. "It'll be easier than phoning for a taxi. I just want to get you home, although I still think you should go to the hospital."

"Yeah, I got that." I force the less bruised side of my face into a smile. To judge by the way Ben's gazing at me, as though it causes him physical discomfort, it's a poor attempt.

"I can't believe Carl did this to you," he bursts out. "I mean, I'm not too keen on the guy, but this…"

"Don't worry about it. Most people are taken in by him."

"You have to go to the police. He can't be allowed to get away with it."

I open my mouth to argue, to explain all the reasons why going to the police would be an utter waste of time, then realise I don't have the energy. I let my head fall against the rough brickwork and stare up at the strip of violet sky far above.

WE'RE SILENT ON the drive home. Ben sits beside me in the back, his concern like a searchlight, making me feel exposed. I rest my cheek against the window and gaze out at nothing. This car, with its smell of damp and slew of empty Sprite cans in the footwell, is so familiar. I can't help remembering all the times Liam and I had sex on this very seat. Frantic, uncomfortable sex. Sex which, for Liam at least, was always tainted with the fear of discovery. It feels so long ago, another lifetime.

Once Liam pulls into our driveway, I expect him to drop us off and leave. My stepbrother, however, invites him in.

"I don't want him here," I tell Ben as he helps me to the front door. I try to sound assertive, but every step sends agony shooting through my ribs and my voice comes out embarrassingly weak.

Ben ignores me in any case. He unlocks the door, then supports me into the living room and onto the sofa.

I slump against the cushions in relief. "Just think how thrilled Mum'll be when she gets home to find bloodstains all over her cream leather."

"Fuck your mum's leather," Ben says.

I snort and clutch my side. "God, don't make me laugh. It hurts too much."

"Sorry. Wait there." Ben gives me a faint smile and disappears into the hallway. I hear him rummaging in the freezer, and a few moments later, he returns with a bag of frozen peas wrapped in a tea towel. "Here."

He leans over me, laying the makeshift icepack against my cheek. I gasp at the cold, but almost at once the throbbing begins to ease. I let out a long breath. "Thanks."

"You need to keep it there, OK?" Ben takes my hand, his grip steady and warm, and presses it against the peas to hold them in place. His fingertips brush my knuckles, a sweet gesture that has my chest tightening. Then he turns to Liam, who's hovering on the threshold. "Would you stay with Taylor? I won't be a minute."

"Uh, sure." Liam nods, though he can't bring himself to look at me.

"I don't need a babysitter," I say, irritated.

"Humour me. You could have a concussion." Ben touches my shoulder. "Back in a bit."

"Where are you…" I start to ask, but he's already gone, the front door banging behind him.

I huff. It isn't as if I can chase after him, demand to know what he's up to. I just have to trust him. Maybe it's stupid when we've known each other for such a short time. Yet I find I do. He didn't force me to go to the hospital, and that has to count for something.

Still without looking at me, Liam crosses to perch on the edge of Martin's favourite armchair by the window. He hunches forward, elbows on his knees, clearly wishing he was anywhere else. That makes two of us. I'd rather endure another of CJ's kicks than be stuck here alone with my ex.

I shift the icepack to cover more of the bruising and tilt the other side of my face into the cushions. If I can't see him, perhaps I can pretend he doesn't exist. Liam, it seems, has other ideas.

"Christ." His voice shatters the illusion, jagged as broken glass. "Taylor, I'm so sorry."

I don't even glance at him. "Easy to say now. What about when you were luring me into that alley so your mates could beat the shit out of me?"

"I didn't know, I swear." He sounds close to tears. "CJ said he just wanted to talk to you. I never thought… If I'd known what he meant to do, there's no way I would've agreed."

"Save your excuses for someone who cares."

"But—"

"Seriously, Liam, I couldn't be less interested if I tried." For months, the hurt and bitterness festered inside me, a septic wound spreading poison to every part of my life. Now I finally have the chance to confront him, all I feel is exhaustion. None of it matters. Not anymore.

Strangely, I believe Liam when he says he's sorry. For all his mistakes, I doubt he wanted to see me get knocked about so badly. The trouble is, his apology has come far too late.

BEN

I PULL THE front door shut behind me and hurry around the side of the house. It's imprinted on my mind—the image of Taylor slumped on the sofa, his arms scraped, black eye already forming. Then there's the way he looked at me as I turned to leave, like I'd tossed him over the stern of the only lifeboat and abandoned him to drown. There's definitely something between him and Liam, something I don't understand. Perhaps I shouldn't have left Taylor alone with him, but what choice did I have? Since he won't let me take him to the hospital, I'll do the next best thing.

When my parents were first married, Mum worked as a nurse in the A & E department of Brookminster General, but she gave up her job before I was born. Maybe she would've gone back to it once Abby started school, although Dad's salary meant she didn't have to. In any case, she'd sold three novels by then and chose to pursue her writing career instead. Of course, her medical training still came in handy for dealing with our bumps and bruises.

As usual, the door to the annex is propped open. I charge in without knocking. "Mum, you need to— Oh."

I stumble to a halt, embarrassed. Mum's seated on the sofa, a half-full wine glass in her hand, but she isn't alone. Toby's dad's lounging beside her. Though there's a respectable amount of space between them, the way their bodies are angled towards each other suggests a certain intimacy. An almost empty Chablis bottle sits on the coffee table, and the kitchen worktop is strewn with foil takeaway containers.

"What is it?" Mum sets down her glass, gaze homing in on my clothes. "Sweetheart, you're hurt. What happened?"

I glance down. My jeans and the front of my shirt are spattered with blood. I hadn't even noticed. I look back up at Mum, shaking my head. "No, not me. It's Taylor. Some guys jumped him in town. He's pretty messed up."

"Oh, God." Shock flashes across Mum's face. Then she's on her feet, calm professionalism taking over. "Don't worry, we'll get him patched up. So sorry about this, Jon."

"Don't be silly." He stands, too, his gaze alert behind his spectacles. "All right if I come with you, establish what's been going on?"

I blink at him, uncomprehending, until I remember Toby's dad is a police officer. Of course he'd want to find out the details. I hesitate, unsure how Taylor will react to Jon's presence. He hadn't responded when I mentioned going to the police. Still, I can't think how to refuse, so I simply lead them both back to the house.

"Taylor was jumped, you say?" Jon asks with real concern. "Do you know the individuals involved?"

Perhaps it isn't my place to tell, but there's no way I'm letting that scumbag get away with it. I intend to make absolutely certain he never comes near Taylor or my sister again.

"One of them was Carl Farmer," I say, "but the others ran before I could get a look at them."

I unlock the front door and show Mum and Jon into the living room. The tension hits me the moment I enter. Liam's staring fixedly out of the window, as though wishing he could pass right through it and disappear. My gaze goes to Taylor. He's on the sofa where I left him, cheek pressed into the cushions, the eye that isn't concealed behind the bag of frozen peas half closed.

He raises his head as we come in. Christ, he looks awful, one side of his face swollen and bloody. Rage squeezes my heart, mingled with a powerful protectiveness. For the first time in my life, I understand the desire to kill another human being.

"Oh, sweetheart, you're in a right old state." Mum rushes to Taylor's side, removing the frozen peas to survey the damage. "Come on, let's clean you up. Can you walk?"

If Mum finds it awkward being in the house she shared with Dad for fifteen years, she doesn't show it. She takes charge in her gentle way, helping Taylor off the sofa and despatching me to fetch clean clothes for him.

I head upstairs, leaving Jon to talk to Liam. Where the other boy fits into the situation, I can't figure out. In the mad dash from The Inkwell and the shock of finding Taylor so beaten up, I hadn't thought to ask Liam how he came to be there. I'd assume he just happened to be passing, except for the fact that there's clearly some history between him and Taylor.

In our bedroom, I unearth an old T-shirt and my softest track bottoms. They'll swamp Taylor's slight frame, but his outfits are so tight they'd surely aggravate his tender skin. With the clothes draped over my arm, I hurry back downstairs and along the hall to the cloakroom.

I knock on the half-open door and slip inside. Mum's at the vanity unit, picking through the contents of the first-aid kit, while Taylor sits on the closed toilet seat in only his boxers. A bandage swathes his right knee, and another is wrapped around his elbow, while several smaller cuts stand out against his complexion.

"OK?" Taylor lowers the flannel he's using to wipe the crusted blood from his face and regards me through his good eye.

A shaky laugh gusts out of me. "I'm pretty sure I'm supposed to be asking you that."

Taylor's crooked grin has my heart doing somersaults. Even battered and bruised, he's beautiful. I set the clothes on the lid of the laundry basket and move to lean against the wall.

"Thanks, sweetheart." Mum smiles at me. She sets out scissors and a roll of medical tape, then turns to Taylor. "Let's have a look at those ribs."

Taylor remains perfectly still while Mum runs her hands over his ribcage, probing with expert fingers. When she reaches the lower left side, he releases a hiss of pain.

Mum eyes him, unusually stern. "You really need to go to the hospital. I don't think they're broken, just badly bruised, but you should still get checked out."

"No point," Taylor says flatly. "They'll only strap them up, same as you."

Mum sighs, looking disapproving, but reaches for the tape. "Brace yourself then. I'll have to make this tight."

Taylor nods, biting his lip. He remains silent throughout the process, but by the time Mum's finished, his face has drained of colour.

"There, all done." She cuts the tape with a snip and straightens, laying a hand on his shoulder. "It all looks worse than it is, although I'm sure it doesn't feel like it. You should probably let your mum know what's happened."

Taylor snorts. "And interrupt her precious holiday? I'm sure she'll be thrilled."

"Sweetheart, she's your mother. Of course she'll want to know, and I'm sure she'd rather hear it from you."

Taylor opens his mouth, expression mutinous, but a soft tap at the door forestalls any argument.

Jon pokes his head around it, His worried gaze finding Taylor. "How're you doing, matey?"

"Yeah, bit better."

"That's good." Jon smiles at Mum before returning his attention to Taylor. "Look, I know you've had a hell of an evening, but when you feel up to it, I'd really like to talk to you."

"I'M NOT PRESSING charges," Taylor says, his tone adamant. He's collapsed once more on the sofa, Mum having dosed him up on the strongest painkillers she could find. The oversized T-shirt and track bottoms make him appear smaller, more vulnerable, but his mouth is set in a stubborn line.

I sit next to him. "You can't be serious."

Taylor glances at me, then averts his gaze with a shrug.

From the loveseat, Jon removes his glasses and polishes them on his shirt. "It's entirely your decision, but you need to think carefully about it. I don't need to tell you those young men have committed a criminal offence. We have more than enough evidence to charge them."

"He's right, sweetheart." Mum looks up from where she's kneeling by his feet, scrubbing at a reddish-brown stain on the leather seat cushion. "No one will force you to do anything you're not comfortable with. You just need to be sure."

"You can't want them to get away with this," I add. "They could've killed you. They might've done if we hadn't chased them off."

"It doesn't matter what I want." Taylor twists to face me, exhaustion in every line of his posture. "Don't you see? CJ's dad's a barrister, a highly successful one. He's famous for getting his clients off, even when they look guilty as hell. He's not going to let his own son get done for ABH or whatever. It would destroy his reputation."

A pensive silence follows this pronouncement. I frown, running a hand through my hair. It comes back to me, how excited Abby had been to discover Carl's dad was this hotshot lawyer. Apparently, he'd been really encouraging when she shared her own plans to study law, had even offered her work experience at his firm once she turned sixteen. Yeah, Carl's family connections would certainly give him a major advantage in court, but does that mean we should just concede defeat?

Mum sighs, abandoning her attack on the bloodstain. "I think that's as good as it's going to get. Ben, sweetheart, do you mind if I pop the kettle on?"

Once Mum's gone to make tea, Jon replaces his glasses and nods at Taylor. "I understand where you're coming from, matey, I really do, and I'm not suggesting for a second that pressing charges would be an easy route to go down, but we have a strong case here. There are witnesses, for one thing. It wouldn't just be your word against theirs."

"Right." Taylor scoffs. "Ben only caught a glimpse of them before they legged it, and no one else is going to vouch for me."

"I will."

We all turn to stare at Liam. He's been so quiet, I'd almost forgotten he was there.

He fidgets, clearly embarrassed by the attention, but he meets Taylor's eyes without flinching. "If you decide you want to press charges, I'll back you up. I've already told Jon everything, and I've agreed to make a statement. I don't..." He swallows, fists clenching on the arms of his chair. "I don't want to pretend anymore."

CHAPTER FOURTEEN

I PROP MYSELF AGAINST the kitchen worktop, keeping the weight off my bad knee. This evening has gone on forever. It took an age for Jon to copy down my statement, since we had to wait for him to call in one of his colleagues to sit in on the interview. After that, Poppy insisted I swallow more painkillers while she issued me with a whole list of instructions. At last, though, my stepbrother shows everyone to the door and the house is quiet.

"Hey, what're you doing in here?" Ben asks when he tracks me down. He's finally changed out of his bloody clothes and has on an old Bhelmead Athletics T-shirt over pyjama bottoms.

By way of answer, I hold up one of the cans of Coke we bought yesterday and take a gulp. Sweetness bubbles over my tongue and down my throat. It tastes all the better because Mum normally refuses to let 'those disgusting fizzy drinks' in the house.

"I could've got that." Ben frowns. "You're supposed to be resting. Mum's orders."

I roll my eyes. "I have a few scrapes, not a broken leg."

Ben shakes his head before grabbing himself a Coke from the fridge. He perches on the corner of the table facing me and cracks the tab. His eyes find mine, soft with concern. "You doing OK? Need any more painkillers?"

"Nah. Your mum gave me enough to knock out a brontosaurus." I offer him a half-smile. "Sorry about this evening. It…well, it didn't exactly go to plan."

Major understatement. I can't help wondering how tonight might've played out if I hadn't been such a prat and followed Liam into that alley. We would've gone for a drink, probably several, then perhaps for something to eat. Ben might be looking at me across a restaurant table right now, rather than a few feet of kitchen tiles. The concern would be absent from his expression, replaced with something I hardly dare put a name to.

Ben quirks an eyebrow. "I know. So inconsiderate of you, getting beaten up like that. Not your fault, silly boy."

"I dunno. I did kind of walk into it." I wince. Talk about gullible. Had I really believed Liam wanted to apologise after all this time? Except…he did come through for me this evening. He backed up everything I told Jon, making no attempt to shrink from his own culpability. It's a year and innumerable taunts and bruises too late, but it still counts for something.

"Stop that." Ben leans towards me, his face earnest. "You didn't do anything wrong. If either of us bears any responsibility, it's me."

I scoff. "Is this the part where you turn out to be the evil mastermind behind the whole thing? CJ only jumped me because you ordered him to, right?"

Ben doesn't smile. He lowers his gaze to the can he's holding, spinning it around and around in his hands.

"Hey." I drop the teasing note from my voice and study him more carefully. "What is it? You can't really blame yourself for any of this. That would be nuts."

"It isn't nuts. I saw the bruise, Tay."

"What bruise?"

But I know. Of course I do. Since the night I came home to find CJ sitting in our living room, I haven't been able to get it out of my mind—Ben standing close enough that I could feel the heat of him, his fingers lingering over the tender spot on my side, igniting a fire inside me.

"It was right here." Ben sets his Coke on the table and closes the distance between us. Just as he had then, he traces the spot a couple of inches above my hip bone where CJ's elbow had landed. I stop breathing. His touch is tentative, as though he's afraid I might break, and yet a tingling current radiates outwards from the contact.

Ben withdraws his hand and rests it on the worktop next to me, his arm millimetres from mine. Every one of my hairs from shoulder to wrist stands on end. His eyes find mine. "You said it was nothing, but I knew something was up. I should've made you tell me."

"Like that would've worked." I stare down at my drink. It's hard to think with Ben so near. His musky scent fills my senses, sending my thoughts skittering in all directions. "Seriously, none of this is on you. I'm the one who let myself be pushed around for months like the pathetic loser I am."

"You're not pathetic."

"Aren't I? I put up with CJ and his mates bullying me for almost a year and never told a soul, all because I didn't think anyone would believe me. I mean, CJ was always the golden boy, captain of the rugby team, favourite with the teachers. Whereas I was this moody kid who wore eyeliner and had too many piercings. No one would've taken my word over his. At least, that's how I saw it. So I kept my mouth shut and let him trample all over me."

"But not anymore," Ben says. "That was a really brave thing you did tonight, agreeing to press charges. I could see it wasn't easy."

"I don't feel brave." I sketch the indentation between two tiles with my bare toe. Every time I imagine what lies ahead—the police questioning, the probable trial, facing CJ in court—I want to crawl under my bed and never come out. I can change my mind. What Jon took from me this evening was only a preliminary statement; I have to go to the station on Monday to sign it. I can still turn back…but I won't. It's time CJ paid for everything he's put me through, and if Liam can find the courage to tell the truth, so can I.

"You scared?" Ben asks.

The side of my mouth lifts in a reluctant smile. "Shit scared, yeah."

"I'm here for you. You know that, right?"

The sincerity in his tone tugs at a place deep inside me. It pulls my gaze up to his, and once there, I can't tear it away. Looking into his eyes is like staring into sun-flecked pools, light and shimmering and bottomless. They brim with so much emotion I could search forever and never decipher it all. My fingers, suddenly clumsy, fumble with my drink. I set down the can before I drop it and grip the edge of the worktop to steady myself. Ben's so close, close enough that I can count the freckles scattered like grains of sugar across his nose.

With his eyes still fixed on mine, he reaches out and touches the swollen side of my face. His fingertips are gentle, a caress of feathers against my skin. My breath lodges in my windpipe.

"Damn, Tay." Ben's voice comes out hoarse, and his expression mirrors the throbbing need in my groin. "You have no idea how much I want to kiss you right now."

The air rushes out of me in a breathy laugh. "It's not like I'm going to stop you."

"But your face. I don't want to hurt you."

"Fuck that. My mouth's about the only part of me that doesn't hurt."

Ben smiles, but still he hesitates. Before he can argue, I slide a hand behind his neck and draw him to me. He groans, the sound resonating throughout my entire body, and kisses me. As our lips meet, the tension that's been stretched taut between us ever since Ben arrived home from Australia drains away. I sink into the warm softness of his mouth, my tongue finding his, tasting, discovering.

Ben's hand moves to the small of my back, burning a hole through my—his—T-shirt. He supports himself with his other hand so he can press me up against the worktop without putting his full weight on me. Every inch of his body moulds to every inch of mine. He's taking obvious care to avoid irritating my injuries while letting me feel just how badly he wants me. It isn't enough, nowhere near, and yet it is. This kiss, gentle and deep and expressing all the longing we've denied these past weeks, is everything.

BEN

I CAN'T STOP looking at him.

As I rummage in the freezer for something to eat and pop one of Linda's frozen meals into the microwave to heat through, Taylor draws my gaze. The pull of him is irresistible. He's seated at the kitchen table, his unbandaged elbow propped on the wooden surface, chin resting on his knuckles. I sense him watching me, his scrutiny like the press of warm fingers against the nape of my neck, and every time our eyes meet, the connection crackles along my nerves.

Somehow I see past the bruises. I'm too intent on the soft curve of his lips, the dark lashes shadowing his cheekbones, his long, slender fingers. The memory of our kiss invades every particle of my being—his mouth, tender and fierce on mine, the way his hands moved over my back, desperate to urge me closer despite the pain. God, how is it possible to want anyone this much? I'd loved Sebastian, or thought I had, but those feelings were always tangled up with guilt, the sense that we were doing something sordid. What I feel for Taylor is different. It's purer, less complicated.

Right, who am I kidding? I pile lasagne onto two plates and carry them over to the table, smiling at my own optimism. However right this feels, I'll wager the entire collection of Star Wars LEGO I keep stored under my bed that Dad and Linda will have something to say about it.

"What's funny?" Taylor asks when I sit across from him.

"It isn't funny. Not really. It's just...what the hell will our parents say about..." I trail off, gesturing between us.

Taylor picks up his fork with a shrug. "Does it matter?"

"Not especially. We aren't doing anything wrong. At least, I don't think we are. I doubt they'll see it like that, though."

"Yeah, well, as you may have noticed, my mother isn't a fan of anything I do, so nothing new there. Why?" His eyes hold mine, dark and intense. "Would you rather we forgot about this?"

I scoff. "What do you think?"

He smiles properly then. It's a sweet, genuine smile that softens his normally deadpan features. I get the feeling you'd have to do a great deal to earn a smile like that from Taylor Solomon.

We're quiet while we eat, but it's a full sort of quiet, overflowing with wonder and complicit glances. Once we've cleared our plates, I dig out some ice cream and we share it straight from the carton.

"So…Liam," I say, as the chocolate melts on my tongue. "What's the story there?"

Taylor grimaces, spoon part way to his mouth. "A very long and tedious one. Sure you want to hear it?"

"Only if you're up to telling. I mean, I could sense there was something between you. Were you together?"

"Yeah." Taylor pops the spoonful of ice cream into his mouth and helps himself to another. Then, his expression neutral, he tells me.

He tells me how they met on the athletics team, about the secrecy and clandestine hook-ups and Liam's terror that his so-called mates would find out. Finally, he tells me about the afternoon Carl walked in on them in a deserted classroom. Liam, confronted with being outed, threw Taylor under the bus, claiming Taylor had forced himself on him. So began Carl's systematic campaign of bullying. As Taylor talks, a burning anger builds in my chest. I'd suspected it was a lie when Abby first passed on Carl's side of the story, but that doesn't make it any easier to hear.

"Jesus, Tay." I thrust my spoon into what's left of the ice cream and glare at it, running both hands through my hair. "Why didn't you tell me? If I'd known, there's no way I would've left Liam here with you when I went to get Mum. Hell, I wouldn't have let the bastard through the front door."

Taylor sets down his own spoon and rests his chin on his hand. When he speaks, his tone bears no resentment, only weariness. "He was scared. No, you don't need to say it. I know that's no excuse for what he did. It... Fuck, it hurt worse than anything's ever hurt in my life. Well, almost anything. Now, though, I'm pretty sure he regretted it the moment it happened."

"And that makes it OK? He spread rumours about you, made your life a misery for months, but it doesn't matter because he was sorry?"

Taylor's gaze snags mine. "You're hot when you're angry. Anyone ever tell you that?" His eyes gleam with amusement... and something darker. Something that, even through the anger, calls to my groin.

"It's not funny." I scowl at him, although I'm fighting a smile. "I hate that he put you through all this."

"I get that, really, and it means a lot. Still, I reckon Liam went some way to making up for it tonight." Taylor stifles a yawn. The eyelid that isn't already swollen shut starts to droop.

I push my chair back and stand, extending a hand to him. "Time for bed. It's been a long night."

Taylor lets me draw him to his feet without argument. I kiss him, slow and lingering, our lips cold and sticky from the ice cream. Then I lead him from the kitchen and up the stairs. In our room, Taylor strips down to his boxers and T-shirt and crawls into his bed, shifting over to make space for me. He adjusts position a few times, wincing as he tries to get comfortable, before settling onto his side.

Without hesitation, I climb under the duvet behind him and spoon his body with mine. I drape an arm over his stomach, careful to avoid his bruised ribs, and Taylor melts against me with a sigh. I'm acutely aware of his body, all solid heat and compact muscle. I want to burrow into him, to touch him and have him devour every micrometre of me with lips and hands, but my exhaustion wins out. It drags at me mentally and physically, anchoring me to the mattress.

I nuzzle Taylor's neck, breathing in his scent—warm skin overlaid with antiseptic and the lavender washing powder Linda uses. "OK?"

"Mmm hmm." His voice, heavy with sleep, carries the hint of a smile. "You?"

"Yeah. Can't quite believe this is happening."

"Any regrets?"

"Seriously?" I huff into his shoulder, sliding my hand under his T-shirt to trace the flat contours of his belly. "I've wanted you from that first day I saw you on the driveway."

Taylor snorts. "Even though I've been a moody shit?"

"Even though."

Taylor's laugh fades into silence. He's quiet for so long I think he must've fallen asleep. Then, his words little more than a breath in the darkness, he says, "Me, too."

CHAPTER FIFTEEN

TAYLOR

I WAKE TO THE soft patter of rain on the bedroom window. Ben's nestled into my back, one arm still around me. I sink farther into him, hovering somewhere between arousal and a sleepy contentment. I could lie here forever, eyes closed, listening to the rain.

Then, like a figure emerging from dense fog, the pain sets in. One by one, my nerves flare to life, the awareness spreading through my entire body until I ache all over. A hiss escapes before I can stifle it.

"You awake?" Ben mumbles into my hair.

"Yeah." I shift, trying to ease the discomfort.

He edges away slightly so I can roll onto my back. My ribs scream in protest, and when I stretch out, my bandaged knee sends a hot dagger shooting up my leg. Ben props himself on an elbow to study me. He winces, gaze travelling over my face.

"That bad?" I ask.

He doesn't answer, but the concern in his expression says it all. Ben reaches out to trace my throbbing cheek. "You OK? Need anything?"

"I can think of one thing." Even through the pain, his touch has my stomach tightening and the blood rushing to my groin. I cup the nape of his neck, drawing his mouth to mine.

The kiss starts off slow, tentative, Ben clearly afraid of hurting me. Yet, as I slide my hands inside his T-shirt and move my tongue against his, he moans, matching my hunger. My various aches swirl away, drowned beneath a tide of desire. I arch against him, tugging at the hem of his T-shirt. I need to feel him, need to feel his skin on mine. Ben gasps as our stomachs graze. He trails kisses down my neck, his mouth hot, greedy. His breathing comes fast and ragged.

A booming bark carries up the stairs. Ben springs off me, sitting up and running a hand through his hair. It's a mess from having my fingers tangled in it. His eyes, still dazed, meet mine. I can only stare back at him and try to slow my thundering pulse. Keys rattle in the lock, followed by the soft murmur of Imogen's voice as she greets Buddy.

"Christ," Ben mutters, "she's back early."

My gaze darts first to the half-open door, then to Ben's neatly made bed. It would be obvious to anyone it hasn't been slept in. We haven't discussed how or when to tell our family about us, but we certainly weren't counting on anyone finding out so soon.

Light footsteps ascend the stairs. With a speed that would have shamed Usain Bolt, Ben launches himself out of my bed and into his own. He's just pulled the duvet up to his chin when Imogen taps on the door.

"Come in," I call, struggling into a sitting position.

My sister pushes the door wider and edges into the room. She studies me for a long moment, assessing the damage. Then, without a word, she crosses to my bed and crawls in next to me, wrapping me in a hug.

"Hey." I tug one of her curls gently. "I'm OK."

Imogen lets out a sound somewhere between a snort and a sob. She reaches up to stroke my battered face, and I'm startled to see the glimmer of tears in her eyes. My sister hardly ever cries, not even when she was eight and sliced open her palm with a Stanley knife.

"I didn't know," she says, her voice barely more than a whisper. "Tobes and me...we knew CJ was a bully, but we never thought... When Jon told us what he'd done..." A single tear trickles down her cheek.

"None of us knew." Ben joins us on my bed, laying a hand on Imogen's shoulder. "But he won't get away with it. Taylor gave a statement. Did Jon tell you?"

My sister nods, casting Ben a watery smile. When she looks back at me, her gaze glows with pride.

I'm SEMI-DOZING ON the sofa, my legs draped across Ben's lap and the TV showing a rerun of *The Big Bang Theory*, when the front door slams.

"Hello? Ben?" Abby rushes into the living room, her hair damp from the rain.

I jerk fully awake, withdrawing my feet onto my side of the cushions. Not that Abby appears to notice. She's too busy gaping at my face, eyes wide.

"Oh my God." Her hand flies to her mouth. "Did...did he do this?"

Seems she can't even bring herself to mention his name. Well, that particular piece of gossip spread faster than Captain Trips. I wonder how many people believe the rumour. Judging by Abby's reaction, she'd half expected it was a lie, or maybe she simply hoped.

I squint at her through my good eye. "What've you heard?"

"That Carl...that he and a couple of others beat you up in some alley in town. Lauren's brother said the police were round at his house this morning, but I thought... I didn't want to... Oh God." Her voice breaks, and she sinks to the carpet beside the sofa, tears coursing down her cheeks.

"Hey." Ben drapes an arm over her shoulders. "None of this is your fault."

She looks up at him, expression pleading. "I thought it had to be a mistake. The Carl I know wouldn't do something like this. He just wouldn't."

"I'm so sorry, Abs." Ben strokes her hair, shooting me a helpless glance. "I know how much you liked him, but I was there. I saw what he did."

Abby absorbs this, her hiccupping sobs barely audible over the telly. I wait for the surge of triumph, the vindication at being proved right. It doesn't come. I watch her struggle with the realisation that the boy she'd been falling for isn't who she imagined, and I feel only pity.

At last, she sniffs and wipes her tears on her sleeve. Her eyes find mine. "You tried to warn me. You told me what he was like, but I wouldn't listen."

Once, I would've brushed her words aside, rebuffed them with a sarcastic remark. Now, I merely shrug. "Don't beat yourself up about it. You're not the first person to be taken in by CJ Farmer, and I'm betting you won't be the last."

"Thanks." A smile trembles at the corners of her mouth. She clambers to her feet, pushing her hair away from her face, and looks at Ben. "Anyway, I came to grab some stuff. I'm going to stay at Lauren's for a bit, maybe until Dad and Linda get home."

"Fine." He pats her leg. "Just drop me a text every now and then to let me know you're OK."

"I will." Abby hugs him. Then, catching me completely off guard, she gives my shoulder the briefest squeeze.

"Well," I say once her feet have pounded up the stairs, "that was…surprising."

Ben laughs, drawing my legs back over his lap. "She's all right, really, my sister."

"Uh-huh?" I flash him a crooked grin. "I've heard her brother's not too bad, either."

THE SECOND SURPRISE of the day comes while we're eating a late lunch in front of the telly. A plate of sandwiches occupies the sofa cushion between Ben and me, and Imogen sits on the floor at our feet, sharing a packet of Bugles with Buddy.

When my mobile rings, I dust the crumbs from my fingers and snatch it off the arm of the sofa. I glance at the screen and grimace. "It's Mum."

My gaze travels over the mess—the dirty cups and glasses on the coffee tables, a toppled pile of books spilling across the floor amidst a sea of crumbs. I have the irrational thought that my mother can somehow see the state of her usually immaculate living room all the way from Marbella and is calling to berate me.

"You'd better talk to her," Ben says, and Imogen nods. "Get it over with."

"I s'pose." I sigh, brace myself for the onslaught, and tap answer. "Hey, Mum."

"Oh, thank goodness I've got hold of you. Abby told us what happened. Why didn't you call us? When Martin and I heard… Taylor, darling, we were so worried. Are you all right?"

Mum sounds fraught, agitated, but not in her normal sharp way. A softness drapes her words, a concern I haven't heard for a long time. And 'darling'? I can't remember when she last called me that. It knocks me off balance and I have no idea how to respond.

"Taylor? Are you there?"

"Yeah, and I'm fine. Really."

"Not according to Abby. She said you look like you've had a fight with a brick wall. Did you go to the hospital?"

"No, but—"

"Taylor, for heaven's sake. What were you thinking? You could have a concussion or internal bleeding or…or anything."

"Mum, calm down. Poppy patched me up. She used to be a nurse, so she knows what she's doing."

"That was good of her." Mum sniffs, the familiar tartness seeping through. "All the same, you should've got yourself checked out. You need looking after, but don't worry. Martin and I will be catching the next flight home."

My heart stutters. I grip the phone as though this will somehow prevent the situation from slipping away from me. It feels so precious, this chance to get to know Ben, for us to be together free from parental eyes. Their return would mean the end of that. I'm not ready to give it up. Not yet.

With an effort, I keep my tone casual. "Really, you don't have to. It's not like there's anything you can do. I'm just supposed to rest. There's no point ruining your holiday. You deserve the break."

"Oh." Mum seems taken aback, even touched, and I know I've struck the right chord. "If you're quite sure, darling. Is Ben taking good care of you?"

"You definitely don't need to worry on that score." I wink at Ben, who flashes me a warm smile. "You just concentrate on enjoying yourselves, yeah?"

"And you take it easy, Taylor, I mean it. Oh, and if that Carl Farmer comes anywhere near you, I want to hear about it. What a vile character he turned out to be. I never liked him."

I stifle a snort. Various disparaging remarks leap to my tongue, but I bite them back. It seems Poppy was right; she might have a strange way of showing it most of the time, but my mum truly does care about me.

BEN

MUM COMES TO check on Taylor later that afternoon. She reproves him for not icing his bruises and despatches me to the kitchen for the frozen peas. When I return to the living room, she has my stepbrother's T-shirt pulled up to expose his taped ribs, examining her handiwork.

As I pass Taylor the tea-towel-wrapped bundle, my gaze lingers on his flat stomach. I recall the smooth warmth of his skin under my hands. His eyes snare mine. Heat blazes between us, and I glance away in time to catch the comprehension that darts across Mum's face.

"That looks secure," she says, easing the T-shirt back down. "I hope my son's taking good care of you."

"He is." Taylor's offhand tone gives nothing away, but the slight twitch of his mouth betrays him.

"Want a cup of tea?" I ask Mum.

She shakes her head. "Thanks, sweetheart, but I won't stop. I just wanted to see how Taylor was doing. You can walk me back, though, if you like."

"Sure." I lay a brief hand on Taylor's shoulder—no sense hiding anything now—and follow her from the room.

The rain has stopped, but a lingering damp hangs in the air. As we start around the side of the house, avoiding the puddles, I breathe in the smell of earth and wet concrete. Mum loops her arm through mine, expression thoughtful. I suspect she's going to ask about Taylor and decide to beat her to it.

"So, you and Jon." I grin at her. "You looked very cosy last night."

"Oh, shush." Mum squeezes my arm, blushing. "It was only a Chinese. Neither of us wants to rush into anything. Jon hasn't dated anyone since his wife died, and I… Well, anyway, we're taking things slowly."

"He seems nice, though."

"He is, very nice, and he clearly dotes on Toby. You can tell a lot about a man from the way he treats his children, I think." At the entrance to the annex, Mum pauses with her hand on the doorknob and smiles at me. "I'm glad you approve."

"I do," I say, meaning it. Suddenly, I need her reassurance. I need to know she doesn't think what we're doing is wrong. We haven't discussed telling anyone yet, but given how close Taylor and Mum are, I don't think he'll mind.

"So, uh…" I take a deep breath. "Taylor and me. We're—"

Mum pulls me into a hug, saving me from explaining. "Sweetheart, I know. I knew the moment I saw you together back there."

"And you're OK with it?"

"Truly, I think it's wonderful. I'm not blind, Ben. I've watched the two of you dance around each other. It was bound to happen sooner or later."

My breath gusts out of me in a rush. I rest my cheek on the top of her head and let the relief wash over me.

"Just promise you'll be careful." Mum puts her hands on my shoulders, forcing me to look at her. "It's possible not everyone will be entirely thrilled about it. You need to be prepared for that."

"Yeah, I know." She doesn't need to spell it out; it's obvious she's talking about Dad. Considering how hard he took it when I came out, I doubt he'll welcome the news of me having a relationship with my stepbrother. Again, it hits me how complicated this whole situation could get.

Just how complicated becomes apparent later that evening.

We've polished off another of Linda's frozen dinners and I'm carrying our dirty plates into the kitchen when my phone chimes. I dump the dishes by the sink, dig my phone from my pocket, and glance at the screen. My stomach lurches. Sebastian.

Tomorrow. Same place. Same time.

I stare at his text, the coronation chicken turning to acid in my gut. What with the events of the past twenty-four hours, I've managed to push thoughts of Sebastian Harcourt and his threats to the outskirts of my mind. Now, they come crashing in on me. My legs feel shaky, and I drop into the nearest chair, unable to tear my gaze from the message. Yesterday, the idea of giving in to Seb's demands, of letting him lure me back into his bed, was abhorrent; today, after a night spent with Taylor asleep in my arms, his body nestled warm and trusting against mine, it's unthinkable.

But what about Dad? He's never been anything but loyal to Harcourts. Does he deserve to lose out on this job because of me? However much I recoil from the truth, there's no denying this situation is my fault. If I hadn't got mixed up with Sebastian in the first place, none of this would be happening.

Perhaps he's bluffing. Seb might be head of HR, but surely staff appointments involve the whole department. Perhaps he's exaggerating his influence, hoping I won't take that chance. It's a comforting thought, and I cling to it.

"Hey." Taylor appears in the doorway, leaning against the frame.

I shove my phone into my pocket. Guilt twists my insides as though I've been caught sexting with another guy. "Hey. Sorry, was just coming. Have you decided on a film?"

Taylor ignores the question. He limps into the room to perch on the table beside me. "What's going on?"

I open my mouth to tell him it's nothing, then close it again. He'd know I was fobbing him off, and I don't want to lie to him. Equally, I have no wish to burden him with my problems; he's been through enough already.

"Text from my ex." I sigh, propping my cheek on my palm. "It's been over between us for ages, but he's having trouble getting that into his head."

Taylor nods, searching my face. It's obvious he wants to ask more, and if he does, I'll have to tell him at least some of it. I owe him that much after he confided in me about Liam. Yet, all he says is, "Seems we both have one of those."

"What?" I bolt up in my chair. "You heard from Liam?"

"Yeah. He asked if we could meet up...just to talk."

"And what did you say?"

Taylor shrugs. "Nothing yet, but we both have to be at the station in the morning to sign our statements. We could go for a coffee or something afterwards."

"You sure that's a good idea? Last time Liam claimed he wanted to talk, you ended up like that." I gesture at his bruises.

"CJ won't dare come within spitting distance of me, not with the police on his back. Plus..." Taylor hesitates. "I think this is something I need to do. Liam and I haven't really spoken since we broke up. There're things we need to say."

I stare down at my lap. I don't like it, not one bit, but there's nothing I can do. Besides, how would Taylor feel if he knew

I'd met my ex the previous evening and would almost certainly be seeing him again tomorrow?

Taylor presses his thigh against mine, waiting for me to look up at him. He holds my gaze. "Sure there's nothing else wrong? You've been kind of quiet. If you're having second thoughts about us—"

Before he can finish, I seize his hands and draw him into my lap. I wrap my arms around him, silencing his surprised laugh with my mouth. Taylor's moan vibrates through my entire body, and I part my lips for his tongue. As the kiss hots up, I vow no one will come between us—not Dad, not my stepmother, and most definitely not Sebastian Harcourt.

CHAPTER SIXTEEN

TAYLOR

I EMERGE FROM THE police station next morning and let out a sigh of relief. The whole process was far less painful than I'd expected. My statement, the one I'd given Jon and his colleague on Saturday evening, had been typed up. All I had to do was check the details and sign it.

"We'll be in touch if we need any more information," the young constable told me with a friendly smile. "I imagine Mr. Farmer will be charged within the next day or so."

He went on to assure me I'd be kept up to date with the progress of the case and advised of any court hearings I might need to attend. Queasiness churned in my stomach at the mention of the trial, but I did my best to ignore it. I'd played my part, and whatever came next, at least I'd have Ben to hold my hand.

I linger in the station car park to wait for Liam. Yesterday's rain has dried up, but the day is cool and overcast. I'm grateful for the long-sleeved T-shirt I'd put on to conceal my bandages. Even without it, though, the thought of Ben would've warmed me right through.

I shake my head at myself, unable to suppress a wry grin. Crazy to think how determined I'd been earlier in the summer to keep my stepbrother at a distance. Now, I can scarcely go a full minute without reliving the pressure of his mouth on mine, his gentle hands exploring my skin. For the billionth time, I curse CJ and his numb-head friends. Thanks to my bruised ribs, I'm having to be careful when careful is the last thing I want to be. I ache to be all over Ben, to lose myself in him until I scarcely know where I am.

"OK?" Liam appears at my side, pulling me from thoughts of my stepbrother.

"Yeah." I glance back at the station entrance. "How'd it go?"

He shrugs, looking away. "Fine, I guess. The constable reckons they'll need to talk to me again at some point, find out more about CJ. Let's get out of here, shall we? The constable said I could leave my car here while we go for a coffee, if you still want to."

"Sure." I peer at him from beneath my lashes. "So long as you don't mind being seen with me in town."

Liam flushes. "I deserved that. If it's any consolation, I've spent the past year despising myself."

He looks so miserable, shoulders hunched inside his hoody. I open my mouth to tell him I'm sorry, that I don't hate him, then close it again. If there's one thing I don't owe Liam Knowles, it's an apology.

"Come on," I say instead. "Let's grab that coffee."

We walk the few minutes to the high street in silence. More than once, Liam does a furtive survey of the people we pass, but each time he catches himself and his gaze returns to the pavement. I suppose it'll take a while for him to kick the habit, to remember there's no longer any point hiding.

When we reach Cafe Ole, Liam insists on paying for my drink. We both order a cappuccino and search for somewhere to sit. The coffee shop is busy with young professionals snatching a caffeine break and shoppers surrounded by bulging carrier bags, but we manage to snag a corner table. As we slide into chairs across from each other, I glance around at the packed café. When Liam and I were together, I would've revelled in the normality of this, of going for a coffee with my boyfriend and not caring who saw.

I refocus my attention on Liam. He's watching me, his hands clenched around his mug, eyes shadowed with regret in his drawn face.

"We should've done this before," he says, echoing my thoughts.

I sip the froth on my cappuccino and lick the chocolate powder from my lips. "You weren't ready. I get that."

His gaze flits to my mouth and away again. "Still, I should've done it. For you. I should've been less of a coward, but instead…"

Liam trails off, his expression haunted and far away. Perhaps he's recalling the afternoon CJ discovered us, his own betrayal of everything we were to each other, and the months of harassment that followed.

I drink my coffee, saying nothing. Liam's sorry, I can see that. I'm even able to muster up some pity for him. Yet he ruined my life that day, caused not only CJ to turn on me but also my so-called friends on the athletics team. He'd stood by while I was repeatedly taunted and shoved into walls, not participating, but never lifting a finger to help. No amount of regret can make up for that.

At last, Liam sucks in a shuddering breath and drops his head in his hands. "I wish I could take it back, what I did. I just panicked. I saw how CJ and the others looked at me, and all

I could think was…these guys have been my friends since primary school. I can't lose them."

"They were never your friends," I tell him, "not really. Friends accept you for who you are. They don't make you feel you have to pretend to be someone else."

"Yeah, I see that now, and even if they were, they're certainly not anymore." His smile is hollow.

"You heard from CJ then?"

"Nah, not a word. Just this one text from Pete."

Liam retrieves his phone from his hoody pocket. He taps the screen before turning it to show me.

You're dead to us, homo.

I grimace. "Charming. Think they figured out you spoke to the police?"

"Probably." Liam shrugs, replacing the phone. "This came through Sunday afternoon, after they'd been questioned. Maybe they saw me running back with Ben, guessed I went for help."

"Be careful, yeah? You know what they're like. The last thing they need is another punchbag."

"I will. I doubt they'll do anything with the police on their case, but I won't take any chances. Besides, I'll be off to uni in six weeks."

"Still set on Leeds?"

"Yeah, fingers crossed." Liam toys with his teaspoon, his gaze earnest on mine. "I wish I'd done things differently that day."

I offer him a lopsided grin. "Yeah, I can see why you'd want to have spent the past year being pushed around by CJ."

"I'm serious. Anything would've been better than watching you get hurt, feeling like the most pathetic piece of shit on the planet, and at least I would've had you. We could've faced them together."

The raw unhappiness in his expression is too painful to look at. I stare down at the table, tracing a finger along a scratch in the wooden surface.

"Taylor." Liam's voice is tentative, but when I look back up at him, his eyes burn into mine. "Losing you was the worst mistake I ever made. I messed up big time, I know that, and I'd do anything to take it back. The way I felt about you, though, that never changed. Is there any chance we could start again? Properly this time. No hiding. No pretending. Everything out in the open."

"Oh." I have no idea how to respond. Once, I would've given anything to hear these words from Liam, but now...

An image of Ben's sweet, open face swims into my mind. Not once over the weekend has he looked at me with anything other than concern or genuine pleasure. There was no doubt, no hint of the shame that twisted Liam's expression whenever he withdrew his mouth from mine, the shame I would pretend not to see. Despite everything that's happened this past year—the bullying, the heartache, the sense of betrayal—I'd go through it all over again to experience this with Ben.

"It's OK." Liam's shoulders sag. "I'm too late. I kind of knew that already."

"I'm sorry, Li. If you'd asked me a few months ago, maybe... I dunno, but—"

"It's fine, really. You've moved on. I get that." Liam smiles at me, one of the saddest smiles I've ever seen. "So, you and Ben, huh?"

I gulp the dregs of my coffee. "Yeah. It's still very new, but yeah."

Liam nods, swallowing as if a sugar lump has become lodged in his throat. When he speaks, his voice is tight. "I hope it works out. You deserve it." He pushes his still-full cup away from him and stands. "Come on, I'll drop you home."

BEN

"Just popping out." I poke my head into the living room where Taylor and Imogen are watching *Pointless.* "Going to walk down to Pardo's to pick up a few things."

Buddy, who's snoozing on the rug, jerks awake at the mention of a walk and wags in anticipation.

"Shall I come with you?" Taylor focuses on me, his good eye drooping with tiredness. Worn out after his visit to the police station and the talk with Liam, he's followed Buddy's example and dozed off and on all afternoon.

"No, you rest up." I force a smile through my nausea. I want to go to him. I want to wrap my arms around him, bury my face in his neck, and hide from the reality of what I'm about to do. But I can't. Not with Imogen here. It isn't that we think she'd mind; we're just not ready to share this with the world.

So, instead of giving in to my longing, I crouch beside Buddy and scratch behind his ears. "Sorry, Bud, not this time. I'll take you for an extra-long walk tomorrow, OK?"

He licks my hand, forgiving as ever. I pat him one last time and stand. "See you in a bit then."

Imogen waves, attention glued to the telly, but I'm conscious of my stepbrother's thoughtful gaze. Taylor knows something's up. Well, of course he does. I've been on edge since Sebastian's text the night before. He can hardly have failed to pick up on it, even with one eye swollen shut.

I stumble along the hall to the front door. Guilt bows my shoulders like a rucksack full of lead. I hate keeping this from Taylor, hate going behind his back, but what choice do I have?

The walk passes in a haze of queasiness and thumping heart. It doesn't occur to me to drive; in the state I'm in, I'd likely wind up consigning poor Esmerelda to the scrapyard. As it is, I barely notice where I'm going and only realise I've stepped in a puddle when my trainers fill with water.

Am I really doing this? I think of Taylor waiting for me at home, aware something's wrong but trusting me enough not to pry, and my gut twists. It's as if an elastic band has attached itself to my innards, attempting to yank me back the way I've come. A voice in my head—my common sense, maybe—tells me I can still change my mind, that I don't have to do this. But I do. From the moment I received Sebastian's summons, my decision was made.

I enter the lobby of The Magnolia, socks squelching, jeans soaked to the ankle. The horse-faced receptionist glances up from her magazine and frowns at my procession of wet footprints on the plush carpet. She's clearly about to demand what business I have tramping over the hallowed threshold of her hotel, but I don't give her the chance. I bring to mind Taylor's air of nonchalance—hips swaying, head held high, thumbs hooked into his belt loops. Then I saunter straight across the reception area and through the archway into the bar.

Sebastian's already here, lounging beyond the curtain of foliage at our usual table. As always, he exudes relaxed sophistication, suit jacket slung over the back of his chair, half-drunk gin and tonic in front of him.

"Hey, baby boy." His gaze travels over me, lingering on my unbrushed hair and faded sweatshirt. Far from seeming annoyed by my obvious lack of effort, his eyes take on a hungry gleam. "So glad you could make it. Sit down and I'll get you a drink. Jack and Coke?"

"No. I… I'm not stopping." I clench my fingers on the edge of the table, trying to disguise the fact that they're trembling.

A predatory smile oozes across his face. "You'd rather we went straight upstairs? I can certainly get behind that idea. At least let me finish my drink, though, before you drag me into bed."

"You're deluded." I'd intended to sound scathing, but the crack in my voice ruins the effect.

Sebastian tilts his head. The smile still plays about his lips, his expression one of polite enquiry. "I'm sorry?"

"If you think…" I grip the table so hard I'm amazed it doesn't splinter. "If you seriously think I'd want you anywhere near me after everything you've done, you must be mad."

There, I've said it. I considered texting him, but that would've been the coward's way out. I needed to look him in the eye one last time, needed to prove to myself that I could. Now there's no going back, even if I wanted to.

Sebastian isn't smiling anymore. He leans towards me, his eyes slits of onyx. When he speaks, his tone drips poisoned honey. "I take it you haven't forgotten what I said?"

"And which part would that be?" I pretend to search my memory. "The part where you said you loved me and would do anything in the world for us to be together? Or how about the part where you swore blind you weren't sleeping with your wife weeks before she got pregnant with your baby? But, no, you mean the part where you threatened to stop my dad from getting a job we both know he deserves unless I have sex with you. My dad who works his arse off for your company, all so you can spend your life drinking champagne and luring naïve young men into your bed."

"Keep your voice down," Sebastian hisses. He peers through a gap in the leaves, checking to see if anyone's glancing at us. "You're embarrassing yourself."

I bark out a laugh. "Really? *I'm* embarrassing myself? In case you've forgotten, I'm not the one who's so desperate he has to blackmail a guy into sleeping with him."

He rocks back in his chair as though I've struck him. Triumph surges through me, intoxicating and powerful, but only for an instant. Under the look he gives me, a look icy with contempt and loathing, it freezes in my chest.

"You think I'm bluffing?" he asks, his voice as slippery as snakeskin. "You think I wouldn't go through with it?"

I try to answer, but my tongue feels unwieldy in my mouth. At home, away from the force of Sebastian's personality, I'd convinced myself his threat was nothing more than a ruse designed to get what he wants, but now...

He must see the doubt in my expression because his lip curls. "I couldn't give a damn about your precious father. He might be a loyal little drone, but there are better candidates out there. Younger, more dynamic candidates. No one stands in my way, baby boy, you should know that. Anyone foolish enough to try will live to regret it."

He means it, every word. I've dared to refuse him, and now he'll have his revenge. The cold truth slams into me, sending a tremor up my legs. With an effort, I swallow my fear and meet his gaze head on.

"Do it then," I spit. "Do your worst, and I hope your conscience keeps you awake every night for the rest of your sordid little life."

In one swift motion, I snatch Sebastian's glass from the table. Then I throw the contents, orange peel and all, into his shocked face.

"Hey, you." I flop onto the sofa beside Taylor and draw him into my arms.

He lays a palm against my cheek, gaze intent on mine. "Hey, yourself. You look better."

"I feel better." I smile at him, melting into his touch. It's true. High on adrenalin and my own daring, I practically flew home. The first thing I did after sailing past the tight-lipped receptionist and onto the quiet street was to block Sebastian's number from my phone. If I have my way, I'll never see or speak to him again.

"Get everything we needed?"

"Huh?"

Taylor raises an eyebrow. "From Pardo's. You were going to pick us up some stuff."

"Damn it." I clap a hand to my forehead. "I completely forgot. Sorry, my head's been all over the place."

"I've noticed." Taylor looks deep into my eyes. It's as though he's hoping to see beyond the surface, right into my soul. "So long as we're OK. I know you're worried how our parents will react, but we'll deal with that, right?"

"Yeah, 'course." I rest my forehead against his. Compared with my confrontation with Sebastian, handling Dad's disapproval will be a breeze. All at once, I want to kiss Taylor so badly my chest constricts. "Where's Imogen?"

"Upstairs getting her things together. She's staying at Toby's tonight, so…" The rest of his sentence hangs between us, heavy with significance.

"So…?" I brush his lips with mine. The contact drags a gasp from Taylor and ignites a flame inside me. Our gazes lock, connected by the promise of things to come. I'm suddenly all too aware that we haven't been properly alone since the previous morning.

Footsteps pad down the stairs and pass the living room towards the kitchen. Taylor pulls away, his mouth quirking in a wicked smile. "Speaking of the parents, Mum called while you were out."

"Oh?" I struggle to reassemble my thoughts. "How was she?"

"Still behaving like she's been taken over by aliens. Wanted to know how I got on at the police station, whether I've been eating properly and getting enough rest. Oh, and she asked me to tell you, thought you'd like to know." Taylor takes my hand, interlacing our fingers. "Your dad got the job."

CHAPTER SEVENTEEN

TAYLOR

I LIE BACK IN the bath with a muffled groan. The hot water stings my cuts and soothes the soreness from the bruises. I'll have to face Poppy's disapproval at removing the bandages and allowing my still-healing wounds to get wet, but it'll be worth it for the luxury of a proper soak.

Immersed up to my chin, my discoloured body obscured beneath a froth of bubbles, I rest my head against the side of the bath and close my eyes. The house settles around me, quiet and empty. Ben has just left on some mysterious errand. He'd appeared in the living room a short while ago, wallet in hand, car keys dangling from one finger.

I lifted an eyebrow. "Don't tell me. You're actually going to Pardo's this time."

Ben's idea of a satisfactory answer was to flash me a secretive smile and assure me he wouldn't be long.

That smile. The memory of it, soft and tinged with mischief, has my mouth curving in response. There's been a subtle shift in him since he came back from his walk. It's as if while he was out, he'd shrugged off his worries about our relationship and tossed them to the gutter. Without that burden, he seems freer, happier than I've seen him all summer. Recalling the way he looked at me, like I held the only solution to a riddle he's wrestled with his whole life, causes a swooping sensation in my belly. Either I'm in serious danger of falling for my stepbrother, or I've taken too many of Poppy's painkillers.

The warm water has lulled me into a pleasurable daze by the time Buddy barks, announcing Ben's return. Fresh and relaxed, I dry myself off and pad back to our room in my towel to pull on jeans and a fresh long-sleeved T-shirt. As I run my fingers through my wet hair, the mirror taunts me with my reflection. I wince. The swelling has gone down enough that I can open my left eye, but that side of my face is a mass of yellow and purple. If I've ever looked worse than I do now, I can't remember.

In a defiant gesture, I grab my eyeliner from the chest of drawers. The simple act of applying it, so much a part of who I am, immediately makes me feel more myself.

I pad downstairs, following the sounds of movement to the kitchen. Ben doesn't hear me come in; he's too busy unpacking several Pardo's carrier bags. I sneak up behind him and slide my arms around his waist. He starts, twisting to draw me against him.

"Hey." He buries his face in my neck with a contented sigh. "You smell good."

The brush of his lips sends goosebumps along my spine. I run my hands over his back, taking in the food shopping on the worktop. A bottle of Prosecco pokes from one bag, a punnet of strawberries from another. "What's all this?"

"Ah, thought I'd make dinner."

"You did, huh?"

"Less of the scepticism, mister. I'm actually pretty handy in the kitchen."

"Of course you are. Is there anything you're not good at?"

"Shush. Mum's never been much of a cook. She'd sometimes forget to eat at all when she got into her flow, so I didn't have much choice."

"Right. So let me guess. You're making fish pie."

Ben shudders. "God, no. It's bad enough that your mum insists on making it every week."

I arch a brow. "But it's your favourite."

"Not anymore. Haven't been able to stomach fish since I got food poisoning in Oz."

I stare at him, outraged. "You mean I've had to choke down a weekly helping of smoked haddock, all so the golden boy can have his favourite meal, and you don't even like it?"

"What can I say?" Ben shrugs, expression sheepish. "I couldn't exactly come clean that first night, not when your mum had gone to so much trouble. I didn't expect her to keep making it."

"Serves you right." I flash him my crooked grin. "Actually, I feel better knowing I'm not the only one who's been forcing it down."

"Watch it, you, or I might change my mind about dinner."

"Yeah? What're we having?"

Ben releases me, going back to unloading the shopping. "Something special to make up for the fact that we never got our date on Saturday. Music, candles, wine…the works."

"If I'd realised you were such a disgusting romantic, Ben Willoughby—" I break off, laughing, and accept the bottle he thrusts at me.

"Shut up and open this." Ben smirks. "And you can pretend all you want. I know you love it."

He's right, damn him.

We're seated across from one another, the kitchen table set with Mum's best white cloth and crystal glasses, Ben's phone playing something mellow and acoustic. It's all kinds of cheesy. Yet when Ben smiles over at me, his face soft in the flickering candlelight, I feel…special. There's no other word for it.

I pop a piece of chicken into my mouth. The tang of lemon and herbs bursts on my tongue. "Man, this is fucking amazing."

"Told you." Ben grins, though he can't hide how pleased he is.

"Seriously. This beats snatching a drive-through McDonald's, which sums up my experience of dating so far."

"Sounds romantic."

"Yeah, well, options are a bit limited when one of you doesn't want to be seen in public."

"I get that." Ben scoops up a forkful of rice, his expression sympathetic.

I look at him, curious. "Is your ex not out, either?"

"Worse. He's married."

"No shit."

"Yeah." Ben pulls a rueful face. "Seb took me for enough fancy dinners, but it was nearly always somewhere out of town. He couldn't risk bumping into anyone he knew."

I reach for my glass and take a sip in an attempt to mask my surprise. Ben's so level-headed, so put together. It's hard to imagine him getting involved with a married man. Then again, love makes us do strange things. I'm proof of that.

"I know what you're thinking," Ben says, "and you're right. It was all one ginormous cliché. He told me his marriage was dead, that he was just waiting for the right time to leave his wife. Next thing I find out, she's pregnant."

Ben's tone betrays no pain, no hint of bitterness. Still, I wince. "I'm sorry."

"Don't be." An edge of flint creeps into his voice. "I had a whole year in Australia to get over it. As far as I'm concerned, Sebastian's ancient history."

"So long as he sees it like that." I remember the text from last night, and protectiveness forms a scaffold around my heart. If that bastard comes anywhere near Ben...

"You don't need to worry. He knows exactly where he stands. I just wish..." Ben spears a bite of chicken but makes no move to eat it. "I wish I hadn't been stupid enough to get mixed up with him in the first place."

"Yeah, well." I reach out to him across the table. "We can all be a bit stupid sometimes. Look at the way I've been behaving."

Ben laughs. He puts down his fork and takes my hand, lacing his fingers with mine. "About that, I've been meaning to—"

Buddy lets out a muted *wruff* from his bed in the utility room, cutting Ben short. Next moment, a key jangles in the front door. We barely have time to exchange a panicked glance when Imogen appears on the threshold.

BEN

I DROP TAYLOR'S hand and snatch up my fork, but it doesn't matter. What with the music, the candlelight and the nearly empty bottle of Prosecco, there's no way this could be mistaken for anything other than a romantic dinner. Imogen absorbs the scene in a single glance, then crosses to pick up the comic lying beside the toaster.

She goes to walk back past us without comment, but Taylor throws out an arm to stop her. "Wait up. Thought you were staying at Toby's."

"Needed this." Imogen holds up the comic before skirting his outstretched arm and making for the door.

"Hey, Imogen?"

She pauses, head tilted, her expression one of mild curiosity. If she'd been shocked to walk in on us like this, she doesn't show it.

"We were going to tell you." Taylor waves a hand, encompassing the two of us. "We were just waiting for the right time."

Imogen scoffs.

"What?" Taylor frowns at her.

She huffs, gaze flicking skywards. "I do have eyes."

"You already knew?" Perhaps I shouldn't be surprised. Imogen has always struck me as far too observant for her own good.

She flashes me a crooked smile, the image of her brother's. "You haven't been exactly subtle. Anyway, saw it coming weeks ago."

"Oh." Seems everyone predicted Taylor and I would end up together. Everyone except us. I scan my stepsister's face. "You don't mind?"

She regards us for a long moment, face revealing nothing. Then she gives us the thumbs up, tucks the comic under her arm, and darts from the room. An instant later, the front door clicks shut.

"Um…" My eyes meet Taylor's. "Are we really that obvious?"

He shrugs. "Looks that way. Then again, my sister doesn't miss much."

"I've gathered." I fork up another mouthful of chicken and chew slowly. Telling Imogen was far easier than I'd feared. Not that I thought she'd disapprove, but I'd been prepared for reserve, for her to echo Mum's caution. Her unquestioning acceptance is unexpected, but I'm glad to have it.

"Whatever you're thinking," Taylor says, "it looks deep."

I shake my head. "Not really. It's just…maybe we're overdramatising this. Maybe our parents won't care."

"I'm not counting on it. At least, not where Mum's concerned, but we'll deal with that when we come to it, right?"

"Yeah." I smile at him, and in this moment, I believe it. If I'm honest, I doubt Dad will like what we're doing any more than Linda, but there's no point stressing over it. Like Taylor says, we'll deal with that when it comes. For now, we have the rest of the week to explore this new path, to see where it might take us.

Once we've scraped our plates clean, I get up to clear them. "Ready for pudding?"

"Hell, yes." Taylor reaches out, resting a hand on my hip. His eyes mark a fiery trail over my chest and down my stomach to my crotch.

My entire body heats up. I almost straddle him right there, needing to feel his tongue in my mouth, his touch on my skin. Not yet. I draw in a steadying breath. After the spectacular failure of our last date, I'm determined not to rush this one, to savour it for as long as possible.

I bat his hand away, grinning. "Behave, Mr. Impatient. I'm about to blow your mind with my culinary creation."

"I'd rather you blew something else, but I suppose that can wait."

"Stop." I harden in response to his words, and a laugh hitches in my throat. "It'll be worth it, trust me."

"I'm holding you to that." Taylor's smirk pushes against my resolve, urging me to crush my mouth on his, to kiss all that cockiness out of him.

With an effort of will that impresses me no end, I dump the dirty plates in the sink and cross to open the fridge. I take out the crystal ramekins, the sole survivors of a set Dad bought Mum for their fifteenth wedding anniversary, and examine my handiwork. Not bad. One of the desserts has sagged on one side, but for a first attempt…pretty good.

"So, what're we having, Nigel Slater?" Taylor asks, tone mocking.

I return to the table, a dish in each hand, and do my best impression of an amateur cook presenting a meal to the *MasterChef* judges. "This evening, I've prepared for you a rich white chocolate mousse served on a crunchy shortbread base and topped with fresh strawberries."

"Idiot." Taylor snorts. He inspects the pudding I set in front of him. "Sweet. You've made the strawberries look like arses."

"God, you're so unromantic. Those are hearts."

"I dunno. I have very romantic feelings towards your arse."

"Shut up and eat." I swat at him, a blush warming my cheeks. I sit back down and pick up my spoon, but my attention's on Taylor, waiting for his reaction.

He scoops up a bite and his eyes go wide. "Wow, this is sooo good."

"Told you so," I say with a wink. I try some myself, although I scarcely taste it. I'm too distracted by the boy seated opposite me.

My stepbrother takes his time. It's obvious from the tantalising way he moves, gaze fixed on me, that he's all too aware of the effect he's having. He slides the spoon into his mouth and sucks on it, his eyes half lidded. After each mouthful, he drags his tongue along his lower lip, caressing, deliberate. I can't look away, can scarcely breathe. The tightness in my jeans is almost painful, throbbing in tandem with my heart.

The moment Taylor licks the last smear of mousse from his spoon, I abandon my barely touched pudding and shove myself away from the table. I extend a hand to him. He ignores it, getting to his feet and pushing me against the worktop. Then he's kissing me, his tongue greedy, invading, and I'm kissing him back, drawing him deep, my body arching to meet his. He tastes of wine and strawberries and the creamy sweetness of white chocolate. I want to drown in him.

"Come on." I moan into his mouth. Without breaking the kiss, I grasp his hips and guide him backwards towards the door.

We stumble along the hall, separating only to tug off each other's T-shirts, which we drop in a heap beside the telephone table. When Taylor's bare skin grazes mine, a hundred tiny shocks sing along my nerves.

In the bend of the stairs, I press Taylor against the wall and drag my lips down his neck to the hollow of his throat, teasing the spot with my teeth. "What would Imogen think if she walked in now?"

Taylor lets out a sound somewhere between a laugh and a gasp. He works at the buttons of my jeans, fingers slipping inside my boxers to close warm and firm around me. I almost lose it right there in his hand. My plan was to take things slow, to make this first time with Taylor last, but I'm too far gone.

"Upstairs," I breathe into his shoulder, "now."

"Yes, sir." Taylor grins, allowing me to spin him around and hustle him up to the landing ahead of me.

In our bedroom with the door shut, we fumble to remove the rest of our clothes, kicking them off where we stand. Taylor turns, eyes heavy with desire. He bares himself to me, even as he drinks me in. My breath catches. It doesn't matter that his skin is an abstract canvas of cuts and bruises. He's stunning, right down to the mole above his navel.

He glances down at himself, grimacing. "Probably not my best look."

I swallow the dryness in my throat. "You're beautiful. It's just…I don't want to hurt you."

"You won't. I trust you." Taylor steps closer. He slides his hands up my sides, confident, commanding, and guides me backwards onto my bed. Then he's astride me, leaning forward on his elbows to recapture my mouth.

CHAPTER EIGHTEEN

I DON'T OPEN MY eyes right away. Too relaxed to move, I lie in the circle of Ben's arms, our legs entangled, his breath a caress against my lips. Distantly, like the murmur of conversation in another room, I'm aware of my body clamouring for attention. My ribs throb, and every bruise, every scrape lobbies to remind me of its existence. Well, they'll have to wait.

I nuzzle deeper into Ben's warmth. My mind drifts, reliving every sensation of last night. I taste the richness of chocolate on my tongue, see Ben gazing at me across the table, his features soft in the candlelight. I hear his words, hot and fierce against my ear as our bodies fused in the darkness, a jumble of mouths and hands and the burning need for closeness. I swallow a groan. With an effort, I open my eyes and find Ben studying me from beneath his lashes.

He smiles, all drowsy sweetness. "Hey, you."

"Hey." I drink in the sight of him, this beautiful boy who has knocked my world askew. He took me apart last night, piece by jagged, imperfect piece, then put me back together in a way that's entirely new. Just looking at him now, flushed and tousled from sleep, has me yearning for him to do it all over again.

"Taylor Solomon." Ben traces my lips with a finger, his eyes darkening. "You have the filthiest smirk I've ever seen."

"Me? Nah. You must be thinking of someone else." I take his fingertip between my teeth and bite gently.

Ben gasps out a laugh. He slides his hands down the length of my back, then grips my buttocks to pull me closer. I grin, draping a leg over his hips. My knee twinges in protest and I flinch.

Worry clouds Ben's expression. "You OK?"

"Yeah. Just a bit sore. Totally worth it."

"It was, huh?"

"Mmm hmmm." I lean in to brush his lips with mine.

Ben sighs against my mouth, reaching up to stroke the bruised side of my face. "What're you going to do about work?"

"Shit." What with everything, I'd completely forgotten that Dean's parents will need to get someone to cover for me this Saturday, maybe longer. Looking like this, I'll send any potential customers screaming from the shop.

"I mean," Ben adds, "you weren't actually thinking of going in?"

I roll my eyes. "Calm down, Dr. Willoughby. Don't get your dick in a twist. I'll call them, let them know what's happened. First, though…" I kiss him again, harder this time, and the outside world disappears for a while.

"So THAT WAS you," Dean says when I call the bookshop later that morning. He lets out a low whistle. "Man, I'm sorry. One of my mates heard CJ was in trouble for jumping some guy, but I didn't know it was you."

"S'all right. Not your fault."

"Still, you should've told me. If I'd known he had it in for you that badly, me and my mates would've paid him a little visit."

"Really, there's nothing you could've done. CJ and me go way back." I smile, touched. His concern means a lot, especially given how awkward he'd been around me at the start of the summer.

"He's an arsehole." Dean growls. "About time he got taken down. You doing OK, though?"

"Yeah. Bit banged up, that's all. Nothing that won't heal." I'm about to tell him I'll need time off work, but Dean gets there first.

"Don't come in until you feel up to it, yeah? We can manage."

"Thanks, man. Appreciate it."

"No worries. It's not like we've been exactly overrun with customers lately, although...hang on a sec."

There's a clunk as Dean sets down the receiver. I shift on the edge of my bed, listening to his brief exchange and the familiar rattle and *ching* of the till.

"Listen," he says when he comes back on the line. His tone carries a hint of that old awkwardness. "I just wanted to say, sorry if I was weird the other day."

"Were you?" I cast my mind back to the previous Saturday. Feels like forever ago. I have a vague memory of Dean asking me when I first realised I was gay, and there'd been something about feeling betrayed.

Dean snorts. "Just a bit, but none of that was aimed at you. My best mate, the one you're filling in for, he kind of dropped this massive bombshell on me and I, uh, I'm not handling it too well."

"Really, it's fine," I say quickly. Dean and I might be on better terms than we were at the start of July, but that doesn't mean he has to confide in me, not when he's so clearly reluctant. "None of my business. You don't have to explain."

"OK. Thanks, man." Dean sounds relieved. "Just didn't want you thinking I was getting at you. Take care of yourself, yeah?"

After we've said goodbye and hung up, I wander downstairs in search of Ben. He's leaning against the kitchen worktop, eating last night's leftovers straight from the dish. The sight of him with his hair rumpled, wearing nothing but a pair of shorts, makes me want to drag him back to bed. Buddy sits at his feet, eyes fixed hopefully on the chicken. Behind them, late-morning sunshine spills through the window. A shaft of it seems to slip right inside me, warming my heart. It banishes the darkness that's lived there for months, all the anger and bitterness, and fills me up with molten gold. It's a perfect August day, I don't have to go to work for a while, and there's the rest of the week to enjoy with Ben.

The happiness must show in my expression because Ben's face breaks into a slow smile. "Everything sorted?"

"Yeah." I bend to scratch Buddy behind the ears. "Dean said to take as long as I need."

"That was good of him."

"He's a good guy. When I first started working with him, I thought he was a bit uptight, but he's all right."

"Sounds like someone else I know."

"Can't imagine who." I grin, my tone offhand.

Ben laughs and waves his fork in my direction. "Come and have some. It's not bad cold."

My stomach rumbles, reminding me how hungry I am. I grab a fork from the drawer and join him at the worktop, spearing a bite. The chicken is chewy and kind of dry. In this moment, however, with Ben smiling at me and the feel of his body still imprinted on every cell of my own, nothing has ever tasted so amazing.

BEN

THE FOLLOWING DAYS with Taylor zip by so fast I'm left dizzy and breathless. Sometimes we're like a pair of kids, revelling in the freedom of our parents' absence. We stay up half the night, talking, charting every detail of the other's body, the ticklish spots and faded scars. Then, after plunging into an exhausted sleep, we wake around noon and eat slices of cold pizza straight from the box. At other times, we behave like some old married couple, popping to the shop for milk, or snuggling up on the sofa with a film and mugs of tea. It's new and exciting and like it was meant to be.

We have the house to ourselves, except for when Abby stops by on Wednesday afternoon to pick up a bikini. Luckily, she finds us with our clothes on and in the kitchen, the oven spewing forth the aroma of basil and melted cheese from Linda's pasta bake.

Still, when Abby pauses in the doorway on her way out, overnight bag swinging from one shoulder, she appraises us with raised eyebrows. "You two look like you've just rolled out of bed."

I glance at Taylor from my seat at the table. We've already agreed to tell Abby about us—it's only fair now Imogen knows—and I suppose this is as good a time as any. Taylor's perched on the worktop, denim-clad legs dangling. When I catch his eye, he shrugs and offers me his crooked smile.

"OK." I take a deep breath and turn back to my sister. "Here's the thing…"

Abby listens, one foot propped against the doorframe. Like Imogen, she shows no surprise and merely smirks. "Took you long enough. Thought I'd have to spend the rest of the summer watching the two of you moon over each other."

Taylor snorts into his can of Coke.

"For Christ's sake." I shake my head. "Not you, too. We weren't that obvious."

Abby lets out a dramatic sigh. "Boys. Always so clueless."

"Hey!"

"No, really. You're perfect for each other. For one thing, you both have terrible taste in men."

I snatch up the tea towel and throw it at her. She giggles, plucking it from the air, and tosses it back at me.

"Right, I'll leave you lovebirds to it." Abby performs a quick survey of the kitchen. Dirty dishes threaten to cascade from the sink onto the floor, while an army of empty drink cans and food containers has set up camp on the worktop. She purses her lips. "I'll be back on Friday to help you clear up before Dad and Linda get home. Our stepmother will have a fit if she sees this lot."

"Never want this to end." Taylor nuzzles his cheek into my shoulder, tone lazy.

It's late on Thursday evening. We're tangled together on my bed, the sheets twisted beneath us, our skin slick with sweat. Dusky light filters through the curtains, giving the room the appearance of being under water.

"Me neither." I run a hand through his damp hair. My body thrums with remembered pleasure, the feel of Taylor on me, around me. I'd give anything to stay here with him forever, just the two of us, safe in our subterranean cave.

"Think we could persuade our parents to stay in Spain for another week?" he asks, his smile wistful.

"I wish." I'm so not ready for this to be over. It feels as though I've barely scratched the surface of this boy, barely glimpsed the web of ideas and emotions that makes up the revelation that is Taylor Solomon. I have the weird sense that I'm preparing to say goodbye to him, which is stupid. He'll still be here, living under the same roof. Yet once our parents walk through the front door, we both know this magical time will be over.

"What're you thinking?" Taylor traces a pattern on my stomach.

I sigh at his touch, my palm coming to rest at the nape of his neck. "Nothing, really. Can I ask you something?"

"Anything."

"It's just…when I first got back from Australia, you seemed so angry. Why?"

Taylor snorts. "You want the list?"

"That bad?"

"Pretty much. I was angry at everything, more or less."

"Tell me," I urge, wanting to know, to understand.

"All right." He puffs out a long breath and rolls away from me onto his back, arms behind his head. "So, you already know some of it. I was angry at Liam for betraying me the way he did, angry at CJ for thinking he had the right to make my life hell, and at myself for letting him trample all over me."

"I totally get that." I prop myself on one elbow so I can watch his face while he talks.

He stares up at the ceiling, expression thoughtful but devoid of heat. "I was mad at Mum for leaving Dad for someone else, for just expecting Imogen and me to go along with it and play happy families. I was angry with your dad, too. He's so bloody nice, has never once called me out for being a shit, and your mum… She's one of the sweetest people I've ever met. She deserves more than being relegated to the annex of her own home, and I hated myself for being partly responsible. Most of all, though, I was furious with my dad for allowing it all to happen in the first place, for buggering off to London and leaving his kids to pick up the pieces. I'm still pissed off at him for that, to be honest. Think I always will be."

"Wow." I digest his words, reeling a little. It's the most I've ever heard Taylor say in one go. "That's…a lot."

His eyes flick to mine, mouth quirked. "Oh, and I was angry at you, of course."

"Yeah, I noticed, but how come?"

"Because you're so fucking fanciable and I wanted you like crazy."

I collapse onto the pillows with a laugh. "That's hardly my fault. Can I help it if I'm irresistible?"

"Trust me." In a quick move that defies his healing bruises, Taylor rolls on top of me and pins my hands either side of my head. His gaze captures mine, wicked and dark. "I'm holding you entirely responsible."

"Yeah?" I look up at him, the air snagging in my throat. "And what're you going to do about it?"

He kisses me, a deep, probing kiss. A kiss that echoes everything I feel right now—all the wonder of getting to know this beautiful, stubborn boy, my longing to hold on to this moment for eternity. I sink into him, drawing him so close I doubt we'll ever be able to pry ourselves apart. Not that I want to. As of tomorrow, everything will change. For now, though, nothing matters but him.

CHAPTER NINETEEN

TAYLOR

I LOAD THE LAST of the glasses into the dishwasher and shut the door with a satisfying snap. Without Mum here to tidy up after us, it's amazing how widely our dirty plates and mugs had dispersed. The dishwasher whooshes into action, and I straighten to survey my handiwork—sink and draining board gleaming, floor and table swept of crumbs. A week ago, I wouldn't have given a shit about the state of the house. Hell, I would've revelled in creating a mess for the sheer pleasure of pissing Mum off. Yet since that frantic phone call when she first heard about the assault, we've formed a tentative truce. It's been kind of restful, not being at loggerheads with my mother. I'm in no hurry to ruin that.

I leave the kitchen and follow the sound of vacuuming to the living room. At the sight of me, Ben switches off the hoover and smiles. "OK?"

"Yeah." I cross to slide an arm around him, gaze travelling over the room. Not a crisp packet or mug ring in sight. "Looks good in here. You'll make someone a great housewife someday."

Ben laughs and pulls me into him. "Shut up. Think it'll pass your mum's inspection?"

"Probably not, but at least she won't have a heart attack as soon as she steps through the front door."

"That's something. My CPR isn't up to my housework prowess."

I grin into Ben's shoulder, inhaling the scent of him. These past couple of days getting to know my stepbrother, existing in our own private world, have been incredible. Now our parents are about to invade that world, and I'd give anything for just one more day.

Feet stampede down the stairs a moment before the girls join us. Buddy trails at their heels, Mum's feather duster in his mouth.

Abby appraises us, standing there with our arms around each other, and wrinkles her nose. "You two are disgusting."

Buddy galumphs into the room and flops onto the rug in front of Ben, dropping the feather duster at his feet.

"I just finished hoovering in here, you great hairy lump." Ben retrieves the duster and waves it at the dog in mock threat. Buddy thumps his tail, clearly delighted with himself.

"Upstairs is tidy," Abby informs us, "and I've had a text from Linda. She said their plane's just landed and they'll be home in an hour or so."

I share a glance with Ben. His expression echoes the longing and regret crushing my windpipe. Very soon reality will barge in with a vengeance, and neither of us is remotely ready.

Abby looks between us. "Are you going to tell them? Not that you'll need to if you climb all over each other like that."

"Yeah." Ben trails his hand down my arm to take mine. "They'll find out sooner or later, and it'll be better coming from us." He speaks calmly, but his shoulders are rigid with tension.

"We're not doing anything wrong," I remind him, squeezing his hand. To the girls, I say, "We thought we'd wait till tomorrow, though. Figured Mum would be more receptive after a good night's sleep." I look to Imogen for confirmation, and she nods.

"So long as you can keep your hands off each other till then," Abby says, gaze fixed on our entwined fingers.

Imogen ducks her head, drawing the curtain of hair over her face, but not before I see her mouth lift in a smirk.

I have the surreal sense that I've slipped into an alternate universe. A universe where Ben wants me every bit as much as I want him and where Abby and my sister are in agreement. A universe where, as the four of us and Buddy settle down to wait for our parents' return, I feel part of a family for the first time since Dad left.

"Taylor, your poor face." It's the first thing Mum says when she walks through the front door to find us assembled in the hallway.

Behind her, Martin takes me in as he hugs Abby, and winces. "You have been in the wars, haven't you?"

My gut squirms in discomfort. After my coolness towards him these past months, I don't deserve his sympathy. Not that my stepdad looks much better. In contrast to Mum, who's tanned and glowing from the Mediterranean climate, he's grey with exhaustion beneath his sunburn.

"It's fine," I mutter, embarrassed.

"It isn't fine." Mum sniffs, pulling me into her arms. For a horrible moment, I think she's going to cry. "You should've let me come home straight away. How could I have left you to go through all this alone?"

Shock clamps my muscles in place. Mum hasn't shown me this much affection in…I can't remember how long. Then my bruised ribs protest and I disentangle myself. "Seriously, Mum, I'm OK. There's nothing you could've done."

"But I should've been here. What sort of mother am I, sipping cocktails by the pool while my own son was in pain?"

Before she can descend into full self-recrimination mode, Abby steps in to kiss her cheek. "Don't worry, Linda, Taylor's been well taken care of. Did you have an amazing time?"

"Wonderful, darling, thank you." Mum perks up, wiping her eyes. "I took loads of photos to show you all. First, though, I'm gasping for a cup of tea. It never tastes quite right when you're abroad. Something to do with the water, I suppose."

While Ben fetches the cases from the car, I offer to put the kettle on. Anything to escape Mum's over-the-top concern for a bit. It's nice to know she cares, really it is. Still, after years of criticism, I'm not sure how to handle it.

Soon we're all gathered in the living room, admiring the holiday snaps over mugs of tea. Abby and I are seated on the sofa either side of Mum, Imogen and Ben at our feet. By unspoken agreement, Ben and I have taken care to sit as far from each other as possible, wary of giving ourselves away. Martin's commandeered his favourite armchair, Buddy curled on the rug beside him, and is watching Sky News with the sound on low.

"And this is Viv and me on a girls' night out in Puerto Banús." Mum scrolls through her phone to what feels like the thousandth photo. She and the wife of Martin's work colleague must've really hit it off because there are seemingly endless pics of the two of them together—clinking glasses of sangria at a beachfront bar, sitting on the side of the pool with their feet dangling in the water, posing arm in arm for the camera like a couple of schoolgirls.

"That's a gorgeous dress," Abby coos. Either she possesses a bottomless well of enthusiasm for ogling other people's holiday snaps or she should be on the stage.

"Isn't it? Viv lent it to me. She and I are planning a weekend in London for some retail therapy once the move's out of the way, and Charles has invited your dad to play golf with him at his club. Viv says…"

I switch off. If I have to hear any more about the Camerons—her designer outfits, his collection of classic cars, their Oxbridge graduate children—I'll say something that'll shatter our fragile truce. Ben catches my eye, faking a yawn, and I smother a laugh behind my hand. I ache to be close to him, to feel the solid warmth of his body, the pressure of his mouth. Fuck, our parents have barely been back an hour and this is already torture.

Ben must share my frustration because he pushes himself to his feet. "Who wants fish and chips?"

"Excellent idea." Martin has been engrossed in the news throughout the photo viewing, but he brightens at the mention of food. "I'll get my wallet."

"That's OK, Dad, you've only just got back. Tay and I will go." Ben looks at me, and I nod. Any excuse to snatch a few minutes alone with him.

Martin waves away his protest. "No, I'll come. I haven't seen my son in a week, after all."

Ben bites his lip, but beyond shooting me a helpless glance, there isn't much he can do. I swallow my disappointment and flash him a crooked grin. We might have to pretend for a while longer, but later, with our bedroom door shut behind us, there'll be no one to see.

Once Ben and his dad have headed out, Abby wanders off to answer a call on her mobile, and Imogen takes Buddy into the kitchen to feed him. Before I can slip upstairs, Mum lays a hand on my arm. "Don't rush off. I want to talk to you."

Instantly, I trawl my brain for whatever crime I might've committed. "Look, if this is about the blood on the sofa—"

"What?" Alarm flares in Mum's eyes, and they dart over the cream leather. Then she catches herself, reaching out to take my hand. Despite the awkwardness of the gesture, it's surprisingly comforting. "No, nothing like that. It's just…I can't get over the fact that I wasn't here when you needed me."

"Mum, we've been over this."

"I know, and Ben's a responsible young man. I'm sure he took good care of you, but, well, I had a lot of time to think while we were away." Mum squeezes my hand, expression full of sincerity. "I realise I've been rather hard on you lately."

I blink. Is my mother actually admitting she may have been wrong? Again, I have that sense of stepping into a parallel universe.

"I was just so afraid," she says. "Your dad was always better at parenting than I was. It came naturally to him. With him gone, I was terrified you'd go off the rails. I could see it happening before my eyes—the make-up, the piercings. I thought it was all my fault. If I'd forgiven your father, if we'd made it work—"

"None of that had anything to do with you and Dad splitting up." Not wholly true since I'd first worn the eyeliner as a fuck-you to her impossible standards. I wanted to punish her for breaking up our family, but my anger and what I've done because of it is on me. "Anyway, how I look doesn't mean I've gone off the rails."

Mum nods. "I'm beginning to see that. I might not approve of all your choices, but I should've given you the space to make them. I'm sorry."

I open my mouth, but no words form. I've never heard Mum apologise, least of all to me, and I have no idea how to respond.

"Can we start again?" Mum asks, her tone tentative. "You'll be off to university before we know it, and I'd hate for us to part on bad terms. If it's one thing this week has taught me, it's that we never know what's around the corner."

Hell, she'll have me blubbing in a minute. I clear my throat against the sudden tightness. "Yeah, I'd like that."

BEN

"So, you got the job." I turn Esmerelda onto the main road and cast Dad what I hope passes for a genuine smile. Much as it's nice he wants us to spend time together, I wish Taylor were the one sitting beside me. "Congratulations."

Dad's sunburnt face grows even redder. "Ah, thanks. Didn't really think I'd get it, to tell you the truth. Lindy was thrilled."

It's an effort, but I manage to choke down my annoyance. "What about you? How do you feel?"

"Well, it's a more senior position, better money. No doubt I've been in my current job too long. This will be a new challenge."

And are those your words, or the ones my stepmother has fed you? I bite my tongue. Much as the way Dad lets Linda run his life infuriates me, his lukewarm enthusiasm eases my conscience. It would be far harder to convince myself I'd done the right thing calling Sebastian's bluff if Dad desperately wanted the job. I haven't heard from my ex since dousing him in his own gin and tonic, and now the position is secure, there's nothing he can do.

"I was glad to give Lindy a bit of good news," Dad says. "When we heard what happened to Taylor…I've never seen her so worried. We were all set to catch the next plane home."

And put an end to our magical week together when it had barely begun. I slow as we approach the fish and chip shop, searching for a parking space. "It's good you stayed. I made sure Taylor was OK."

"I know you did. That meant a lot to Lindy. To both of us. I think that's the only reason she agreed to finish the holiday, knowing you were there to take care of Taylor. I told her how responsible you are, that she could trust you."

Warmth blooms inside me. The compliment comes out of nowhere and means all the more for it. "Thanks, Dad."

I pull into a vacant space and turn off the engine. Before I can reach for the door handle, however, Dad lays a hand on my shoulder.

"I realise I don't say it enough. Never been great with words, me." He shifts, clearly awkward. "This situation hasn't been easy, not on any of you, but you've done your best to make it work. Lindy and I appreciate it more than we can say, and, well, I'm proud of you."

When we get home, I find Taylor alone in the living room.

"Hey." He greets me with his lopsided smile.

I want to kiss him so badly my chest hurts. Only that afternoon, I would've given in to the urge without a second thought, and I curse our parents for erecting this invisible barrier between us.

"Hey." I flop onto the sofa beside him, allowing my thigh to press against his. Taylor returns the pressure, a show of solidarity as much as longing. "Sorry about earlier. I didn't think Dad would insist on coming with me."

"S'all right. Knew it wouldn't be easy once they got back."

"Understatement. Do you have any idea how much I want to kiss you right now?"

"Some." That crooked grin again. God, if he keeps this up, I'll jump him and to hell with the consequences.

"Dad took the food into the kitchen," I say to distract myself. "Your mum's just warming the plates in the oven. Is it me, or is she in an unusually good mood?"

"It isn't you. She's being kind of weird, to be honest. Don't faint, but she actually said we could eat in front of the telly."

"You're kidding."

"I know, right? And while you were out, she went all mushy. Said she'd been too hard on me and could we start over." Taylor shakes his head, looking stunned.

"Wow." I laugh. "It's not just your mum, either. The mushiness must be catching. In the car, Dad was all 'I'm so proud of you', and he hardly ever says stuff like that. I didn't know what to say."

Taylor snorts, resting his shoulder against mine. "We should send them on holiday more often, you reckon?"

"Definitely."

"Maybe…"

"What?" I angle to face him.

"I was just thinking. Maybe we should tell them, catch them while they're in a good mood."

I'm quiet, considering his words. Part of me is reluctant to spoil the atmosphere, which is more relaxed than it's been since I came home from Australia. On the other hand, in their current mood, our parents might be more receptive. The clatter of plates drifts along the hall from the kitchen, and Linda calls for the girls to come downstairs.

Taylor must pick up on my hesitation because he touches my arm. "We don't have to. It was only an idea, but we can wait till tomorrow. I just thought—"

"No, you're right." I sit up straighter and take his hand. "We might not get a better chance. Let's tell them."

"Tell who what?"

We jump and turn towards the doorway. Linda's standing there, a plate of fish and chips in each hand, and her expression is utterly devoid of mushiness.

CHAPTER TWENTY

T HAT GOOD MOOD we'd counted on? It evaporates so fast I'm left wondering whether the past couple of hours were a figment of my imagination.

"Would either of you like to explain what's going on?" The acidity has returned to Mum's tone. I could almost believe it never went away. Her gaze zeros in on our entwined fingers, but neither of us lets go.

I meet Ben's eyes. He offers me a shaky smile and tightens his grip on my hand. I squeeze back, trying to reassure him. We were about to tell our parents, anyway. We just didn't intend for them to find out quite like this.

"Taylor?" Mum hurls my name at me as though it's an insult. "If you don't start talking right this minute…" She doesn't need to elaborate; the threat comes through loud and clear.

I shrug, aiming for nonchalance. "Would've thought that was obvious."

Pink patches appear in Mum's cheeks. Maybe I could've put that better, but…seriously? She'd walked in on us holding hands, for fuck's sake. Before she can respond, two sets of light footsteps sound on the stairs and the girls materialise in the hallway behind her.

"What's going on?" Abby asks.

Imogen catches my eye over Mum's shoulder. She flicks a glance towards Ben, one brow raised. I nod once, and she grimaces.

"Ah, girls." Mum rounds on them, her words overly bright. She thrusts the plates into their hands. "Change of plan. Why don't you take your food upstairs and eat in your rooms?"

Abby accepts her fish and chips, twisting to peer into the living room. "If this is about Ben and Taylor—"

"It isn't up for discussion." Mum drops the chirpiness. "Upstairs. Now. Both of you."

"But—"

"Now, Abigail, I mean it."

Ben and I exchange a startled look. Mum's never snapped at my stepsister, not in all the months we've lived here. Abby rocks back a pace, as if Mum has thrown the battered cod at her head. Imogen touches Abby's arm and motions along the hall. Abby shoots Mum a glare, her mouth set, then follows Imogen from view. A moment later, an upstairs door slams.

"Everything all right out here?" Martin appears with two more plates, concern creasing his round features.

"No, Martin, it isn't." Mum folds her arms, as formidable as I've ever seen her. "Put the food back in the oven, please. We need to talk."

Martin blinks, plainly confused, but does as he's told. Mum remains on the threshold, body rigid, staring fixedly at the fireplace. It's like she thinks the sight of us will scar her retinas. My gaze finds Ben's, and he strokes a thumb over my palm.

"OK, I'm here." Martin returns, minus the plates, and pats Mum's elbow. "Lindy, shall we sit down?"

Mum jerks her head, a gesture that's part agreement, part impatience. She crosses to perch on the arm of Martin's favourite chair, her every muscle pulled taut.

"So, what's this all about?" Martin lowers himself onto the cushions and looks over at Ben and me. For the first time, he notices our clasped hands and his eyes widen.

"That," Mum says, each syllable edged in steel, "is what I'd like to know."

Ben takes an audible breath. "Taylor and me, we're… together."

"Don't be ridiculous," Mum snaps.

Her dismissal instantly gets my back up. "Why ask if you don't want to hear the answer?"

Ben presses his leg against mine in silent warning. He turns to our parents. "It's true. We've liked each other for weeks and got together while you were away."

"I don't understand." Martin's forehead wrinkles. It's like he's struggling to figure out the punchline to a crude joke. "This isn't possible."

"Of course it isn't." Mum lays a hand on his shoulder and glares at us. "This nonsense stops right here."

The blood rushes to my head. My anger is a living thing. Its pulse thunders in my ears, against my temples, behind my eyes. I surge to my feet, tearing my hand from Ben's. "You can't do that. You can't just pretend everything we feel doesn't matter because you don't like it."

"Watch me." Mum makes to stand, but Martin grasps her arm.

"Let's calm down." He looks from Ben to me and back again. His expression reminds me of Buddy when he begs for a slice of toast. "There has to be some mistake. I mean, you boys are virtually brothers."

"Stepbrothers." Ben corrects him. "That isn't the same thing."

"You're still family," Mum says, verging on hysteria.

I scoff. "Only because you ditched Dad and married someone else. You don't get to punish us because you fucked up."

Mum's face floods with colour. She yanks herself from Martin's restraint and stands to confront me, eyes blazing. "How dare you judge me! You have no idea what I went through with your father, none whatsoever."

"Fine. Then you have no right to judge us, either."

"For God's sake, Taylor, you must see how wrong this is. You really expect us to stand by and let this happen?"

"It isn't illegal." Somehow, Ben manages to speak calmly. He comes to my side, resting his palm on my back in solidarity. "Taylor and I aren't breaking any laws."

Mum shakes her head as though to dislodge a mosquito whining in her ear. "That's not the point. What you're doing… it's immoral, disgusting."

I flinch. She may as well have seized the crystal vase from the nearby coffee table and flung it at me. What Ben and I have is the purest thing in my life. The idea that anyone, that my own mum, could view it as something unclean… For the second time in as many hours, emotion clogs my throat.

Ben slides his arm around me, anchoring me against him. He directs his next words at his dad. "You can't stop us. Whatever you think, you have no right to keep us apart."

"We have every right." Mum jabs a finger into Ben's chest. "Honestly, I'm surprised at you. I thought you were more responsible."

"For the last time, we haven't done anything wrong!" My voice cracks. I've been mad at Mum before—fuck, I've spent my entire life being mad at her—but I've never hated her as much as I do in this moment.

"I've heard enough." Martin's on his feet now, his face crimson. "Whatever's been going on while we were away, it ends here, understand?"

"But, Dad—" Ben blurts, just as I say, "You can't just—"

"I said enough!" Martin's roar is so unexpected, so completely out of character, we fall silent at once. He glowers at us, his breathing laboured. "Now, listen up. You may be adults, but you're living under my roof and that means you follow my rules. This…this relationship is over. No arguments. No excuses. Do I make myself clear?"

BEN

"I suspected your dad would take it like this," Mum says as she pours boiling water into three mugs.

I'm slumped on the sofa in the annex, head still reeling from the row. Taylor sits beside me, pale and shell-shocked, his face a stony mask. He's barely said a word since we left the house, letting me fill Mum in on what happened. For all his defiance, his claims not to care what Linda thinks, he's clearly taken her reaction to heart.

Mum brings two cups of tea over to us, pushing one into Taylor's unresisting hands and offering the other to me.

I take it, grateful for anything that isn't a recrimination. "They were so...angry. I mean, it's not like I expected them to be thrilled, but they completely lost it."

"It was a shock, that's all." Mum fetches her own mug and settles on the footstool on my other side. "They'll come round, I'm sure, once they've had a chance to get used to the idea."

"They won't." Taylor's voice is jagged, as though he's swallowed a mouthful of broken glass. His fingers clench convulsively around his mug. "You didn't hear them, the things they said, the way they looked at us like we were something dirty."

"Sweetheart, I'm sorry." Mum leans over to touch Taylor's knee, her eyes full of sympathy. "I honestly don't know what to tell you, other than...give it time. This has been a lot for them to take in. They're bound to need a while to adjust."

"Why, though? It's not like you have a problem with it."

"No, but it's different for me. Try to see it from your Mum's perspective. I'm sure all she wants is for you to be one big happy family, for her children and Martin's to be like brothers and sisters. Now, here you are, changing the rules." Mum gives us a rueful smile.

Taylor shakes his head. "You're seriously sticking up for her? She's the one who put us in this position. She can't complain because it didn't work out the way she wanted."

"Taylor's right," I say. "We didn't plan any of this, but the way Dad and Linda were talking, it's like they think we can just turn off our feelings and pretend they never existed."

Resentment boils in my gut. They'd dismissed our relationship without a thought, brushing it aside as though it meant nothing. I want to rage against the unfairness of it. Surely, given how they broke up two families to be together, they of all people should understand. I almost point out as much but bite my tongue. Mum hardly needs reminding of the force that ended her marriage.

Mum takes a sip of her tea. "We tend to dismiss things we'd rather not face up to. If we pretend something doesn't exist, we hope it'll go away."

"They won't split us up, however much they might want to." I look to Taylor for confirmation.

He meets my gaze, and the fierceness in his eyes makes my heart constrict. "You know it."

His resolve calms me, and I turn back to Mum. "Dad said we can't be together while we're living there, but he can't stop us, can he?"

Mum opens her mouth to answer, then closes it again.

"What?" I say, stung. "You agree with him?"

"Sweetheart, you know I don't, but, well, he is right up to a point. It is his house, and while you're under his roof, you have to live by his rules, however short-sighted they might be." She softens her words with a smile. "Come on, you'll both be off to uni soon. Then you can do as you please. Surely you can cut your Dad and Linda some slack until then."

My heart urges me to argue. Our relationship isn't a shameful secret that needs to be hidden away. My brain, though, can see the sense in Mum's words. I glance at Taylor. He grimaces but lifts one shoulder in resignation.

I sigh and gulp the last of my tea. "I s'pose."

"You'll be fine," Mum assures us, voice warm. "Everything will work out in the end, you'll see. Let me get you both another cuppa, give you the strength to face the music."

She collects our mugs and heads into the kitchen area, skirting a stack of cardboard boxes I hadn't noticed before. Curious, I take a proper look around. The coffee tables are bare of their usual ornaments and photo frames, while the shelves of the bookcase, normally crowded with Katie Fords and Sheila O'Flanagans, gape like toothless mouths.

"You been having a clear-out?" I call over the rasping hiss of the kettle.

"Sorry?" She glances over, following the direction of my gaze. "Ah, no. I…well, I wasn't going to mention it, what with everything else going on, but I'm moving out."

"Oh." I digest this, momentarily distracted from my own troubles. "Thought you were waiting until the sale went through."

"That was the idea, but something came up, and I decided to go for it. From what your dad says, the buyers are in a good position, and he doesn't foresee any complications. I have a bit of money put aside to tide me over till then." She refills our mugs, gaze on her task. "This situation has gone on long enough. It isn't healthy for any of us."

The smile she darts over her shoulder is anxious, as though expecting me to protest. As if I would. It's only a mystery to me how she's stood living here for as long as she has.

"Where will you go?" I ask. Then it hits me, and a grin spreads across my face. "Wait. You're moving in with Jon, aren't you?"

"What? No, of course not." She laughs. "It's far too soon for that. I scarcely know the man. No, Jon has a friend who does up properties to rent, and he's just finished working on a flat a few minutes' walk from the high street. I went to view it the other day and it's ideal. I can move in whenever I like."

I get up and cross the room to hug her. "That's great, Mum."

"Thanks, sweetheart." She squeezes me very tight. "And don't you worry about a thing. It'll all sort itself out, I promise."

WE PAUSE ON our way back to the house, dawdling in the deeper shadow beside the wall, both reluctant to return to the condemnation that's waiting for us. I lean against the rough brickwork and draw Taylor's body into mine, wrapping my arms around him.

He rests his head on my shoulder, his hands sliding up the back of my T-shirt to rest on my bare skin. "Is your Mum right, do you think?"

"What about?" I bury my face in his hair, inhaling the scent of apple shampoo.

"About them coming to terms with us. In time."

"I dunno, Tay. Seems kind of unlikely, but...maybe. One day."

"But it won't matter, right, either way? You meant it when you said we wouldn't let them split us up?"

There's an uncertainty in Taylor's tone, a vulnerability I haven't heard before. It has me wanting to track down everyone who has ever hurt him and make damned sure they never do it again.

"Hey." I tilt his chin up, hoping he can read my sincerity in the dark. "It'll take more than a bit of disapproval to come between us, you know that."

Taylor kisses me. Beneath the gentleness, his lips contain a core of tungsten. I sink into him, holding him close, savouring every precious moment of being with him, because there's no telling when we'll have this luxury again.

CHAPTER TWENTY-ONE

TAYLOR

MUCH LATER, I lie on the sofa bed in Martin's study and stare into the blackness. Even without the springs digging into my back, sleep would've been impossible. After all the shouting and harsh words, the house is unnaturally silent. I'm aware of every creak, every breath of wind beyond the window. At each sound my heart jumps. I half hope to feel Ben sliding under the covers beside me, wrapping me in his strength and wonderful Ben scent, but of course, he doesn't come.

Given their reaction, I wasn't exactly shocked when our parents banished me to the study. Nor did it come as a surprise when I was the one evicted while Ben got to keep our bedroom. It belonged to him first, after all. He protested, bless him, pointing out that the sofa bed would be harder on my bruises, but I told him it was fine. The idea of getting into another fight with Mum was way too exhausting, and it wasn't as if I expected to sleep much.

I shift on the lumpy mattress, a pointless attempt to get comfortable. More than anything, I wish we hadn't told them. For some reason—a moment of insanity, perhaps, or just plain stupidity—I thought being open and honest with them would earn our parents' respect. What a fucking joke.

If we'd only kept quiet, I'd be with Ben right now. We'd be alone in our own private darkness, all teasing hands and hot whispers, while Mum and Martin snoozed on in blissful oblivion. I've grown used to falling asleep in Ben's arms, the warmth of him nestled against my back. My entire body aches with his absence. For what must be the tenth time, I consider slipping along the landing to our room, just for a few minutes... but I can't. If I know Mum, she'll be expecting that, lying awake ready to catch me in the act. It isn't worth it, not even to feel Ben's mouth on mine.

A faint scrabbling snaps my attention to the study door. As I squint through the dark, it edges open with the soft scuff of wood on carpet. I hold my breath, every nerve tingling in anticipation of Ben's touch. Then something cold and wet nudges my hand. I exhale, torn between disappointment and gratitude.

"Hey, Bud." I stroke the dog's silky head. We'd returned from the annex to find the kitchen deserted and Buddy huddled in his bed in the utility room, ears drooping. What must he have made of all the tension and raised voices? Overcome with guilt, I scoot over and pat the space beside me. "Come on then."

Buddy must recognise an unmissable opportunity when he sees it, because he bounds onto the bed at once and settles down with a contented huff. Mum will lose her shit when she finds out, but so what? She's already determined to keep me from Ben; there's nothing worse she can do. The thought offers me a twisted sort of comfort.

I roll onto my side, curling around Buddy's cushiony bulk, and drape an arm over him. Gradually, his reassuring presence and snuffling snores lull me, and I drift into an uneasy sleep.

"CHRIST, THAT'S BETTER." Ben slumps onto the park bench with a sigh. His whole body relaxes as though he's sunk into a hot bath after running a marathon. "If I'd had to spend another second in there, I would've gone mad."

"Tell me about it." I detach Buddy from his lead and sit beside Ben, close enough that our thighs touch. Away from the oppressive atmosphere of the house, the tension drains from my shoulders.

Martin shut himself in his study after breakfast and hasn't emerged since. Wish Mum had done the same. Instead, she's spent the morning prowling from room to room, tight-lipped and sharp-eyed, denying Ben and me the chance to share so much as a private glance. In the end, Abby arranged to go into town with Lauren, and Imogen sought refuge in *Secrets of the Solar System*. I invited her to come for a walk with us, but she rolled her eyes and pointed me towards the door. I didn't protest; alone time with Ben will be hard to come by from now on.

Predictably, Mum pounced as we were about to slip out through the front door. She grasped my elbow, mouth set in a grim line. "Oh, no. You two aren't sneaking off anywhere, not together."

"Try and stop us." My glare spat enough venom to paralyse a lesser mortal. I wrenched myself free, slamming the door behind us. Once we were outside, there was nothing she could do, not without continuing the argument on the driveway and making a scene in front of the neighbours.

"OK?" Ben rests a hand on my leg.

"I am now." I smile at him. Despite everything—the drama and my own exhaustion, the fact that I ache all over—I mean it. Our parents might have the right to dictate what goes on within their walls, but they have no control over what we do beyond them. They can't keep us apart, however much they wish it were otherwise.

Ben returns my smile, expression soft behind his fatigue. He slides an arm around me, and I subside into him. Together we watch Buddy amble around, pausing to sniff at random patches of grass. Like us, he's in disgrace after Mum discovered he spent the night on the sofa bed. We had to liberate him from his solitary confinement in the utility room.

It's a dull afternoon, air heavy and close, the clouds gobbing out the occasional spot of rain. But for the three of us, the park is deserted. A strange hush hangs over everything, like the yawning silence between one explosion and the next. I drink it in, savouring the temporary peace.

"They can't keep this up, can they?" Ben asks. "Being mad at us, I mean."

My mouth twists. "I can't speak for your dad, but knowing my mum, I wouldn't bet on it."

"Yeah, not sure Dad'll ever forgive me, either, whatever Mum says."

"Your mum's the best. Wish she was mine."

"Now that really would be incestuous."

We double up, leaning into one another. It feels good to laugh, to let all the pent-up tension bubble out of me. I'm still grinning when Buddy lumbers over. He nudges the front of my hoody and glances up at me, expectant.

"OK, boy." I chuck him under the chin before reaching into my pocket for the tennis ball.

"You do know you're fighting a losing battle," Ben says.

"We'll see." I flash him a wink and hurl the ball as far as I can across the park.

Buddy plods after it with all the speed and enthusiasm of a decrepit old man on his way to the dentist. When he reaches the ball, he scoops it up in his jaws and flops onto the grass, tail wagging.

Ben snorts. "Told you so."

I poke my tongue out at him. Sticking my fingers in my mouth, I let out a piercing whistle. "Fetch, Bud, there's a good boy."

Buddy's only response is to glance in my direction, tail thumping even harder.

"Lazy dog." I shake my head and start over the grass to retrieve the ball myself, while Ben cracks up behind me. "Drop, boy."

Buddy deposits the ball on the ground. I pick it up, tossing it back towards the bench. He sets off once more to snatch it up, then promptly lies at Ben's feet and looks over at me with obvious pride.

Ben's eyes sparkle as they catch mine. "I'd give it up if I were you. We've been trying to teach him to fetch since he was a puppy, but he soon learned it's much more fun to make us do the running about for him."

We take it in turns throwing the ball for Buddy and chasing after him to reclaim it, until he collapses from the exertion, tongue lolling. Ben takes my hand to draw me onto the bench with him. His arms encircle me, lips finding mine, warm and fierce and full of urgency.

"I hate this," he murmurs into the kiss. "I hate feeling like we're doing something wrong."

"I know. Me, too." I bring up a hand to cradle the side of his face, the stubble rough against my palm. "I'm sorry."

Ben pulls away slightly, his gaze locking with mine. "What for? None of this is your fault."

"It kind of is. I was the one who suggested we tell them. I thought they might respect us more for being honest with them, but we both know how that turned out. Now we're having to skulk about like criminals."

Ben shakes his head. "They would've found out sooner or later. It's better they heard it from us. If they won't accept it, that's their problem."

"S'pose." I trail my fingers down his cheek and trace the outline of his jaw. "I just wish September would hurry up."

"In the meantime, let's make the most of this," Ben says, pulling me closer.

Lost in the feel and taste of each other, it's a few moments before we become aware of the distant ringing. With obvious reluctance, Ben disentangles himself and fishes his mobile from his jeans pocket.

"Hey, Abs, where are—" He breaks off, listening. Even from where I'm sitting, I can hear his sister's voice, shrill and indistinct. "Whoa, slow down. I can't... OK, we'll be right there."

"What's up?" I ask as soon as he hangs up.

Ben looks up at me, his forehead creased. "That was Abby. She says we need to come home. Something's happened."

BEN

THE SHOUTING REACHES us even before I have the key in the lock. I exchange a worried glance with Taylor.

"It can't be anything to do with us," he says, clearly trying to convince himself. "Not this time."

"No," I agree. All the same, as I open the front door, my stomach roils with queasiness.

"Do you think I'm a complete idiot?" Linda's anger blasts from the living room, bringing us up short in the hallway. "No explanation? No nothing? What aren't you telling me?"

Whatever Dad says in reply, he speaks too quietly for me to make out the words. Still, the plea behind them is obvious.

"Ben, up here."

Abby's urgent whisper tugs my gaze upwards. My sister beckons to me from behind the bannisters where she and Imogen are crouched, plainly eavesdropping. Taylor releases Buddy, who slinks away into the kitchen. Then the two of us hurry up the stairs to join the girls on the landing.

"What's going on?" I drop to the carpet next to Abby, while Taylor takes the spot beside Imogen.

"It's been horrible." Abby's eyes glimmer with tears. "Dad had a call from the HR department at Harcourts. Apparently, there's been a mix-up with the job."

"What sort of mix-up?" But even as I ask the question, I know. The truth settles in my gut, heavy and distasteful, like a helping of Linda's fish pie.

"Not sure, exactly, but it sounds like Harcourts made a mistake when they offered it to him. After I got back from town, someone phoned to tell him he hasn't got the position, after all."

"And Mum went mad," Imogen adds. With her face devoid of its usual irony, she looks incredibly young.

As though to illustrate her point, Linda's voice rises to a shriek that carries easily up the stairs. "Well, I'm sorry, Martin, I just don't believe it. No one retracts the offer of a job without good reason. You must have done something to put them off."

"Oh, shut up." Abby hugs her knees to her chest, glaring through her tears. "The cow, taking it out on Dad. It's not his fault Harcourts screwed up."

"Can they really do that?" Taylor wonders. "Offer someone a job and then take it back? Seems kind of unethical."

Abby hisses like an enraged swan. "What else can you expect? Those stuck-up pricks don't give a toss what this will do to Dad."

"They shouldn't be allowed to get away with it."

"They can do what they like." My tone comes out flat. "It's not like it was official. Nothing's been signed."

Taylor frowns, but another outburst from downstairs drowns his response. "So you're just going to lie down and let them trample all over you? Maybe it's little wonder they changed their minds. They must've decided to give the job to someone with more backbone!"

Abby sucks in a sharp breath, and Imogen covers her mouth, eyes wide. I can't take any more. The others can listen in if they want, but I've heard enough. I push to my feet and slip along the landing to my room.

With the door shut to block out Linda's tirade, I yank my mobile from my pocket and jab a finger into the screen until

I find the number I want. The phone vibrates against my ear; I realise I'm shaking. It rings once…twice…three times, then…

"Hey, baby boy." Sebastian's voice, cocky and drawling as ever, drips from the receiver. "Knew you wouldn't be able to stay away."

"You bastard." Anger clogs my throat. I can barely get the words out.

Sebastian's lazy chuckle caresses my ear. Once, that chuckle would've melted my insides into a churning geyser of desire; now, it makes me want to punch him in his smug face. "You seem a little tense. Don't worry, though. I know a few tricks to cure that."

"You're sick." I pace, unable to keep still, stalking from the bookcase to the window and back again. "Sick and delusional. You honestly think I'd want to come anywhere near you after what you've done?"

"And what's that? What have I done that's so terrible it gives you the right to phone me at work and hurl abuse at me?"

"Seriously? You're going to play the innocent after all your threats? My dad's just had the opportunity of a new job taken away from him, and why? Because you couldn't handle the fact that I don't want you anymore. You're pathetic."

"Say whatever you like." Sebastian stifles a yawn. "Rant and rave and call me every name under the sun. You'll have a hell of a job proving anything."

A sharp retort leaps to my tongue, but I bite it back. For all his lies, the scheming and blatant blackmail, his last statement rings true. I lower my phone, bring up Sebastian's texts. Nothing incriminating there. To an outsider, they'd read as innocuous, nothing more sinister than arrangements to meet up. No, my ex will have disguised his tracks well, masking all evidence of his involvement.

Sebastian continues speaking, a muffled squawk issuing from the earpiece, but I'm done. I cut the call, flinging my phone across the room. It bounces off the wall and falls to the carpet with a soft thump. Arrogant, conniving dickhead. It's bad enough he went through with his petty act of revenge, but to turn around and pretend he's done nothing wrong... Still, what did I expect? An apology? Yeah, right. I doubt Sebastian Harcourt has ever apologised for anything in his life.

A wave of exhaustion crashes into me. My legs buckle, and I collapse onto the edge of Taylor's bed, dropping my head in my hands. My anger drains away, and a leaden guilt thuds onto my shoulders. I'm to blame. For everything. I shouldn't have dismissed Sebastian's demands so lightly, should never have antagonised him. Better yet, I shouldn't have got mixed up with him in the first place. But I did, and now Dad's paying for it.

I'm still sitting there, hunched forward with my elbows on my knees, when a door bangs somewhere below. Feet stomp up the stairs, followed by the slamming of a second door, then... silence. Seems the shouting has stopped, at least for now.

A few moments later, the bedroom door opens. Taylor slips inside, closing it behind him. He crosses to sit beside me on the bed and lays a hand on my back. "You OK? You disappeared on us."

I shrug, too mired in my own shame to take any comfort from his touch.

"Mum's finally run out of steam," he says. "We had to duck into Imogen's room or she would've caught us."

I nod, don't have the energy to do anything more. Taylor studies me, his expression soft, and I look away. However much he might think he understands, he has no way of knowing what I've done.

"Were you speaking to someone?" Taylor rubs the small of my back. "You sounded upset."

I stare at the scuffed toes of my trainers. "Sebastian."

"Your ex? What did he want?"

"He didn't. I called him."

"Oh." Taylor's hand drops to rest on the bed between us. When he speaks, his tone is neutral. "How come?"

I hesitate. Once the truth is out, I won't be able to take it back. Still, I have the overwhelming urge to confess, to have someone else look at me with the accusation and disgust I feel towards myself.

I straighten, meeting Taylor's gaze. "There's something I need to tell you."

CHAPTER TWENTY-TWO

TAYLOR

IN THE BRIEF silence that follows Ben's words, he simply looks at me, his expression racked with guilt and unhappiness.

"OK." I draw my knees up to my chest, wrapping my arms around them as if to protect myself from…I'm not sure what. "I'm listening."

Ben studies his hands. A splinter of dread stabs at my gut. I know what he's about to say. Why else, with our family in bits around us, would he have called his ex? Despite everything Sebastian's done, the way he fractured his heart, Ben's still drawn to him. He's still the first person Ben turns to when things get tough.

I thrust the suspicion away, bury it beneath a debris of hurt and doubt in the darkest corner of my mind. Less than an hour ago, the two of us were tangled together on a park bench. I remember how Ben looked at me, his eyes soft with tenderness, remember the searching pressure of his mouth. Ben cares about me; I know he does. But what if that isn't enough? What if all this with our parents has put things into perspective for him, made him realise this isn't worth the hassle? Wouldn't be the first time, after all. Liam abandoned me as soon as our relationship threatened to get rough, along with my so-called friends on the athletics team. Fuck, even my own dad buggered off and left me in the wreckage of his marriage. Story of my life, apparently.

Ben sucks in a shaky breath. "Damn, Tay, this is all my fault."

"What is?"

"The job… Your mum going mad… All of it."

"How'd you work that one out?" My arms lose their death grip on my knees. I'd prepared myself for a variation on the 'it's not you, it's me' speech. I can't help being relieved.

"Sebastian," Ben says. "He's sort of been blackmailing me. Trying to, anyway."

It spills out of him, the truth about his ex's twisted attempts to lure him back into his bed. As he talks, Ben's fingers clench in his lap, squeezing so hard I'm afraid the bones will snap. Anger builds inside me, all churned up with protectiveness towards my boyfriend and frustration at my own helplessness. I want to reach out to him, to take his hands in mine and smooth my thumbs over his knuckles until his grip relaxes. The rigid tautness to his back and shoulders, however, warns me against touching him.

Ben raises his head to meet my gaze, expression hollow with misery. "And now Sebastian's used his influence to make them change their minds about giving Dad the job, and it's all because of me."

"That's crap." My voice comes out sharper than I intend. "It's hardly your fault he's a vindictive arsehole." Unable to sit still, I push myself to my feet and pace the strip of carpet between the beds. "We can't let him get away with this."

Ben massages his forehead. "I don't think we have a choice. There's no proof, like Sebastian said."

"There has to be a way. Your dad could take it to the employment tribunal or something."

"Yeah, right. Even if he'd signed anything, which he hasn't, no one's going to accept my word over one of the Harcourts."

I want to argue, to remind him how he urged me to stand up to CJ and his lawyer dad. Ben looks so defeated, though, I don't have the heart. Deflated, I lower myself onto the bed across from him. "Either way, you can't beat yourself up about it. What Sebastian's done…it isn't on you."

"Isn't it?" Ben raises an eyebrow. "I should've stopped him, done something, anything. Instead, I just let it happen."

"What could you have done? Other than give in and sleep with him." My mouth quirks, but when Ben doesn't respond, I drop the smile. "I mean, you didn't actually consider it."

"What? No, of course not. I…no." He shakes his head, but a guilty flush stains his cheeks.

I stare at him. "You did, didn't you? You actually thought about doing it. That's why you didn't tell me."

"No. Damn it, Tay. I didn't tell you because, well, look at you." He waves a hand, taking in my ribs and battered face. "Maybe I figured you had enough going on at the moment."

"Fair enough." I cross my arms, gaze steady on his. Common sense warns me against pushing the issue, but I ignore it. "So you didn't think about going to bed with him? Not even for a second?"

"For Christ's sake." Ben slams his fist into the mattress. "I don't know, all right? Give it a rest."

His words detonate between us, leaving a yawning crater in their wake. I can't look at him, can't speak through the tightness in my throat. I shrug and angle my body to stare out of the window. A fine drizzle has begun to fall, smearing the glass with tear tracks. Downstairs, Buddy starts to bark. The noise goes on and on, unnaturally loud in the silence. Next door's cat must have wandered into the garden again.

My brain has frozen. Ben's words echo in my ears, but I can't process them. I sit there, arms hugged to my chest, queasiness gnawing at my stomach. All the while, I'm aware of Buddy's incessant barking.

A door bangs open, and Mum's voice carries along the landing, tinged with hysteria. "If that blasted dog doesn't shut up this minute…" Her feet pound away down the stairs.

I risk a peep at Ben, and his eyes meet mine. The dark smudges beneath them stand out against his pallor.

"Look," he says, sounding more tired than I've ever heard him, "Tay, I—"

And then Mum screams.

BEN

I FLING OPEN the bedroom door and hurry along the landing, Taylor close behind me. The girls burst from Imogen's room as we reach it, and the four of us almost trip over one another in our race to get downstairs.

"What's happened now?" Abby wonders, her question tight with fear. The same fear that has encased my heart in ice.

It's probably nothing. Linda's found Buddy using one of her best blouses as a blanket again. No cause for alarm.

I stumble to a halt in the kitchen doorway, the others crowding around me. Abby lets out a stifled gasp. The fear expands to press cold and hard against my ribcage. Linda's kneeling on the tiled floor beside Dad, who's slumped against the cupboard under the sink. Buddy's sitting nearby, silent now, gazing at Dad with anxious eyes.

"Martin?" Linda's saying, tone frantic. "Martin, can you hear me?"

"What's going on?" I hurry to crouch on Dad's other side. His face is pale, almost grey. "Linda, what's wrong with him?"

She glances up at me, pupils dilated. "I don't know. I just found him like this. Martin?" She turns back to him, giving his shoulder a gentle shake. "Talk to me, darling. Tell me what's wrong."

Dad tries to pull himself up, but subsides against the cupboard door, features distorted with pain. He forces the words between laboured breaths. "Chest… Can't…breathe."

"Oh, God." Abby's voice cracks. "What should we do? Linda, we have to help him."

Our stepmother's hands twist in her lap. Yet when she looks up, her expression is resolute. "Someone fetch Poppy. She'll know what to do. And call 999. Tell them we have a suspected heart attack."

I'm on my feet at once, but Taylor's already heading out, pulling his phone from his pocket. He retreats along the hallway, and then the front door snaps shut.

"It's OK, Martin." Linda grips his hand. "You're going to be fine. Try to relax."

Dad rolls his head to look at her, fighting to draw air into his lungs. "So…sorry. Know…I'm a…disappointment."

Abby shakes with quiet sobs. Imogen, eyes huge and dark in her stricken face, puts an arm around her. I simply stand there, paralysed with shock and my own inability to help.

"Marty, no." Tears sparkle on Linda's cheeks, and she bats them away. "Of course you're not a disappointment. You must never think that."

"But the job… Let you down… No backbone…" Dad's words dissolve in a fit of coughing that racks his entire body.

Linda strokes his arm, more tears escaping from beneath her lashes. "Don't talk now, darling. You need to save your strength."

The front door clicks once more, and Taylor reappears. "Poppy wasn't in, but the ambulance is on its way. The woman I spoke to said to keep him quiet and give him an aspirin."

"I'll get it." I start towards the cupboard where Linda keeps the medication. It's a relief to have something practical to do.

"No." My stepmother's sudden vehemence pulls me up short. She releases Dad's hand and rises to her feet, determination in every line of her slender frame. "I'll get it. The rest of you…out."

"What?" Abby gapes at her. "No way. I'm staying with Dad."

"You'll do as you're told. You heard what the despatcher said. Your dad needs to be kept quiet. It won't do him any good to have you all standing over him." Jaw set, she pushes past me to fling open the cupboard.

I stay where I am. Rage ignites the fear inside me, and it roars to life in a thousand white-hot sparks. "He's my dad. You have no right to send me away."

Linda rounds on me, the box of aspirin in her hand. "I have every right. Do you honestly think you being here is any help to your dad after the way you and Taylor upset him with your ridiculous carryings on?"

"The way we upset him?" I glare at her. "What about you, ranting and raving at him, making him feel like a failure for something that wasn't even his fault?"

"How dare you! Your father lay awake half the night worrying over what you've got yourself into, what people will say when they find out this has been going on under his roof."

"Really? Because I heard you two talking, and it sounded to me like you were the one keeping him awake with your petty, small-minded—"

"Stop it." Abby steps between us. "Just stop. It's not fair on Dad. He's had nothing but stress since he came back from holiday, and now look what's happened."

She flees from the room, shoulders heaving. Imogen casts us both a reproachful look, then follows. There's a tense pause, broken only by Dad's shallow breathing. Buddy whines softly.

Linda purses her lips, probably to stem the flood of accusations. She crouches beside Dad, her back to me, and speaks with strangled calm. "Someone should wait outside to show the paramedics where to go."

"I'll do it," Taylor offers, but I shake my head.

"No, I will." With a disgusted glance at my stepmother, I brush past Taylor and stalk along the hallway. In the curve of the stairs, Imogen has her arm around Abby, who's crying into her shoulder. Neither of them pay me any attention as I fling open the front door.

It's still raining. The persistent drizzle crawls down my neck, soaking through my sweatshirt. I scarcely notice. A deadening chill has settled over me, seeped into my very bones. I cradle my arms to my chest. I can't get it out of my mind, the image of Dad gasping for breath on the kitchen floor, his face ashen.

Do you honestly think you being here is any help to your dad after the way you and Taylor upset him with your ridiculous carryings on?

Linda's words bounce around my brain, reverberating like a never-ending echo. I'd lashed out, tried to deflect the blame onto my stepmother. In my heart, though, I can't shake the sense of responsibility. Dad's inside right now, fighting for his life, all because of me. My relationship with Taylor, my refusal to take Sebastian's threats seriously…everything has come about through my actions. *If Dad doesn't make it…* I shy away from the thought; it's too horrific.

Soft footsteps crunch behind me. I don't need to turn to know it's Taylor. Still, I can't bring myself to face him.

"This isn't your fault." His voice is careful, measured, as though he's unsure of his reception.

I focus on the drops of water pinging off the gravel. "Isn't it?"

"'Course not. There must be a load of stuff going on we don't know about. You can't blame yourself."

Easy for him to say. It isn't as if anyone he cares about is in danger. Taylor's never made any effort to conceal his feelings towards Dad, resenting him for still being here when his own father hightailed it to London.

"Ben?" Taylor touches my shoulder. It's the merest whisper of fingertips, but I flinch. He drops his hand, and when he speaks, his tone has lost all inflection. "You can't even stand to look at me, can you?"

I swing to confront him, anger forcing its way through my misery. "What do you expect? My dad's in there having a heart attack because of us. We knew this…this thing between us would cause trouble, but we went ahead and did it anyway. You might not give a damn about anyone else, but I do."

Taylor's face shuts down. That's the only way I can describe it. All expression, every trace of emotion, retreats somewhere deep inside him, until only a mask remains. I'm reminded of the sullen boy he'd been when I first came home from Australia. Feels like a millennia ago.

We wait on the driveway, silence forming a canyon between us, while the rain continues to fall. At last, from a distant part of the city, there drifts the keening lament of sirens.

CHAPTER TWENTY-THREE

TAYLOR

ONCE EVERYONE HAS left for the hospital, I drag myself upstairs. The silence is a physical force, pressing in on me. I had no business going with them; Mum and Ben made that abundantly clear. Besides Imogen, who paused on her way out to squeeze my arm, no one seemed able to look at me. They hold me at least partly responsible, or else they believe my coolness towards Martin these past months bars me from sharing in their concern. Maybe they're right. I don't belong.

When I push open the door to our room, the memories body slam me and I have to steady myself against the wall. I see the two of us tangled together on the bed, morning sunlight nudging through the curtains to strike sparks off Ben's hair; feel him stir in my arms seconds before his eyes flutter open to gaze at me, expression drowsy and soft.

Loss squeezes my chest. The pain is so awful I can scarcely breathe. I haul in air, fighting the surge of nausea, and screw my eyelids shut. Another image surfaces to blot out the rest. I'm back on the driveway waiting for the ambulance. Ben regards me, the anger and accusation obvious even through the blur of rain. His voice replays in my head, unrecognisable in its rawness. He may as well have been a stranger.

Fists clenched, I force the recollection aside. Against my better judgement, almost against my will, I reach into my jeans pocket for my mobile. I stare at the screen, desperate for a call from Ben, a text, anything to let me know he doesn't hate me. The phone remains blank and silent in my hand. Of course it does. Like my wounded feelings are his top priority at the moment.

Disgusted with myself, I drop the phone onto the bedside cabinet and move into action. My school backpack is tucked away on the top shelf of the wardrobe where I'd shoved it the instant my final exam was over. I pull it down and begin cramming in everything I can—underwear, T-shirts, a spare pair of jeans. Doubt I'll be returning any time soon.

After forcing the zip closed, I pause to take one last look around this room where so much has happened. For a brief spell, a matter of weeks, I felt at home here. Not anymore. Rucksack slung over my shoulders, I head downstairs and out through the front door, shutting it with quiet finality behind me.

By the time I reach the train station, I'm soaked to the skin and my brain has sunk into a weird detachment. I buy a one-way ticket to London and huddle in the corner of an empty compartment. Bag tucked under my feet, cheek resting against the window, I stare blindly out at the rain-washed platform until the train chugs away.

There's something hypnotic about it, the lurching sway of the carriage, the rhythmic clatter of wheels on the track. I think of the others, imagine them sitting in a hospital waiting room, heavy with that clinical smell and the sombre hush of the very ill. Has there been any news? Probably too soon yet. I ache to be there, to hold Ben's hand and reassure him everything will be all right. But what if it isn't? I recall Martin slumped on the floor, face grey and clammy, battling to draw air into his lungs.

What if he doesn't make it? But I can't think like that; the idea is too horrible.

The train terminates at Waterloo, which is just as well. In my disconnected state, it takes me a while to realise we've stopped. By some miracle, I locate the right platform for the Northern Line and catch the next train.

Ten minutes later, I emerge into the drizzle outside the South West London station. Though it's barely evening, charcoal clouds have stolen most of the daylight. Streetlamps shimmer through the rain, their orange glow giving the unfamiliar streets a dream-like quality. Or maybe I'm the one who isn't entirely real. I blink, trying to clear the fog from my brain. What to do next? As I stand there, uncertain, people move around me on the pavement, talking, laughing, while traffic speeds past on the main road. They all have somewhere to be, a purpose to fulfil.

Directions. I need directions. I reach into my back pocket for my mobile to bring up Google Maps. The address has lain crumpled in a secret drawer of my mind for months, though I'd never intended to use it. Except…my phone isn't there. Confused, I search my other jeans pockets, then the pockets of my hoody. Nothing. Damn, it must've fallen out on the train. I've already retraced the first few steps towards the carriage, when the truth hits me. Back at the house, I'd taken my phone out to check for messages, then thrown it on the bedside cabinet. I must've forgotten to pick it up before I left. Fuck it. Of all the idiotic things to have done.

The strength drains from my legs, and I lean against the nearest brick wall for support. I feel panicky, disorientated. It's as though I've climbed halfway up a cliff, only to realise the safety line has been cut. I massage my forehead. *Think, Tay.*

This is hardly the end of the world. Crazy as it seems, people did manage without mobile phones. You'll just have to do this the old-fashioned way.

The first person I approach isn't from the area, so has never heard of the address I'm looking for, and the second doesn't speak English. I have better luck with the third, a middle-aged lady weighed down with shopping bags. She spends five minutes giving me a precise series of directions, but either she was thinking of a different street entirely, or I somehow take a wrong turn. Either way, I walk the pavements for what feels like an age, each road blurring into the next, until at last, I stumble onto the one I want.

It takes another eternity to find the right block of flats amidst an endless procession of identical modern buildings. By this time, my bruised ribs feel as though they're on fire. The straps of my rucksack cut into my shoulders and my clothes, which had dried out on the train, are once more drenched. On any other day, I might've hesitated, crippled with shame over my behaviour this past year. As it is, I'm too exhausted, too utterly hollowed out to feel anything other than relief as I press the bell for number eleven.

There's a brief delay, just long enough for me to wonder what I'll do if no one's home, and then a voice comes over the intercom. "Hello?"

It's so familiar, lazy and warm and with that subtle flavour of Istanbul. The sound of it pierces my numbness, bringing a lump to my throat. For a terrible moment, I'm sure I'll break down right here on the steps of this anonymous apartment block.

I swallow, but still my words come out as a croak. "Hey, Dad, it's me."

BEN

I'M TRAPPED IN a nightmare. I can't escape it, no matter how hard I struggle to wake up. The previous summer, when I fled to Australia with a backpack full of broken dreams, was the worst I'd ever felt...until now. At least then, there hadn't been the added pain of knowing I was to blame. I hunch forward on the leather sofa in the waiting room and rest my head in my hands. Guilt and dread tear at me, a constant reminder of all the bad decisions that led to this point.

Linda didn't want us to come to the hospital. She turned to us before following the stretcher into the ambulance. Worry pinched her features, and she had her arms wrapped around her thin body as if to keep it from shattering apart.

"There's no need for us all to go," she said. "It isn't as if there's anything you can do. I'll call as soon as there's any news."

None of us responded, but Abby's glare spoke volumes. No way we were sitting at home, not knowing what was happening. As the ambulance pulled away, Abby and I exchanged a look through the rain. Neither of us said anything; that look said it all. We both knew we had to be there, on the spot, in case Dad... Well, just in case.

Mum's Renault came into view along the road, passing the ambulance in the other direction. She skidded to a stop on the driveway and leapt out, face anxious as she hurried towards us. Once we filled her in, she immediately took charge, insisting on driving us to the hospital. While the girls joined the Pardo's carrier bags in the back, I collapsed into the passenger seat, thankful I wouldn't have to drive. Given the state I was in,

I wouldn't have trusted myself behind the wheel. Taylor hadn't come with us. He used the excuse that someone needed to feed Buddy, but I could tell he felt his presence was unwelcome.

"Your dad will be fine," Mum assured us as she guided the car through the Saturday afternoon traffic. "Brookminster General has a wonderful cardiac unit. He'll be in the best possible hands."

I nodded, throat too constricted to speak. All I could think was, *but what if he isn't?*

At the hospital, Mum led us through the maze of departments with names like Garnet and Sapphire and up a flight of stairs to the Acute Cardiac Care Unit on the first floor of Opal. There, she settled us in the small visitors' lounge and went to see what she could find out.

"They're running tests," she told us, sitting beside me on the sofa, "so it could be a while before we know more."

Mum explained about the blood tests and ECG, which would help determine whether Dad had suffered a heart attack and the severity of it. Her words scarcely registered. *He's still alive.* The single fact lodged itself in my mind, and I clung to it as though it were a lifebelt.

Mum got up to leave soon after that, saying she didn't want to tread on Linda's toes. Before she headed out, she hugged Abby and Imogen in turn, then drew me to my feet.

"Call me," she said, squeezing me tight, "as soon as there's any news or if you need a lift home. I'll be right here."

That feels like forever ago. I've lost track of how long we've sat here in this lounge that tries so hard to be cosy. As if any cheerful paintings of farmyard scenes or the out-of-date magazines on the coffee table could soften the blow when your world falls apart.

We have the room to ourselves. Other than the rain pattering against the window and the distant ringing of a telephone, the cardiac unit is smothered beneath a blanket of subdued calm. It's unnervingly quiet. At first, my head snaps up at every squeaking footfall in the corridor outside. Yet as the minutes drag by and still there is no news, I sink into a hopeless lethargy.

The girls sit across from me, pale and silent, Abby's head resting on Imogen's shoulder. Every time I look over at the two of them, drawing what comfort they can from one another, loneliness drags at me. I wish Taylor were here, his fingers gripping mine—fierce, loyal, an anchor to hold me steady. I stomp on the longing, grind it into dust. I mustn't think about Taylor, not the delicious slide of his skin against mine, or the way his mouth—that full, sensuous mouth—quirks when he's amused. Most of all, I mustn't think about the hurt that flashed across his expression before the barrier came up. That belongs to the past. It's over, forbidden, something that should never have happened and which can never happen again.

My mind swings once more to Dad. I shy away from that last glimpse of him, his eyes glazed with pain as the paramedics loaded him into the ambulance. Instead, I think back to the father of my childhood, long before I came out to him and that awkwardness grew between us.

I remember the autumn shortly after Abby was born, when it rained so heavily the river flooded and much of Brookminster was under water. Dad and I put on our wellies and set out to explore this magical city of streams and tributaries, everything shrouded in a ghostly hush, the houses and trees sprouting from a fairy-tale lake.

I remember my fifth birthday, Dad taking me to the park to ride my new bike, my special big-boy bike without stabilisers. He walked behind me, holding me steady until I found my balance. Then, when I fell off and cut both my knees, he carried me home on his shoulders, singing silly songs all the way to distract me from the humiliation.

I remember the Christmas when I was eight, the excitement of unwrapping the largest present under the tree to reveal the seven-hundred-piece LEGO *Millennium Falcon*. Though he's always been hopeless at anything technical, Dad spent the next week helping me put the model together, brick by painstaking brick, only to discover at the end that there was a piece missing.

Memories that once felt so insignificant, so commonplace they were hardly worth remembering at all, flash before my eyes like clips from a family video—being tucked up on the sofa, skin itchy with chickenpox, while Dad read to me from Roald Dahl's *Revolting Rhymes*; Abby and me helping him wash the car on a bright spring morning until Abby threw a wet sponge at me and the whole thing deteriorated into a three-way water fight; Dad spending hours with me at the kitchen table, quizzing me on Stalin's Five Year Plan and the periodic table in the run-up to my GCSEs. He'd do anything for anyone, my dad, and it's only now that I realise how little he ever asked for in return. He wanted so much for us to be happy, for the six of us to be a family, and what had he ended up with? Nothing but arguments and stress.

In a distant part of my brain, I'm aware of footsteps approaching. I take no notice, dismiss it as another false alarm, until Abby shoots to her feet.

"Linda?" Her voice shakes as much as the hand pressed to her mouth. My sister sounds more frightened than I've ever heard her. "What is it? What's happened?"

I follow her gaze, and my heart stops. Linda's standing on the threshold, clutching the doorframe as if to keep herself upright. She doesn't speak. She simply looks at us, silent tears streaming down her cheeks.

CHAPTER TWENTY-FOUR

TAYLOR

DAD'S WAITING FOR me on the second-floor landing. His face works when he sees me, and I'm afraid he's about to cry.

"It's good to see you, matey. You have no idea how good." He pulls me close, hugging me so tight my ribs scream in protest, then holds me at arm's length. His gaze rakes my bruises. "Christ, what happened? Who did this to you?"

I lean into his warmth, inhaling the beloved Dad smell of Dunhill and Marlboro Gold. Only now can I admit to myself how much I've missed it, missed him. I open my mouth to explain but find I can't speak.

Whenever I pictured this moment, I was always angry, hostile, demanding to know how he could've abandoned us. Yet something fundamental has shifted inside me. As I watched Martin fighting for breath on the kitchen floor, it hit me just how easily that could've been Dad. All at once, my hostility of the past year seemed childish.

"Actually, that can wait." Dad smiles at me. It's a smile of such love, I'm ashamed I could ever have thought he wanted to leave. "Come on, let's get you inside and dried off. Then you can fill me in."

Arm slung over my shoulders, Dad guides me into the flat and along a beige-painted hallway with a worn carpet. I steal glances at him from the corner of my eye. He's thinner than I remember, his hair longer, spilling over the collar of his polo shirt in a way that would've had Mum reaching for the scissors.

"Welcome to my humble bedchamber." Dad opens a door with a flourish, the side of his mouth quirking in a wry grin.

He flicks on the light and ushers me in ahead of him. The room is narrow, a single bed pressed against one wall, a wardrobe and dressing table along the other. I move to stare out of the window at the far end. Cars whoosh past on the road below, the rain turning their headlights a dirty yellow.

"You have anything to put on?" Dad asks. "Or I can lend you something."

"That's OK. I brought some stuff." I let my rucksack fall onto the cream duvet cover and unzip it to show him the mess of clothes.

He smirks. "Nice packing. The bathroom's just next door. Hang on, I'll get you a towel. Anything else you need?"

"Don't think so. Thanks, Dad."

"Hey, what're dads for? I'll be in the living room across the hall. Come and find me when you're ready."

He disappears, returning a moment later with a folded towel. Then he leaves me to it and closes the door softly behind him.

It's a relief to get out of my wet clothes. The towel is kind of scratchy but still comfortingly warm against my cold skin. As I change into a fresh T-shirt and jeans, my gaze travels the room. It's amazingly tidy. No dirty laundry tossed in a corner, no odds and ends scattered over the dressing table. Twenty years of living with Mum must've rubbed off on him.

To judge by the dining chair tucked beneath the dressing table, facing Dad's trusty Asus, he's using it as a desk. Next to the laptop, the only personal touch besides the wax jacket slung over the back of the chair, sits a wooden photo frame. I immediately recognise the picture. Dad snapped it the day he took Imogen and me to Little Hampton. I must be about twelve, Imogen seven. We're holding ice creams, both of us grinning and dusted with sand, the sea shimmering blue-grey in the background. Life seemed so much simpler back then.

I gather my wet things and go in search of Dad. He's in the kitchen area at one end of the open-plan living space, filling the kettle.

"Hey." He smiles over at me. "Just dump those in the washing machine and I'll rinse them through for you. Coffee?"

"That'd be great." I bundle my damp clothes into the machine, then wander the long room while Dad makes coffee.

The flat isn't what I expected. Not that I often let my thoughts stray to Dad's new home, but when I did, I sort of assumed he and Clive would've reverted to their uni days. I'd imagined a student squat, pizza boxes stacked on the coffee table, the floor littered with beer cans and Xbox controllers. This is nothing like that. It's functional, ordinary, all scuffed tan leather and dark furniture. The only thing in the room that looks new is the sixty-inch telly mounted on the wall above the fireplace.

"Here." Dad joins me, carrying two steaming mugs. "Sit yourself down. You look done in."

I collapse onto the nearest sofa and accept the drink he hands me. Heat seeps into my fingers, though it does little to thaw the chill inside. He's right; I'm exhausted, worn out by all the emotion of the past twenty-four hours. Still, I'm too on edge to relax.

The intense quiet of the flat strikes me. Since leaving the house, I've been focused on nothing but the need to get away.

Now, it occurs to me to wonder how Dad's flatmate will react to me turning up out of the blue. "Dad, where's Clive?"

"Away for a few days. Gone walking in the Lake District with his lady friend. He'll be back Tuesday evening." Dad settles on the sofa at right angles to mine and regards me over the rim of his mug. The shrewdness in his gaze reminds me forcibly of Imogen. "So, what's happened?"

The question almost makes me smile. What's happened? What hasn't happened, more like. I have no idea where to start. Stalling for time, I take a too-big gulp of coffee and burn my tongue.

"I mean…" Dad's mouth twitches again in that ironic half-smile. "I'm chuffed to bits you're here, really chuffed, but something tells me you wouldn't have come all this way in the rain just to say hi to your old dad."

I drop my eyes. "Look, I'm really—"

"No, don't apologise. You've been angry with me, and I get it. Christ, I've been pretty bloody angry with myself." He runs a hand through his shaggy hair. "Does your mum know you're here?"

I snort. "Like she could give a toss where I am."

"Why'd you say that?"

"Because it's true."

Falteringly, often having to force the words past the lump in my throat, I tell him everything. I tell him about the break-up with Liam and the bullying I've endured for the past year, which culminated in me getting the shit kicked out of me. I tell him about Ben, our feelings for each other and how Mum and my stepdad reacted when they found out. I explain about Martin's job offer being retracted and how we later discovered him collapsed on the kitchen floor. Finally, I describe Mum's outburst, the fact that she clearly blamed Ben and me and how, as we waited on the driveway, Ben could scarcely bring himself to look at me.

Dad lets me talk. He doesn't ask questions, doesn't prompt me when I pause to compose myself. He simply listens, expression full of sympathy, until the words dry up.

"Wow." Dad releases a long breath, shaking his head. "You really have been through the mill, haven't you?"

I stare into my cooling coffee. "I don't know what to do. I feel like this is all my fault."

"Of course it isn't your fault. Any number of things can cause a heart attack, if that's even what it was. It would take more than a silly argument to set one off."

"But supposing…supposing Martin dies? Ben will never forgive me. Fuck, I'll never forgive myself." My voice fractures.

"Right." Dad straightens, rubbing his hands together. "Here's what we'll do. First, I'll ring the hospital, find out how your stepdad's doing and get a message to your mum." He holds up a silencing finger. "Yes, I know you said she won't care, but I happen to think she'll be incredibly worried when she realises you're gone."

Actually, I'm pretty sure my absence would be a relief to her—if she's even noticed. Still, I'm too weary to argue the point.

"Then," Dad says, "I'll rustle us up something to eat. How's that sound? Don't tell me you haven't missed my famous corba."

"Sounds good." In truth, my stomach feels too twisted up with nerves and unhappiness to eat anything, even the comforting Turkish soup which is Dad's speciality. I don't have the heart to protest, though, not when he's trying so hard. As he pulls out his phone to look up the number for the hospital, I lean into the squashy leather and wonder how I could've cut myself off from him for so long.

BEN

"I'm sorry." Linda brushes the tears from her cheeks, only for more to take their place. "I'm so sorry."

She blinks as though struggling to wake from a nightmare and looks around at the three of us. Imogen has got to her feet beside our stepsister, one hand resting on Abby's back. Their expressions reflect my own terror. He's dead. The horrible certainty drops like a slab of concrete onto my sternum, crushing the air from my lungs. He's dead, and my life will never be the same.

Then, through her tears and obvious exhaustion, Linda smiles. "It's all right. He's going to be all right."

The sound Abby lets out is part gasp, part sob. The next moment, she's in Linda's arms, the two of them laughing and crying, holding on to one another for support. Imogen sags onto the sofa as though every nerve in her body has been cut. She catches my eye and beams. I try to grin back, but my facial muscles appear to have seized up.

He's OK. Dad's OK.

I stay where I am, chin cradled in my palms, and let the relief wash over me. It spreads to every part of my body, sweeter and more warming than a shot of butterscotch schnapps. Still, even as the tension releases its grip on me, my sense of responsibility separates me from the others. I don't deserve to share in their happiness.

Linda folds onto the sofa across from me, between Abby and Imogen. Dad's resting now, she tells us. He's still quite poorly but stable. He'll be kept in for a few days for observation and so the doctors can monitor his progress.

"Can we see him?" Abby asks.

Linda shakes her head. "Not tonight, darling. Your dad's very tired, needs his rest. I suggest you all go home and get some sleep. You can come back and see him tomorrow. I'm sure he'll be more up to visitors by then."

I half expect Abby to protest, but she doesn't. Either she can see the sense in our stepmother's words or she's simply too drained to argue. She leans her head on Linda's shoulder. "What about you?"

"I'll stay here, just for tonight. I'd hate for your dad to wake up alone. He's in a very nice private room, and there's an armchair I can sleep in. I'll be fine." Linda smiles around at us. With her hair dishevelled and her mascara smudged from crying, she looks nothing like her immaculate self. For the first time, I feel a rush of genuine affection towards her.

Linda glances my way, but only for an instant. She strokes Abby's hair. "Do you think your mum would give you a lift home? I know it's late. Or I have money for a taxi."

"That's OK. She said she would." My sister straightens and stands. "I'll go and call her now."

"Thanks, darling. God, I'm desperate for a coffee. Imogen, would you see if you can track down a drinks machine? The one on this corridor is out of order."

Once the girls have left, silence suffocates the room. I can't bring myself to look at Linda, can't face seeing the accusation in her eyes. Dad might be out of danger, but nothing alters the fact that my actions helped put him there in the first place.

"Ben?" Linda's tone is uncertain, almost unrecognisable.

I swallow. Something large and solid sticks in my throat. Across from me, the leather sofa creaks. Linda gets up, crossing the lounge to sit beside me.

"Ben, look at me." She takes my hands in hers, squeezes them tight.

With an effort, I lift my gaze. Her eyes are shining with fresh tears, but her expression holds no recrimination. There's only regret and a fierce earnestness.

"I'm so sorry." Her voice cracks. "What I said to you, all those terrible things, I didn't mean them. I was just so scared. If I'd lost your dad, I don't know what I would've done. Of course I blamed myself. I was so awful to him about the job, and I kept thinking, what if that's the last thing he remembers? But I should never have taken that out on you. Never." She grips my hands, face full of sincerity. "Can you ever forgive me?"

LATER, IN THE passenger seat of Mum's car, I stare down at my phone. My text taunts me from the screen, the text I've spent the past ten minutes agonising over and can't bring myself to send.

Dad's OK. On our way home. Sorry for everything.

The words are trite, inadequate. They don't come close to expressing the confusion of emotions inside me—my remorse at the way I behaved, the overpowering sense of relief. The heart attack hadn't been connected to the weekend's events, Linda assured me as we sat in the visitors' lounge. Rather, it was caused by a build-up of cholesterol in the arteries leading to the heart. It could've happened at any time, had certainly been threatening for months.

"So if it's anyone's fault, it's mine for feeding him all those crumbles and sponge puddings. I was so concerned with taking care of him, wanted to make him happy, and all the time…" Linda dashed away her tears, expression growing determined. "Well, not anymore. From now on, your dad will be on a strict regime of healthy food and exercise."

I sigh and delete the text. There's too much to explain in a single brief message. As soon as we get home, I'll sit Taylor down and apologise. I'll beg if I have to, get down on my knees, whatever it takes to earn his forgiveness.

When I open the front door, Buddy trots into the hall to meet us, tail windmilling. Besides the glow spilling through the windows from the security light outside, the house is in darkness. Mum shepherds Abby and Imogen into the kitchen, saying we could all do with some hot chocolate, but I don't follow. Instead, I slip upstairs and along the landing.

Wary, unsure of my reception, I edge into our room. Like the rest of the house, it's in blackness. "Tay?"

No response.

I flick on the light, but even before it illuminates the room, I know it's empty. The hollow silence tells me he isn't here. I hesitate on the threshold, noting the sock dangling from an open drawer, the wardrobe doors hanging ajar. It's as though Taylor was in too much of a hurry to shut them. Then I spy his mobile on the bedside cabinet and let out my breath. He can't have gone far without his phone.

I retreat, peering into the bathroom and Dad's study where Taylor had been banished last night. I even check the en suite off the master bedroom, but there's no sign of him.

Downstairs, I poke my head into the kitchen. The girls have slumped into chairs at the table while Mum stands at the worktop, spooning chocolate powder into mugs. "Have you seen Taylor?"

"No, sweetheart. I assumed he was upstairs." Mum removes a saucepan of hot milk from the hob. "You look exhausted. Come and sit down."

"In a minute. I want to find Taylor, let him know Dad's going to be OK."

I move from room to room, switching on lights as I go, my unease morphing into fully fledged anxiety. He hasn't crashed on the sofa, isn't hunched over the dining room table. Nor is he huddled by the radiator in the cloakroom. I return to the kitchen, a horrible queasiness in my gut.

"He isn't here," I say, trying to subdue my panic. "I've looked everywhere."

"I'm sure there's no need to worry." Mum presses a cup of hot chocolate into my hands. "He must've gone to a friend's."

I catch Imogen's eye. Her expression mirrors some of my own concern. I curl my fingers around the mug, seeking comfort from its warmth, finding none. Mum might not think Taylor's absence is cause for alarm, but she doesn't know what passed between us, how hateful I'd been. Plus, thanks to Carl Farmer, he doesn't have any friends left, not unless you count Liam.

A shard of glass slides into my chest. It was obvious the one time I met Liam that he still has feelings for Taylor. What if my harsh words forced Taylor to question our relationship, helped him realise this thing between us is too brittle to withstand any serious pressure, and he's gone running to his ex?

Buddy, who's been eyeing Imogen's hot chocolate, gets up and ambles over to the back door. He whines, and I cross to let him out. I'm suddenly desperate for fresh air, to be alone. I follow Buddy onto the patio, pulling the door shut behind me.

The rain has stopped, and the air smells clean and damp. While Buddy sniffs his way around the flowerbeds, I stare into the night and wonder where my boyfriend is now—if he's even still my boyfriend. His absence chisels away at my heart, carving a Taylor-shaped hole. There's so much I planned to say to him—that I'm sorry, so incredibly sorry about Sebastian and for the things I said; that I want so much for this, for us, to work, no matter the obstacles. Most of all, I intended to tell him how, even though we haven't known each other very long, I'm pretty sure I'm falling in love with him.

CHAPTER TWENTY-FIVE

TAYLOR

I STIR, REACHING FOR Ben beside me. Then I remember, and the loss thuds into my stomach. When I peel my eyes open, the walls of Dad's bedroom waver into focus. I offered to sleep on the sofa, but Dad insisted I take his bed, and I was too wrung out to argue.

Grey daylight bleeds through the thin curtains. I roll over to glance at the clock radio on the windowsill. Nearly eleven. Wow. Conditioned from years of getting up early to run, my body rarely lets me lie in. I must've needed it. After the events of yesterday, I fully expected my thoughts to keep me awake till dawn. Instead, worn out by the emotion of it all, I'd blacked out the moment my head hit the pillow. Still, as I stretch, I feel as though I've barely slept at all, muscles aching, my brain muggy.

Dad moves around the flat. Muffled sounds filter through the closed bedroom door. He was amazing last night, telephoning the hospital for news of Martin, throwing together a red lentil soup and making no comment when I only sipped at it. The whole time, he kept up a stream of cheerful talk in an obvious attempt to distract me. Again, I wondered how I could've shut him out of my life all these months.

I'm tempted to stay where I am, to simply pull the duvet back over my head and sleep the day away. Dad deserves more than that, though. With a colossal effort, I fling off the covers and drag myself out of bed. Pulling on the jeans and T-shirt I've slung over the back of the chair, I wander across the hall to the living room.

"Look who it is." Dad glances up with a smile. He's sitting at the small dining table, a mug of tea and the sports pages in front of him. "Sleep OK?"

"I reckon." I rub my knuckles into my eyes, which are sore and gritty with tiredness. "Sorry. Didn't mean to lie in so late."

Dad chuckles. "I looked in on you a couple of times, but you were completely zonked. Seemed a shame to disturb you. What would you like? Tea? Toast? Cereal? Bacon? Eggs? Sausages?"

"Just tea, thanks, but I can make it."

"That's all right. It's nice to have someone to take care of. I've missed it."

I know he isn't saying it to make me feel bad. All the same, guilt pinches my side. I flop onto the sofa while Dad pushes his chair back and heads into the kitchen.

"Anything you'd like to do today?" he asks, putting the kettle on to boil.

"Don't you…?" I hesitate. It occurs to me I don't have a clue whether Dad's found a new job or if this is still a painful subject. "Don't you have things you need to do?"

"Nope. I'm my own boss these days, just doing a bit of freelance web design work."

"That's great, Dad."

"Yeah, well, keeps me out of trouble. I also get to choose my own hours, so today I'm all yours." He tosses teabags into two mugs. "What do you think? We could see the sights, visit the Science Museum, grab some lunch. Whatever you like."

"Um, sure. Any of those sound good." I try to summon some enthusiasm, but it rings false even to my ears. The idea of traipsing around London fills me with the impulse to superglue myself to the sofa, and my stomach spasms at the mere suggestion of food. Dad's trying so hard, however, I feel I have to make a token effort.

"On the other hand," Dad pours boiling water over the teabags, casting me a shrewd look, "we could veg in front of the telly, pig out on junk food and generally catch up."

I smile despite myself. Dad has always been able to read my mood far better than Mum. "Is that OK? I mean, if you'd rather go out—"

"Of course it's OK. I'm just happy you're here. Besides, I can tell you're not up to it." He brings the tea over, hands me a mug and sits next to me on the sofa.

I take a sip. Hot and strong with the merest splash of milk. Just the way I like it. No matter how many times I tell her, Mum always makes it too weak. "Thanks, Dad. Sorry to be such a downer."

"Don't be daft. Still fretting about Ben?"

I do this weird kind of half-nod, half-shrug. The mention of his name causes a tightness in my throat, and I swallow another mouthful of tea.

"I'm sure you don't need to worry," Dad says. "It was one hell of a shock for him. People often say things they don't mean when they're upset."

I'm silent for a while, staring out of the living room window. Yesterday's rain has stopped, but the sky hangs low and overcast. I want so badly to believe him, to put Ben's coldness down to his fear for Martin, but Dad doesn't know the whole story. I haven't told him about Sebastian; it isn't my secret to share. Yet I can't shake the suspicion that I've simply been a rebound crush, that Ben's still in love with his ex, despite everything he's done.

"I don't know," I say at last. "I think he might decide being with me is more trouble than it's worth."

"Then he doesn't deserve you. If he cares about you that much, he won't abandon you just because things have got tough."

"You did." The words burst from me before I can think them through. Once they're out, though, I realise they needed to be said.

Dad's gaze drops to his hands—the strong, capable hands that put up the bookshelves in my bedroom and helped Imogen build model train tracks. For the first time since I turned up on his doorstep, the mask fractures. Sadness shows through the cracks, and suddenly he looks much older. "I never abandoned you, Tay. Whatever else you think, I need you to know that."

"It felt like you did." His regret tugs at me, but I refuse to let him off the hook.

"I know." Dad massages his forehead. He meets my eyes, his own alight with sincerity. "Fact is, I was ashamed. I failed you all, you and Mum and Imogen. There was this part of me that thought you'd be better off without me."

"So you ran off to London?"

"Hardly ran. Crawled away with my tail between my legs, more like. Besides, I didn't have a whole lot of choice. I had no house, no job, no money. When Clive offered me his spare room, it seemed like the best option. The only option, really."

I don't respond, can't decide how to feel. The rational half of my brain can appreciate the logic of what he's saying, but nothing changes how alone I've felt this past year.

"Taylor?" Dad touches my shoulder, waiting until I look up at him. "Listen, you and Imogen are the most important people in the world to me. I still think I did the best thing I could at the time, but I went about it all wrong. I see that now. I should've put my own shame aside. I should've made it clear, wherever I might be, I was here for you, that I'd always be here, no matter what. I thought you knew, but I should've made sure. I failed you. I take full responsibility for that, and I'm sorry."

In the face of his remorse, the last of my resentment crumbles to ash. My eyelids prickle and I blink hard. "It's OK, Dad, I get it. Anyway, it isn't all your fault. I shouldn't have been such a brat, should've talked to you when you phoned."

"Forget it." Dad drapes his arm over my shoulders, pulling me into his side. "You're here now. that's all that matters."

BEN

"HERE WE ARE." Linda sets a tray on the table and pulls out the plastic chair across from me. "I got you some cake as well. You didn't eat much at home."

"Thanks." I curl my hands around the mug of tea, ignoring the cellophane-wrapped brownie. The thought of eating has my stomach clenching in rebellion.

Silence descends between us. Despite our truce of the night before, sitting alone with my stepmother in the hospital canteen feels strange. Only now do I realise how pivotal Dad's been to our relationship, the gravitational force pulling us all together.

And we almost lost him.

Every time I remember how close he came to slipping away from us forever, bands of ice tighten around my heart. He's OK, I remind myself for the thousandth time that day. Dad's going to be OK.

I glance around the busy canteen, at the dreary day beyond the tall windows and the people occupying the other tables, frazzled-looking grown-ups struggling to entertain fractious children. I can't think of anything to say. Perhaps we already said everything we needed to last night.

"Your dad's so much brighter today," Linda says, sipping her tea. She betrays no hint of the awkwardness I feel. "He's really looking forward to seeing you."

"Is he?" I recall his bewilderment and disgust when Taylor and I told him about our relationship and can't hide my scepticism. Much as I'm anxious to see my dad, to confirm with my own eyes that he's OK, part of me dreads it. That's why I didn't protest when Abby and Imogen claimed first visit.

"Of course he is." Linda smiles at me, though there's a definite reserve behind it. She might not blame Taylor and me, but she isn't happy about us either. She pushes the plate across the table. "Come on, darling, you really should eat something."

This is rich coming from her. Except for a solitary piece of toast, she's eaten nothing all day. She arrived home from the hospital late that morning, pale and rumpled but in good spirits. The three of us, puffy-eyed and still in our pyjamas, were in the living room, slumped in front of the telly. Buddy trotted over to greet her, tail going crazy.

As we watched on in amazement, Linda dropped to her knees and wrapped her arms around his neck. "You're my good boy. Yes, you are. My good, clever boy. God." She looked up at us with tears in her eyes, one hand on Buddy's head. "What would we have done without him? He saved Martin's life."

Then she pulled herself together and went to have a shower, returning ten minutes later to fuss over us. She plied us with bacon sandwiches and mugs of tea and promised we'd be able to visit Dad that afternoon. I took my tea upstairs with me to get dressed, hoping Linda wouldn't notice I hadn't eaten anything.

I should've known better.

Because it's easier than arguing, I free the brownie from its cellophane wrapper and take a bite. The sponge congeals to the consistency of wet mud in my mouth. I force it down with a gulp of tea. It sticks in my throat, a marble-sized lump, before it's swallowed up by the black hole Taylor's absence has opened inside me.

The relief at learning he was with his dad has long since mutated into remorse, knowing I was the one who drove him away. Christ, I need him so badly—need to see him, to have him close, for him to tell me I haven't ruined everything.

Linda chatters on about the new diet and exercise regime she's planning for Dad, God help him. Eventually, though, she checks her watch and suggests we head up to the CCU before the girls tire him out. I push my barely touched cake away and follow her from the canteen.

At the door to Dad's room, she lays a hand on my arm. "No need to look so worried. He really is much better."

I nod. She's misunderstood the cause of my anxiety, but I don't correct her. Uncertainty plays tug-of-war with my gut. What if Linda's wrong? What if, after everything that's happened, I'm the last person he wants to see?

"Tell your dad I'll be up in a little while." Linda presses my arm and steps away. "I'm going to ring Taylor."

She hesitates, expression quizzical. Perhaps she's waiting for a reaction, or else for me to ask her to pass on a message. I consider it but dismiss the idea almost at once. How can I possibly condense all I want to say into a few words? Instead, I take a deep breath and open the door.

Dad's sitting up in the high bed, propped against a mound of pillows. With the tubes and wires sprouting from various parts of his anatomy, he resembles some weird kind of android. The girls occupy the chairs on either side of him, Abby chatting away to the accompaniment of the heart monitor.

"Ah, here's my boy." Dad gives me a tentative smile. He does look better, still tired and drawn but without that frightening greyish tinge. He clasps Abby's hand and reaches out to pat

Imogen's knee. "Do you two mind if I have a private word with Ben? It's been lovely to see you both."

"We're just glad you're OK," Abby says, bending to kiss his cheek. "We'll be back to see you later."

Imogen nods, waggling her fingers in farewell as the two of them get to their feet. Then they disappear into the corridor, leaving Dad and me alone.

I move over to the bed and take Abby's vacated seat. "How're you feeling?"

"Oh, you know. Not too bad, considering." Dad casts me a sheepish glance. "Sorry I gave you such a scare. I've been overindulging, apparently."

"That's all right, so long as you promise not to do it again." I manage a weak smile, but my voice sounds forced.

Dad chuckles. "Not much chance of that with Lindy on the case. Nothing but bracing walks and rabbit food for me from now on."

"I'd stay here as long as you can then, make the most of it."

"I might just do that. Don't tell Lindy, but I'm finding it rather peaceful."

"Your secret's safe with me."

We share a complicit look. Dad averts his gaze first, toying with the cannula in the back of his hand. We're quiet for a while, the hush broken only by the beeping of the heart monitor.

"Listen," Dad says at length, "we need to talk about Taylor."

I've been expecting it, steeled myself for it. All the same, my stomach plunges. Whatever he's about to say, I have a feeling I won't like it. "Dad, we don't have to do this now. We can wait till you're better."

"No, I think this needs to be said. Otherwise, it'll be there, hanging over us." His attention drifts to the window behind me. "The thing is, I'm not happy about it. As far as Lindy and I are concerned, we'd rather you put this whole episode behind you and pretend it never happened."

I open my mouth to point out that love doesn't work like that. You can't just switch it on and off at will, no matter how convenient that might be for everyone else. He and Linda should know that more than most. Before the protest can spill out, I sink my teeth into my tongue. The last thing Dad needs is to get into a row.

Nevertheless, he holds up a hand to forestall me. "I can see what you're thinking, and you're right. Much as we wish you'd put an end to this, we know it isn't realistic. You're both adults, and in a few weeks, you'll be heading off to university. There's nothing either of us can do to stop you seeing each other."

I stare at him, some of my dread ebbing away. This conversation isn't taking quite the inflexible line I'd imagined.

Dad confronts me with an obvious effort. "That said, Lindy and I want it made abundantly clear we're opposed to this relationship. We won't tolerate it under our roof."

"But—" The word escapes before I can prevent it.

Dad silences me with a frown. "This isn't up for discussion, Ben. We might accept this is going on, but we won't have it rubbed in our faces. That means no sharing a bedroom, no public displays of affection, not while you're in our house. As far as we're concerned, it isn't happening. We don't want to see or hear anything about it. Is that understood?"

He sags against the pillows, plainly exhausted. Still, his eyes remain firm and serious on mine. My head reels. I don't know what to say, what to think. It could've been worse, I suppose. I was prepared for an ultimatum—*Stop seeing each other or be cut off from the family forever.* These ground rules of Dad's have to be preferable to that, right? Yet the idea of concealing such an important part of our lives leaves a sour taste in my mouth.

"Ben?" Dad's tone carries a warning.

It costs me every gram of restraint I have, but I choke down my resentment. "Yeah, I get it."

"Good lad." Dad grasps my shoulder, looking relieved. "Lindy will be talking to Taylor, explaining the situation, so there's no need for us to say any more about it."

I focus on my knees, afraid of what might show in my expression. Of course, all this will be irrelevant if I can't convince Taylor to forgive me. I ache to speak to him, to have him reassure me we'll be OK, but not over the phone. When I apologise, I have to look him in the eye, let him see how much I mean it. If there's any hope of salvaging what we have, I'll need to do it face-to-face.

CHAPTER TWENTY-SIX

TAYLOR

FOR WHAT FEELS like the hundredth time, my eyes stray to the clock mounted on the wall across the restaurant from our corner booth.

"Ready to make a move?" Dad asks.

I turn back to find him regarding me, an amused arch to his eyebrows. I offer him a sheepish smile. "If that's OK."

"'Course. If you're sure I can't tempt you to some pudding…"

I shake my head. I've already forced down a few slices of pizza, which lie heavy and congealed in my belly. "You have some, though, if you want."

"Best not. Need to watch my waistline." Dad pats his perfectly flat stomach.

I snort. From the old photo albums dating back to Dad's schooldays, I know he's always been lean and angular like me.

"Besides," he adds, "we mustn't keep your young man waiting."

"Not sure he's mine anymore." I pick up a napkin, crumpling it in my fist. Then again, perhaps he never had been. Not really. He certainly sounded distant on the phone that morning, as though we were speaking from opposite ends of the Milky Way.

The ringing filtered through the closed bathroom door as I was getting out of the shower. When I emerged, a towel draped around my hips, Dad was waiting to hand me the cordless. "For you."

I looked at him, questioning. His expression gave nothing away, so I took the receiver and wandered with it into Dad's bedroom. "Hello?"

I expected it to be Mum. She'd want to find out when I was coming home or maybe delight me with another charming lecture on how my relationship with Ben wouldn't be tolerated in her house.

"Hey, it's me."

At the sound of Ben's voice, my legs gave out, and I sank onto the edge of the bed. It was quiet, tentative. Still, the force of it knocked the wind out of me. For a few moments, I couldn't breathe.

"Tay, you there?"

"Yeah." The air gusted from me in a shaky sigh. "Yeah, I'm here. How… How's your dad?"

"Much better, thanks. They're keeping him in for a bit to monitor him or whatever, but the doctors say he's on the mend."

"That's amazing news. Really."

"Yeah." Ben let out his breath. "He had us all scared for a while there."

Silence stretched across the distance between us. Forty-eight hours ago, it would've seemed impossible Ben and I could ever be short of things to say to one another, and yet here we were. My heart twisted. I didn't expect him to call. Hell, after the way we left things, I thought he never wanted to speak to me again.

"Look," he said at last. His words were strained, as though they cost him a great effort. "We need to talk."

"OK." My grip tightened on the receiver. I braced myself for him to end it then and there, already experiencing a phantom of the pain I knew would follow.

"But not over the phone," he went on. "Would it be all right… Could I pick you up this afternoon? You don't have to come home with me, not if you don't want. I need to see you."

I thought about refusing, insisting we talk then. What was the point in delaying the inevitable? Might as well get it over with, like ripping off a plaster. Yet I agreed to wait. Perhaps it was pathetic, but I'd wanted to cling to my tiny shred of hope for a few hours longer.

Dad gets up from the table, laying a hand on my shoulder. "I'm sure he's still yours, but let's go and find out, shall we?"

We leave the little Italian place and begin the short walk back to the flat. Summer has returned in full force, driving away the rain and cloudy skies of the past days. The London streets are crowded with people enjoying the warm weather. A cluster of laughing young women pass us on the pavement, shopping bags from Zara and Monsoon bumping against tanned legs. Across the road, half a dozen or so kids huddle in the bus shelter, puffing on illicit cigarettes. I'm right here, in the midst of all this thriving energy, and yet I feel apart from it. Envy turns my lunch to acid—envy at their happiness, their uncomplicated enjoyment in the sunshine.

Dad flings an arm over my shoulders. "So, off to uni in a few weeks. I can't believe my little boy's all grown up."

"Give over, Dad." I manage a weak grin, elbowing him in the ribs. I remember how, at the start of the summer, I'd been desperate to leave, had counted down the days to my escape. Then, as my feelings for Ben grew, I'd looked forward to the two of us setting off together, able to lead our own lives. Now, with everything up in the air between us, I can't see beyond the next few hours.

"You're welcome to stay, you know," Dad says, "for as long as you like. Until you need to leave for uni."

"What about Clive?"

"He won't mind. You remember how easy-going he is. Besides, he spends half the week at his girlfriend's these days."

It's tempting, the idea of seeking refuge with Dad, free from the judgement and awkwardness that awaits me at home. Yet whatever comes of my conversation with Ben this afternoon, I know hiding isn't the answer. Dad needs to get back to his work, and I have to return to reality, however uncomfortable it might be. Plus, I miss Imogen and Buddy. I even miss Abby, impossible though it would've seemed a week ago.

"Thanks, Dad. I think I should get back, though, at least for a bit, start sorting out my stuff for uni."

Dad gives me a sideways hug. "Sounds like a plan. Just keep in touch, yeah? And know you're welcome any time."

"I will." The cold weight pressing down on my chest lifts a fraction. It's been great, this brief interlude with Dad, spending some quality time with him, catching up on all the months we've lost. Never, not for anything, would I have brought about the events that had me boarding that train. Still, if one good thing has come out of them, it's that they forced me to see sense.

We round the corner onto Dad's road. My heart stalls, then accelerates to a thousand beats per minute. All at once, the pavement feels uneven and riddled with potholes beneath my feet. Or perhaps I've simply forgotten how to move, because I'm stumbling, tripping over my own trainers.

Ben's there, waiting for me outside the entrance to Dad's building. With the distance between us and the sun behind him, it's impossible to make out his expression. I have the urge to run to him, to hurl myself into his arms and never let him go. Instead, I haul in a ragged breath, shove my emotions somewhere deep inside and make my careful way towards him.

BEN

"WHERE ARE WE?" Taylor glances over at me from the passenger seat.

I pull the car into a parking space along the grass verge and switch off the engine. "You'll see."

He raises an eyebrow but follows me out of the car and across the narrow lane to the olde-worlde pub. I found it during a Google search that morning. The moment I saw the photos of The Cottage, all thatched roof and walls trailing honeysuckle, I knew this was the place.

Rather than going in through the front entrance, I lead Taylor along a gravel path that skirts the side of the pub. The peace of the Brookshire countryside drapes itself around us. Save for birdsong and the crunch of tyres as the occasional car passes on the dirt track, there isn't a sound to be heard. In the walled garden at the back, I leave Taylor seated at a table in a patch of afternoon sunshine and head inside to buy drinks.

None of this has played out as I expected. I had it all planned, exactly what I was going to say, the apology, the explanations. In the end, though, I didn't need to say any of it.

"Tay, I'm so, so sorry," I said the moment we were alone in the car. I turned to look at him, pouring all my remorse and sincerity into that look, all the love. I needed him to see it, to understand.

Before I could launch into the speech I'd prepared on the drive to London, he shook his head. "It's OK. I get it."

I paused, thrown off my stride, and scanned his face for any sign that he was fobbing me off. "Really?"

"'Course. You were worried about your dad. I…" He studied his hands, biting his lip. "I should've cut you more slack."

I let out the breath I'd been holding for days. My stomach unclenched, some of the anxiety seeping from me. Perhaps things would be OK, after all. "It wasn't your fault, any of it. Yes, I was worried—God, I was scared out of my mind—but I shouldn't have taken it out on you. It wasn't fair."

"Seriously, it's fine." Taylor made as if to reach out to me, then clearly thought better of it. For all his assurances, there was a tautness in him, a wariness to his expression that belied his words.

"What is it?" I asked. That anxiety crept back, closing icy fingers around my heart. He might not have gone running to Liam after our row, but perhaps my harshness had killed his feelings for me, the feelings that were still so new and untested.

Taylor stared ahead through the windscreen, as though determined to avoid my eyes. He locked his fingers together in his lap, squeezing so hard I was afraid his bones would crack. "I need to know…about him…Sebastian."

"Sebastian? What do you mean?"

"If there's anything between you… If you think you might still be in love with him, just tell me. I'd rather know."

"Tay," I said, then stopped. The idea was ridiculous, a billion miles away from the truth. If not for the pain visible through the chinks in Taylor's calm, I would've laughed. I massaged my forehead. "Why would you even think that?"

He shrugged. "All last week, when we were getting together, you were seeing him and you never told me."

"Only because he was blackmailing me. Christ, you really think I'd want anything to do with him after what he did to

Dad? OK, so I met up with him a couple of times, but every second I was there, I could hardly stand to look at him. That last time, I chucked his drink in his face."

"Seriously? Well, that proves it. You must still be in love with him." Taylor's voice was deadpan, but the corner of his mouth quirked in a shadow of that crooked grin.

"Shut up." I gripped his hands in mine and gazed into his eyes—those beautiful, brown eyes, vulnerable without their armour of make-up. "Whatever I felt for Sebastian, it died a long time ago, back in Australia. What you and I have is different. I think… I think I'm falling in love with you."

"Yeah?" That smile widened, and he entwined his fingers with mine. "You don't think this might be more trouble than it's worth?"

I released a sound somewhere between a huff and a laugh. "I think it'll be a whole lot of trouble, but I also think we're worth every bit of it."

I return to the garden and set our beers on the picnic table, sliding onto the bench across from Taylor.

"Cheers." He takes a long pull from his glass and regards me over the rim, eyes warm and full of something dark and intense that has heat uncoiling in my groin.

I swig a mouthful of my beer. It's crisp and cold and slips easily down my throat. Seated opposite Taylor with the sun pleasant on my back, safe from the disapproval waiting for us at home, I feel happier than I thought possible a couple of hours earlier.

"What?" Taylor tilts his head, expression quizzical.

I realise I've been staring. Actually, I can't tear my eyes from him—the toned leanness of his arms; the slender fingers that have explored every inch of me; his full, sensuous mouth. He's really here. Much as I hoped with every cell in my body that I'd be able to make things right between us, I hadn't truly believed it.

I smile at him, strangely shy. "I just…I thought I'd lost you."

"Nah." Taylor's hand finds mine under the table. "You'll have to try harder than that to get rid of me."

I unleash a shaky laugh and squeeze his fingers. We sit quietly for a while, hands clasped, exchanging glances between sips of beer, savouring one another and the drowsy stillness of the summer afternoon.

"I like your dad," I say. "He reminds me of you."

"Really? It's no wonder he and Mum split up then. You've seen how well we get on." He props an elbow on the table, his grin half wry, half wistful. "I'm glad I went."

Taylor doesn't add how much he's missed his dad. He doesn't need to. When I watched the two of them together, their bond was obvious.

He shoots me a rueful look. "It's going to be tough, isn't it, living at home?"

"Your mum gave you 'the talk' then."

"Oh, yeah. How did it go? 'If you're determined to continue with this relationship, we can't stop you, but it will not be permitted under our roof.'"

His imitation of Linda is so spot on, his emphasis on the word 'relationship' so thick with disdain, it has me snorting beer from my nose.

His eyes snare mine, the expression in them growing serious. "We'll get through it though, won't we, until we leave for uni?"

"'Course we will." I stroke my thumb over the smooth skin of his palm. "It'll just about kill me, not being able to kiss you whenever I want, but we'll manage."

"It's killing me right now, to be honest." Taylor flashes me a wicked grin, his gaze settling on my mouth. The blatant hunger in that look has me aching for him—for his lips, his hands, his hard, lean body. "How long before we're expected home?"

"Actually…" I linger over the word. "Come on. I have something to show you."

Taylor tilts his head but lets me draw him to his feet and into the little pub. Rather than heading to the bar, I lead him through a door and up a steep, spiral staircase. The ancient boards creak and dip under our feet. When we reach the first-floor landing, I dig a key from my pocket and unlock a door to our right, stepping aside to let Taylor go in ahead of me.

Taylor revolves on the spot, thumbs hooked into his back pockets. He takes it all in, the quaint cottage bedroom with its bluebell-patterned wallpaper and vase of fresh flowers on the mantelpiece above the open fire. Then he turns to me, a slow smile spreading across his battered face. "You booked this?"

"Just for tonight." I close the door behind us and turn the key. It locks with a satisfying click. "Thought we should make the most of it, before—"

I don't get to finish. Taylor moves close, pressing me into the door, his hands coming up to cradle my face. Then he's kissing me, and it's hot and fierce and greedy, all probing tongue and urgency. I moan into his mouth, gripping his waistband to force him harder against me, aware of nothing but my need for him, his need for me.

"Want you," he murmurs against my lips. His hands are everywhere, tangling in my hair, running the length of my spine, tugging at the zip on my jeans. "All of you."

"God, yes." I edge him backwards towards the bed, already reaching inside his boxers. My mouth rakes his shoulder, his neck, his throat.

As we tumble onto the marshmallow-soft mattress, everything else fades away. Our parents' disapproval, the difficult weeks that lie ahead…none of it is important. In this moment, nothing matters but that we're together, right here, right now.

"Damn you, Ben Willoughby." Taylor gasps against my ear, his breathing fast and ragged. "I have a horrible feeling I'm falling in love with you, too."

CHAPTER TWENTY-SEVEN

Taylor

I SQUEEZE MY WASHBAG into the bulging suitcase and straighten, casting a final look over the bedroom I've slept in for the past year. This will be the last time I set foot here. I'll be back in November to give evidence at CJ's trial, but by then, Martin will have completed on the sale and he, Mum and the girls will have moved into their new home.

The six of us went to view the house a few weeks ago. It's smaller than this one, a three-bed semi with a courtyard garden and a garage Mum has plans to convert into an en-suite bedroom. Ben caught my eye at this, both of us clearly wondering the same thing. Was this a sign that our parents were beginning to accept us? Of course, we should've known better. The hope barely had a chance to sprout before Mum crushed it to pulp.

"Any stuff you're not taking to uni, you boys can keep in there," she told us, "and when you visit, you can take it in turns sleeping on the sofa bed."

Oh, well. I'd shrugged, not caring all that much. It's a nice house, welcoming despite its shabbiness and seventies wallpaper, but I couldn't picture myself living there.

My gaze sweeps the room, searching for anything I've forgotten. It already appears abandoned. The chest of drawers has been cleared of my usual paraphernalia, and the wardrobe gapes open to reveal rows of skeletal hangers, their carcases picked clean. The nostalgia catches me off guard. I didn't expect to feel anything other than relief at the prospect of leaving, and yet…

My eyes linger on the mattresses, now bare of sheets. Ben and I had lain for hours on these beds, tangled up in each other's arms, languid with pleasure and discovery. For a precious few days, this was our sanctuary. Here, we were free to explore one another, to marvel at this thing between us before everything went to hell.

These past weeks, I've once more become the room's sole occupant. Ironic, really. When Ben came home from Australia, I would've traded my collection of first-edition Tolkiens to have the space to myself. Then, when I finally got my wish, I could think of nothing but the yawning emptiness in the bed beside me where my boyfriend should've been.

After Poppy moved out, though, Mum and Martin decided there was no need for me to continue sleeping on the sofa bed and transferred Ben into the annex. They dressed it up as a treat—"It'll be just like having your own place, give you a real sense of independence." Yet they also made sure to stress that it was still part of the main house and would therefore be subject to the same stipulations.

We went along with it, as we went along with all the rules they laid down for us. Mostly. We may have caved a couple of times, stolen the odd kiss in the privacy of the annex, frantic with longing and the need to be close. Fuck, we're not made of stone. On the whole, though, we've been the model of restraint.

It hasn't been easy. Seeing Ben every day, playing the role of stepbrother when I wanted nothing more than to be with him, to lose myself in him, has been pure torture. Still, we got through it. Somehow. Now, for a while at least, we get to leave all this pretence behind.

The A' Level results were announced the week following Martin's heart attack. I got those three 'A's I worked my arse off for, securing me a place at City to study English Lit. And Ben will be in London, a mere Tube ride away, albeit not where he'd originally planned. Then again, a lot of things have changed over the course of this summer.

Satisfied I've packed everything, I close the suitcase on the clothes and other odds and ends that will be travelling with me into my new life. I'm struggling to zip it shut when the bedroom door opens. Imogen slips inside, Buddy ambling at her heels. She crosses to perch on my bed, adding her weight to the lid of the case so I can fasten it.

"Cheers." I flash her a grateful smile. Dropping to my knees beside Buddy, I wrap my arms around his solid bulk and rest my cheek against his fur. "I'm going to miss you guys."

My sister looks at me, eyebrow raised.

"Hey." I frown in mock outrage. "I mean it. I expect you to text every day."

She smirks at that, her expression knowing.

"What's that for?" I ask.

She snorts and tucks her legs beneath her. "Like you'll notice whether I text or not. You'll be way too busy getting off with Ben."

"Since when does my sister have such a dirty mind?"

"Since she was forced to watch you gazing at Ben as if you might rip his clothes off at any minute."

"Can't blame a boy for looking." I give her knee a playful slap. "Seriously, though. I'll only be a train away. Not that far. Let me know if you need me, yeah?"

Her eyes meet mine. She nods and reaches out to touch my cheek.

I catch her hand, gripping it tight. "And you'll be all right here, coping with Mum without me?"

She nods again, squeezing my fingers, and I believe her. Unlike Martin and me, who have only begun inching towards a truce, Imogen connected with our stepdad from the outset. Plus, despite their differences, she and Abby have continued to grow closer. As for Mum, she might never truly understand her children, but the fear of losing Martin has sanded her sharpest edges. She's as efficient and controlling as ever, but a little softer, less critical.

Right on cue, her voice drifts up the stairs. "Taylor, you'd better get a move on. Ben's waiting to leave."

Imogen and I exchange an amused glance. Then I give Buddy one last pat and push myself to my feet, seizing my suitcase by the handle. I smile at the pair of them. "Come and see me off?"

BEN

I LOAD THE last of our boxes onto Esmerelda's back seat and lean against the passenger door, face tilted to the sun. Despite its warmth, the air is cool and fresh and tastes sweet on my tongue. It's the taste of promise, of freedom.

Abby comes to stand next to me, her head on my shoulder. "Wish you didn't have to go. You only just got back."

"I know." I put my arm around her. In truth, so much has happened this summer, so much has changed, it seems far longer than a few months. I feel like a different person, someone with a plan, who knows what he wants to do with his life.

One August afternoon shortly after Dad came out of hospital, Taylor and I escaped the house to take Buddy for a walk. Sitting on our favourite bench in the park, I said, "I've been thinking about uni, what I'd like to do."

"Yeah?" Taylor glanced sideways at me. His shoulder pressed against mine, solid, comforting.

I took a deep breath. This was the first time I'd spoken the idea aloud. "I... I'd like to train as a paramedic."

"Really? Because of what happened with your dad?"

"Yeah. Seeing him like that, knowing he needed help and not having a clue what to do... I never want to go through that again."

Taylor smiled at me, expression soft. "I think that's great. You'll be amazing at it."

"Thanks." I took his hand, relishing the rare moment of contact. "This feels like the right thing to do."

When we got home, we went straight onto my laptop to research courses. I fully expected to have to wait until the following year, perhaps get a job in the meantime, but I was lucky. A prospective student had missed out on their required A' Level grades, creating a space on the Paramedic Science course at St George's. I applied, just on the off chance, and was accepted. It means I'll be farther from Taylor, an hour-long drive rather than a five-minute one, but we'll manage.

Raz will be in London, too, starting his second year at UCL. I met up with him and the rest of the lads when they got back from Thailand. Things weren't the same between us. Maybe we'll never recapture the easy friendship we had before, but I'm determined to be a better mate from now on.

I give Abby a squeeze. "At least I won't be on the other side of the world. You can visit any time."

Her eyes gleam with sudden excitement. "And you can give me a guided tour, take me to a party."

"What? And set you loose on all those unsuspecting young men?"

"Oh, I'm off boys. Lauren and I have made a pact to steer clear of them for a while."

"Very wise. Boys are way too much trouble."

Abby scoffs. "You don't mean that."

"S'pose not." I grin. For all the discord my relationship with Taylor has caused, all the obstacles we're likely to face in the future, I wouldn't give him up for anything.

As if sensing my thoughts, Abby says, "It won't always be like this. They'll accept it eventually. They'll have to."

Taylor emerges from the house then, Imogen following. He struggles towards us under the weight of his suitcase and sets it down with a sigh. "This is the last of it."

"Just as well, otherwise you'd be walking." I smirk at him. Hauling the case into the boot, I squash it in amidst the black bags of clothes and towels, duvets and pillows. The back seat is already crammed to bursting with boxes of books, crates of DVDs, laptops, bedside lamps, and everything else we'll need to start this new phase of our lives. This is really happening. Seeing it all there, packed up and ready to go, brings the reality home to me as nothing else has.

I've just slammed the boot shut when Dad and Linda come out to see us off, Buddy attached to my stepmother like an extra shadow. It would've seemed impossible before Dad's heart attack, but ever since the morning Linda returned from the hospital, woman and dog have been inseparable. While Linda might still grouch about the hairs on the carpet, these days, her tone is more one of exasperated affection. I'm glad. At least I can head off to uni knowing Buddy will be well loved.

"All set?" Dad makes an uncertain motion as if to pull me into a hug, settling for laying a hand on my shoulder. Things have been strained between us these past weeks, but he's trying. We both are.

"Think so." I ignore the awkwardness and hug him. After all, I won't see him again until Carl's trial in November, and if it's one thing this summer has taught me, it's that you never know what lurks around the corner. "Take care of yourself, Dad, won't you? No overdoing it."

He chuckles, patting my back. "I doubt there's much danger of that, not with Lindy here to keep an eye on me."

I laugh, conceding the point. Though Dad still tires easily, Linda's new regime of exercise and nourishing food has brought a healthy colour to his cheeks. Dad's decided, once he's well enough to go back to work, he'll hand in his notice and look for a position elsewhere. Much as he enjoyed his job, he says returning to Harcourts after the fiasco of his failed application would be too humiliating. So even if Sebastian's deluded enough to believe we still have a chance, which I doubt, he no longer has any hold over me.

I release Dad and glance over at my stepmother. Strange to remember how much I resented her earlier in the summer, begrudging her intrusion into our family. Over the last month, however, I've got to know her better, come to appreciate the big heart that lies beneath all that briskness.

"Just bear in mind," she's in the process of lecturing Taylor, "you're there to study, not to attend wild parties."

"Right, because I've always been such a party animal. Hardly a night goes by when I'm not staggering home drunk in the early hours."

"That may be so, but university's a whole different situation. I was a student myself once, don't forget."

Taylor looks at his mum with new interest. "Oh, yeah? What did you get up to in your uni days?"

"Nothing whatsoever that concerns you. I just want you to be careful." She gives him a swift peck on the cheek, then turns to me. "I'm relying on you to make sure my son stays out of trouble."

It's the first time either of our parents has mentioned the fact that Taylor and I will continue to see one another in London. Perhaps it's wishful thinking on my part, but her acknowledgement strikes me as a positive sign.

"I'll do my best," I promise. As always when he's close by, Taylor draws my gaze, but I resist his pull. Soon I'll be free to gaze at him as much as I want, to touch him, kiss him, feel his body against mine. The thought has my heart racing and my skin flushing with heat.

While Dad shakes Taylor's hand, wishing him well, Linda reaches on tiptoe to kiss me. "Do take care of yourself, Ben. It's been lovely getting to know you."

Considering how I've become involved with her son, it's possible she isn't being entirely sincere. Still, I appreciate the effort.

I hug Imogen next, coming to Abby last. She clings to me for a moment, crushes me so hard I'm amazed my ribs don't splinter.

"Be good." I release her with a playful shove. "And look after everyone for me. Once we're settled in, you and Imogen can come up for the weekend."

Abby brushes a stray tear from her cheek but manages a watery smile. "And you look out for a hot boy for me."

"Hey, thought you were off boys."

"Only till the right one comes along. I'm not planning to join a convent."

"There's an idea," Dad says. "Yep, I think nun would be an excellent career choice."

Abby sticks out her tongue at him, and we all laugh. Buddy thumps his tail. In this moment, the seven of us sharing a joke in the morning sunshine, there's no disapproval, no tension. We feel like a proper family.

I check the time on my phone. We should probably get going, especially since I told Mum we'd drop in and see her on the way. She's another one I don't have to worry about leaving behind. Now she's settled in her new flat, enjoying her independence and the budding romance with Jon, she's happier than I can remember in years.

I glance over at Taylor. "Shall we head off?"

He responds with a thumbs up. Amidst a final flurry of hugs, I slide behind the wheel and wait for Taylor to climb in beside me. Our eyes meet. The restraint that's been his shield these past weeks begins to crack, allowing the excitement to shine through, the same excitement kindling in my own stomach. I have the urge to take his hand, to feel his fingers warm and solid in mine, but I'm also aware of Dad and Linda nearby, waiting to see us off. There's no rush. Soon we'll have all the time in the world.

"Ready?" I ask.

"Yeah." Taylor's face breaks into a slow smile. It's a smile full of hope and love and things as yet undiscovered. The most beautiful smile I've ever seen. "Let's go."

With my heart full to overflowing, I start the engine and pull out of the driveway. As I swing the car onto Fairfield Avenue, I turn to get a final look at the house that's been my home for most of my life. It isn't as much of a wrench as it might've been, not with Taylor seated beside me and the future shimmering bright and mysterious ahead of us.

We wave one last time to our family gathered on the drive, and they raise their hands in farewell. Dad has an arm around Linda, while Buddy's tail wags an enthusiastic goodbye. Then I put my foot down, urging Esmerelda towards the motorway and whatever university has in store.

THE END

CLAIM YOUR FREE STORY

Thank you so much for reading. If you enjoyed this book, you can join my readers' club to get a free and exclusive short story in my *Boys on the Brink* series. Simply go to

https://jamiedeacon.com/readersclub

and enter your email address. You'll then receive a welcome email from me with links to download your story in your preferred format.

You'll also be signed up to my newsletter where I share updates on my writing, post giveaways, and generally indulge my passion for the world of YA LGBTQ+ fiction. You can unsubscribe at any time and your data will be kept safe and secure.

Happy reading and I look forward to connecting with you!

Jamie

PLEASE LEAVE A REVIEW

It's no exaggeration to say that, to authors, reviews are invaluable. Just a line or two expressing your thoughts can be such a help in spreading the word to like-minded readers. So, if you enjoyed this book, please consider leaving a review on Amazon or your online bookstore of choice. It would mean more to me than I can say.

ABOUT THE AUTHOR

Jamie Deacon is an award-winning author of young adult LGBTQ+ fiction with a passion for weaving stories about friendship, falling in love and finding the courage to be true to yourself. Their debut novel, *Caught Inside*, won two Rainbow Awards and was nominated for a Lambda Literary Award, a Bisexual Book Award and a Next Generation Indie Book Award.

Jamie was born with Retinitis Pigmentosa, a degenerative eye condition that left them registered blind by their mid-teens. Now only able to view their surroundings in light and shadow, Jamie creates vivid settings inside their head and brings them to life through the magic of words.

Jamie lives with their childhood sweetheart close to the River Thames in Berkshire, England. When not curled under a blanket with a book, they enjoy British comedy, are a huge dog lover, and get way too competitive at family games nights.

To find out more about Jamie and their books, you can visit https://jamiedeacon.com

BOOKS BY JAMIE DEACON

BOYS ON THE BRINK SERIES

Caught Inside
https://jamiedeacon.com/caught-inside

Forbidden Steps
https://jamiedeacon.com/forbidden-steps

Defensive Play (Novella)
https://jamiedeacon.com/defensive-play

Off Course (Short Story)
https://jamiedeacon.com/off-course

STANDALONE TITLES

The Music of Unexpected Things
https://jamiedeacon.com/the-music-of-unexpected-things